Mistletoe
in
Maisonville

Also by Lisa Herrington

The Renaissance Lake Series

The Fix

Fall Again

Million Reasons

Standalone Books

One Starry Night

Mistletoe in Maisonville

LISA HERRINGTON

Mistletoe in Maisonville

Lisa Herrington

Writerly House Publishing

Mistletoe in Maisonville

Published by Writerly House Publishing
www.WriterlyHouse.com
www.LisaHerrington.com

This is a work of fiction. Characters, names, places, and events are products of the author's imagination. Any similarity to events or places, or real persons, living or dead, is purely coincidental.

ISBN: 978-0-9990626-3-0

10 9 8 7 6 5 4 3 2 1

Chapter One

Felicity Storey had just replaced the last light bulb on the string lights outside as her best friend Evie Mae Shepard walked toward her with tears in her eyes. "We aren't going to make it," Evie said, flopping down at one of the small iron table and chair sets.

"It's only been one month," Felicity replied, scared to death of what failing would mean.

They'd both graduated from college last May. Instead of going the traditional route, they'd borrowed money from Evie's evil classmate, wanna-be loan shark Isaac Keller, and signed an impossible contract without reading the fine print.

Espresso to Geaux had been a midnight secret for Evie for as long as Felicity could remember. Neither girl had much money, but their dreams had been rich. Growing up in the quaint little water town of Maisonville was to blame. After all, they saw plenty of people have their wildest dreams come true after moving to the small town. Why couldn't it happen for two girls that had grown up there?

The town was nicknamed Renaissance Lake because most people who moved to Maisonville would begin again with a great, new season in their life. Of course, it had a wonderful retiree population, but there were quite a few twenty-somethings that were moving back to town and beginning again too.

It was why a pop-up food truck masquerading as a coffee shop was a great business idea. But Evie's parents refused to let her try something so bold without her college degree in hand first. Brennan and Kristy Shepard hadn't gone to college but had worked hard to provide for their family. Kristy was a hairdresser and worked out of their home, while Troy had a small garage and worked on cars of all makes and models.

Evie's older brother, Mitch, had grown up with the gift of repairing anything he set his mind to and then joined his father's business, helping build quite a remarkable reputation for their integrity, honesty, and skills. But none of that was good enough for the baby girl in the family, and Evie had counted the days until she had her business degree in hand.

Felicity had always wanted to write novels. She'd even written pretty good stories and published them online in high school. But she'd been raised by a strong, hard-working single mother, who was a secretary for twenty years. Asha Storey also cleaned houses on the side to make ends meet. She wouldn't hear of her intelligent, beautiful daughter not getting a college degree. After all, who could make a living writing fiction?

Both girls had worked in a popular coffee shop while in college at ULL, the University of Louisiana at Lafayette, honing their skills. At least, that was the case for Evie. Felicity just needed the money, and working with her best friend was as good as she could get back then. But in the middle of the night, when her studies were done, and she should've been sleeping, Felicity read books about plotting and story structure beyond what she was getting in school.

Now six months post-graduation, they lived in the small pool house behind Evie Mae's parent's home. They ate every meal with either Felicity's mom or Evie's family. All of that just to pay back the exorbitant interest accruing with Baby Shark, Isaac Keller. "I can't tell my parents the loan details, or they'll kill me," Evie cried.

"We could always tell, Mitch," Felicity said.

Evie shook her head. "Are you crazy? He'd lecture us for life because that's what he would get after murdering Sharknado."

"You're right. I know you're right, but what else can we do?" Felicity had known Mitch was overprotective, but she and Evie had spent every penny of that loan buying the used food truck and refurbishing it with Mitchel's help. It had turned out beautiful, and once they'd found a semi-permanent place to park it, Felicity's mom had donated the supplies for a makeshift back patio for people to sit and drink their beverages and hang out. They couldn't believe how painting the truck black and modernizing the interior, plus adding outside seating, turned out. When Isaac Keller saw what they'd accomplished, he salivated at the idea of keeping it for himself.

They should have known better than to sign a contract with him before having their parents look it over too. Isaac was the child prodigy of his sleazy dad and his shifty businesses. Sure, Mr. Keller was wealthy, but he'd made money from owning strip clubs and those quick loan places in New Orleans where they prayed upon people down on their luck. He would brag to Evie that they were providing much-needed services to the community, thinking she would one day go out with him. But Isaac made their skin crawl. Especially when he referred to his dad as a shark in the business world, hence the nickname Felicity had branded him with, Baby Shark.

"There has to be something we can do," Felicity said, trying to console Evie.

"I have an idea, but you're not going to like it."

Felicity shook her head. "We aren't stripping if that's your plan. Or selling pics of our feet online."

Evie laughed at her crazy friend. Sure they'd been drinking while staying up all night baking goods for their coffee shop when she suggested those things a couple of weeks ago. Who knew wine was so good with cookies?

"No, I know. I was looking on-line for jobs."

Felicity rolled her eyes. She and Evie were open sixteen hours a day and then spent another three or four baking goods or prepping for the morning rush. They were running on fumes.

Evie showed Felicity the job ad on her phone. "This is legit. It was on linked-in and posted by a reputable head hunter."

The ad read:

Looking for a "Ghostwriter" for a large manufacturing company's CEO.

This person will write speeches, social content, video content, and more-

Must also be willing to travel with the CEO.

Must have a strong interest in humanitarian efforts.

Compensation is competitive.

"What the heck, Evie? How can I work as a ghostwriter and the coffee shop?"

"That's just it. You can't. But one of us has to bring in more money, and right now, I can handle things here while you go get this job so we can pay the Keller Shark."

Felicity looked at the ad again. She'd never worked as a ghostwriter, but how hard could it be? Of course, there was no guarantee Felicity would get the job. She might not even get an interview.

Evie Mae watched as Felicity reread the ad. It wasn't an ideal situation, but it seemed to be their last hope. As Felicity handed the phone back to her friend, she nodded. She would at least try to help save their business.

Evie smiled. "Great. I knew you would do it, which is why I already called them, and you have an online interview in the morning."

"I might not get this position, you know?" Felicity removed her ponytail holder and rubbed the back of her head, which was now a little tender from having worn her hair up all day.

"We aren't going to put that negativity into the universe, Felicity. Do you hear me? Manifesting only positive vibes for our successful future is how we conquer things."

Felicity didn't want to tell her best friend since kindergarten that manifesting their future was what got them into the mess they were in with Isaac Keller in the first place. But as she looked around at the great business they'd built out of a basic worn out used food truck, she was too proud to have regret. She would rock that interview and get to the next level, no matter what she had to do.

But a zoom meeting at seven in the morning, after she'd stayed up all night researching ghostwriting, manufacturing companies, and baking four dozen amazing muffins, had her second-guessing herself when the bubbly woman welcomed her to the interview.

"Good morning, Ms. Storey-- long pause, then awkward face. "Um, Ms. Storey, you have something on your face right here," the job recruiter whispered as if they were meeting in person instead of over Zoom.

When Felicity grabbed her phone and looked at her face, there was pumpkin cream cheese filling smeared across her right cheek. "Thank you. Sorry, I was baking this morning."

Just when she thought the perky woman would thank her for her time and rush through the interview so she could throw Felicity's resume into the garbage, the lady lowered her eyes and said, "Oh, you're an early morning baker too? That. Is. awesome!"

Dang, Evie and her manifest your own destiny nonsense. Evie was going to positively manifest Felicity into the next round of cross-examinations or, as the job recruiter called it, meeting the boss.

Chapter Two

F elicity checked the address on the building against her GPS. It was correct. She was at *1 Canal Place* and needed to find somewhere to park. An inexpensive place, at that. She circled the block and saw the fee rate on the sign outside of the nearest parking garage. She couldn't be sure the company would comp her parking, and she didn't have twenty dollars to spare.

Evie had made it clear they weren't going to make enough money to pay their loan at the end of December to Baby Shark, if they didn't tighten their purse strings. Which meant every penny went into supplies for the coffee shop or the loan. Period.

Their luck had to come through eventually. Right? Just as she drove past the side of the multi-story building again, she finally caught a break. A huge town car pulled out from a larger than usual parking spot on the street in front of the building. She could absolutely slide her used Honda Civic in there. Thank goodness, it would be about fifteen dollars cheaper than the garage. She put on her blinker and began pulling into the perfect spot as she said in a sing-songy voice,

"Princess parking," which was the rule between her and her best friend whenever they got the spot closest to the door, anywhere.

But before she actually could slide into her space, an obnoxious black Suburban with tinted windows began backing into it and her car. She quickly threw her car into reverse but as she looked up, there was a city bus coming up behind her. That was when the land crusher crashed into her before settling into the only parking space within three city blocks of this building.

"No," she groaned and laid her forehead down on the steering wheel. She'd gotten there half an hour early so she wouldn't have to rush. Would she even make the interview now?

The driver of the offending SUV popped out shaking his head at her. "Not today, mister," she stepped out of her car and threw her hands up in the air as he flashed her a crooked grin.

"Forgot your glasses today?" she asked as she kept trying to remember that she had an important job interview waiting upstairs.

"Come on, sweetheart, didn't you see me parallel parking first?"

"Don't call me sweetheart. And you know I was here first, with my blinker on because you whipped around me and then backed up."

A police officer who'd apparently been across the street, came running over as if she and the guy were going to get into a fight. "Hey, hey, now. Let's all calm down," the young officer said as he gave them a stern look.

"Did you see him hit me?" Felicity asked but the policeman shook his head, no. "You can't tell me this fancy building doesn't have cameras," she added pointing at the building she needed to be walking into right now.

The other driver no longer smiled at her as he said, "Look lady, you're going to get me fired." Then he looked at the policeman. "You can see I'm clearly in the spot and she hit the corner of my vehicle."

"That's not--" before she could finish with that's not true, another man, a very handsome man with light brown hair and expensive sunglasses, stepped out of the SUV. He was wearing a charcoal colored suit with a red tie as he slipped his phone into his suit pocket. He stepped over to the police officer and shook his hand, never glancing Felicity's way.

She didn't hear his name but heard him explain that it was his car and driver. "I'm afraid I was on my phone when it happened, but there should be security footage."

"Now you're in trouble," Felicity pointed at the driver who was glaring her way.

The man in the suit finally looked at her. "Settle down there feisty one, I've got this."

Felicity couldn't believe the suit told her to settle down. In the history of the world has anyone calmed down because someone told them to calm down? She had an interview she was now going to be late for but here on the street in New Orleans at eight in the morning, audacity was at an all time high. She stepped in front of suit, facing the police officer and an arms reach from the rude driver who's face was now beat red as he looked like he was minutes away from cardiac arrest. She was not going to take the blame for an accident that wasn't her fault, especially since she'd lowered her insurance to only cover liability to save money.

"It seems like you are listening to everyone here except the person who was victimized. Is that because I'm a woman, Mr. Policeman? I have rights you know? And this, this, irritating man right here zoomed around me as I put on my blinker and began pulling into that spot! He not only didn't use his blinker but he bullied my little car by knocking us out of said premium spot with that giant gas guzzling monstrosity."

9

She heard the suit smirk, "Mr. Policeman," was he seriously going to make fun of her? She turned around and shushed him which made him smile even more. What the hell was going on around here? Did none of these people have more important things to do than make her miss her interview? Evie was going to kill her if she missed it and how would she explain that she'd been hit for trying to take the princess parking that was legally hers?

When Felicity turned around the police officer looked annoyed at her as he pulled out his notepad and started writing. "I will need to see your driver's licenses, car registration, and insurance, please."

"What? This wasn't my fault. That was my spot. I got there fair and square. He hit my car!"

The police officer held up his hand for her to stop. "Miss--"

"Felicity Storey," she answered him begrudgingly.

"Miss Storey, I wasn't just talking to you."

She looked up to see the other driver already handing his documents over. He looked so smug that she wanted to slug him in his crooked teeth.

Suit reached over and thanked the officer, then asked if he needed anything else from him because he was late for a meeting.

Of course. Like she didn't have someplace else better to be.

Suit told the rude driver he would see him upstairs and nodded at Felicity who turned her head and ignored him.

It took another half hour before the police officer finished writing down all of their information and then she still had to move her car because the jerk who had hit her refused to move. So much for princess parking. Felicity sure didn't feel like a princess anymore.

She was officially late for her interview and after all of that still had to pay twenty dollars because the only place left to park was the super expensive parking garage.

As she walked into the lobby where she had her 8:30 A M

sharp, interview the secretary fake smiled at her as she called Mr. Ira Sutton to tell him his 8:30 had finally shown up at almost nine.

Felicity wanted to walk right out as the woman kept looking up and staring at her. There weren't any other candidates in the lobby and it took twenty-five minutes before the secretary spoke to her again saying, "Ira will be out to see you in a few minutes."

So, it's Ira now, not Mr. Sutton? Maybe the secretary had a thing going on with her boss. Maybe she didn't like the idea of a female writer interviewing for the job and traveling around with the CEO? Felicity had made up an entire scenario of how the secretary was having a hot affair with Mr. Ira Sutton, CEO, and how the tawdry affair was known through out the office and even to the cheating secretary's husband. Then a leggy strawberry-blonde came walking out. *Were all the women there attractive?*

Felicity wasn't dog meat. Sure she only wore a little mascara and tinted lip gloss most of the time but she had blue-green eyes and good skin. Besides her hair was thick and wavy, some said her best feature, and that morning her natural auburn highlights were glossy and on point. She didn't have on stiletto's like strawberry shortcake over there but she had borrowed a cute green dress from Evie Mae that accentuated her figure in a professional way.

The handsome man walking behind strawberry, she couldn't call her shortcake anymore because she was really tall, was only a couple of inches taller than her but he was all smiles as he said they would be in touch and then he warmly introduced himself to Felicity.

"Hey, I'm Ira Sutton. You ready?"

Felicity gave him her best smile as she nodded and followed him back into the inner sanctum of the office. It was a nice modern looking area, with large cubicles with sleek looking desks and chairs. But Ira Sutton didn't work out in that area with the masses, he led her into a private office with two large desks across from each other then through to another even fancier office that overlooked part of downtown and the river.

"Please have a seat, Ms. Storey. Can I get you anything? Water? Coffee?"

Were all CEOs that nice? Perhaps this job really was meant for her. He seemed so laid back and perhaps traveling wouldn't be such a chore?

"No, thank you," she said as she watched him pull out a printed copy of her resume.

"Well, alright lets get right to it."

Felicity sat forward in her seat as Ira Sutton pulled out the large leather chair that looked a bit too big for him and sat down. "Mr. Sutton, if you don't mind, I'd like to first apologize for being late."

He gave her the funniest grin, "Oh, don't worry. I have already heard all about it. Something about someone trying to steal your princess parking spot?"

There was something about the way he smiled at her that made her nervous. How did he know what had happened or that she called it princess parking? And why was he being so nice to her? Over the phone they had made such a big deal about being on time and she'd been half an hour later than scheduled.

It was then that she heard the irritating voice of that rude driver and then The Suit, telling him to lower his voice. She turned around and could see the back of handsome suit guy standing there and scolding the driver before he fired him.

When Felicity turned around to look at Ira Sutton, she thought his face would split from smiling so big. Then Suit walked in the door and Ira stood up from the desk and handed her resume over. Ira winked at Felicity before he headed toward the door, Hudson Frost this is Felicity Storey. Felicity Storey this is our CEO, Mr. Hudson Frost.

Felicity watched Suit, Hudson Frost, walk around the desk. Had she shushed him out on the street in front of the police officer? And had he just fired his driver before he walked into the room with her?

When he sat down at his desk and finally locked eyes with Felicity, she was pretty sure this CEO was about to hand her the interview from hell.

Why did she let Evie talk her into this anyway? She could run the coffee shop and Evie could get a job. Everything in their lives for the next two years didn't really hinge on this going well.

Did it?

Chapter Three

Felicity sat back in her chair as she studied Hudson Frost, CEO. He looked older in his sunglasses. More handsome too, she thought and smirked because she was absolutely lying to herself. He pierced her with his dark eyes and she wished she knew what he was thinking.

"Miss Storey," was all he said and then looked down at her resume again. "So your name is Felicity Storey and you're a writer?"

She bit her bottom lip to keep from making the smart mouth comment on the tip of her tongue. What was wrong with her? Why did she feel the need to argue with him? Was it the way he'd dismissed her when he'd stepped out of the SUV that morning and walked directly over to the policeman? Or maybe it was the way he told her to settle down. Whatever it was, she truly needed this job and had to swallow some of that dang pride.

He looked at her expectantly and that was when Felicity realized he meant for her to answer the question.

"Sorry. I thought that was rhetorical. Yes, my name is Felicity Storey and I am in fact, a writer."

He grinned and she knew he wanted to get into it with her too. The tension in the room was palpable.

"Tell me Miss Storey, what have you been doing since you graduated in May?"

The way he kept emphasizing her name, *Storey*, made her want to yell *"What is your deal?"* at him.

Instead, Felicity took a deep cleansing breath before she answered, "My best friend from school and I opened a small coffee shop and it took most of the summer to get things ready for the opening."

"Maisonville?" he asked, looking down again at her resume. Had he not looked at it until now?

"Yes, I grew up there."

"You're not talking about Espresso to Geaux are you?"

Felicity stared at him for a bit too long before she answered him. "You've been to my coffee truck?"

He smiled and that time it warmed up his golden brown eyes. "The first week it opened. My folks have a house on the river and I have to tell you, we were thrilled when you guys started. Good coffee and that croissant donut was amazing."

The croissant donut had been her idea after seeing an ad for one in New York. She didn't make them every morning but at least once a week she fried them up on the spot.

"So things aren't working out with your partner, Miss Storey? Why are you looking for another job?"

This was the strangest job interview she'd ever been on and honestly, the most important one. It must be the reason all his questions felt so personal. "Evie, my business partner and I need to get ahead of some bills for the business. I really am a writer, it's my first love and so I was the logical choice to leave."

"So you aren't looking for a long term position?"

"Why would you think that?" *Felicity tried to smile, she really did, but his question didn't make sense. She was applying for a full time position and didn't that imply she was looking for long term employment?*

"Once you get ahead of those bills as you put it, then I presume you will want to get back to the coffee truck business?"

"That was honestly, Evie's dream. But I didn't have any other offers at the time."

He still didn't look convinced and she needed to turn this around. *Come on, Storey, you need this job,* she chanted in her head.

Locking onto his stare, she smiled that time, genuinely. "Mr. Frost, I'm captivated by story and an extensive reader. I've spent the last two days learning as much as possible about your company's manufacturing business but couldn't find much of an online image anywhere. The job posting mentioned I would need to handle your email correspondence, speeches, social media, and video content. But we could work on starting a youtube channel for you or the business. I successfully did all of that in college but when Evie and I came up with the coffee truck idea, I began documenting the entire process and between you and me, scripted it perfectly to draw more views and build excitement for our opening. By the time we were ready to launch, other social media influencers called and wanted to be a part of the grand opening. It was free advertisement, helped us build our brand, and we were able to blow out our opening projections, especially in our small town."

Hudson Frost flashed a movie star grin at Felicity and her stomach instantly felt hollow. She bit her lip to keep herself grounded in the moment.

"We've never looked at social media content as strongly as I would have liked. You have my attention, Miss Storey. Where would you start with a YouTube channel?"

Yes, she was back in the running, she could feel it. "People love to feel connected. While I couldn't find the origin story about the company, we could dig into it and see if it was worth using. I know the company has deep humanitarian interests and we could focus on it, maybe use employees and how they are making a difference."

He was sitting forward in his chair now and giving her a serious look. It made her a bit nervous but she pushed on. She was a great writer,young and ambitious. Writing social media content was easy for her and as a side hustle she shined in that arena.

"Of course, that's just off the top of my head. We could brainstorm and really come up with the image or brand you would like to put forward for the company."

He examined her resume for a fourth time and didn't look at her when he said, "I travel extensively and expect my ghostwriter to accompany me. How do you feel about traveling and will your significant other be okay with you working right up to the holiday?"

"I love to travel," she said a little too quickly. The furthest she'd ever traveled was the one time she went to Orange Beach, Alabama with Evie Mae's family, but she was sure she would love to travel if she ever got the opportunity. She kept grinning like a fool and then remembered the second part of the question. "I don't have a significant other, just a mom who will work every day except Christmas. She won't mind."

He nodded and she no longer could tell if this was going her way or not. Hudson Frost might be a young CEO but he had a game face that didn't give anything away.

When he abruptly stood, she did too. "I apologize for my driver's behavior this morning. But-"

How had she already forgotten about the crazy accident with his SUV that morning? Of course he wasn't going to hire her. He'd just fired his own personal driver for the accident. This interview was just to save face in the event she tried to complain about being overlooked because of the fender bender.

"Miss Storey?"

She looked up to see his concerned expression, "You okay?"

She never could hide how she felt and at that moment the disappointment over not getting a job that she might have loved, was there. She nodded at him but knew she didn't look convincing.

"I was saying that I apologize for my driver's behavior. But when security pulled the tape, he clearly and illegally whipped around you so he could snag that parking spot. It was clear on the video that he did in fact, hit your car and the accident was his or rather our fault."

While she'd temporarily forgotten all about the accident there wasn't much else he could have said that would have been better. She nodded back at him for fear she wouldn't say the right thing. Especially since she wanted to cheer in the air that she was right and they'd been wrong at the scene. Not to mention she wouldn't have to worry about not having full coverage insurance because his insurance would have to pay for it.

"I'll have Ira let you know when he gets in touch with our insurance so we can take care of the damage to your car."

"Thank you," Felicity said, before she followed him into the outer office he turned around surprising her.

"And Miss Storey, you could have parked in the garage. We validate."

She didn't know what to say, was he still mad about the incident? He was impossible to read but at least the interview had mostly been painless.

So what if she didn't get the job. She had come close. She could feel it. Next time, she told herself and then tried to focus on the positive. At least she wouldn't have to worry about the damage to her car.

Standing in front of Ira Sutton, she could now see clearly that he was Hudson's very capable assistant. He smiled her way and then toward his boss.

"You were right, Ira. Set it up for tomorrow morning," Hudson said cryptically to his assistant and then turned toward her and reached out his hand.

She shook his hand firmly, something Evie Mae's dad had taught them both to do and made them practice with him and Evie's brother.

Hudson gave her a sly smile and then thanked her for coming in. Before letting go of her hand he leaned in and whispered, "The building security cameras are state-of-the-art. If you are on the street out front, even inside your car, they can hear what you're saying." He stepped back, turned, and left without another word, leaving Felicity speechless.

It wasn't until Ira stood up and called her name that Felicity realized she was watching Hudson walk back into his office.

When she turned to look at Ira, he smiled. "Don't be embarrassed. We all loved that you called it princess parking. The female security guard typed it into the computer screen so the spot is officially named that from here on out.

Felicity shook her head. It wasn't the first time she'd embarrassed herself and certainly wouldn't be the last. She'd learned a long time ago to just roll with it.

Evie would always say that if your going to do the walk of shame, hold your head up high and do it like a boss. She liked the way that sounded and worked at being comfortable in her own skin, especially since her bitter breakup last year.

Ira handed Felicity a folder with some company information. "The good news is that you're making it to the last round of interviews. If you want this job, Felicity Storey, it is yours for the taking. I think he really liked you. He never interviews a candidate himself."

Ira got her attention with that little tidbit of inside information. She knew she liked Ira Sutton from the moment she'd met him. "Hey, Ira? How many of us are coming back tomorrow?"

Ira winked at her. "Just two, you and Sierra Colson who you saw me walking out this morning."

Strawberry not shortcake made it to the final round too.

Felicity thanked Ira and told him she would see him in the morning. Now she had to spend the forty-five minutes driving back to Maisonville trying to figure out how to tell Evie everything that had happened.

Chapter Four

W hat happened to your car, Fe?" Evie asked before
Felicity could get inside the food truck and put on
an apron.

There was a line of seven people in front of Evie Mae
and another five waiting for their orders, but she could talk and
whip up a latte in her sleep.

Felicity tied the black apron with Espresso to Geaux written
in what looked like white chalk paint and began pulling out
pastries and donuts to help fill the orders.

"You won't believe the morning I've had," she explained as
they took the rest of the orders and got everyone taken care of in
less than fifteen minutes.

Once the crowd was gone, Evie cut her eyes to examine her
friend. "You didn't go on that interview, did you?"

"Of course, I did. Mr. CEO, I'm too sexy for my suit, was in
the SUV that hit me."

Evie shook her head, horrified to hear the rest of the story.
Felicity didn't leave out one single detail.

"So, are you and the leggy blonde going to have to fight to the death over the position or what?"

It didn't matter whether she had a death match coming up tomorrow with Strawberry not Shortcake, Evie expected her to pull out all the stops for this job.

Sipping an Americano with pumpkin whip, Felicity leaned back against the butcher block counter that Mitch Shepard had sanded and sealed by hand until it was perfect. "I don't want you to get your hopes up, Evie. I mean, Ira seemed to really like me and must have picked me from the crowd if the cryptic comment from Frost was any indication. And Ira did say the job was mine for the taking. But that woman was something else. Like beauty queen pretty and I'm not sure if I can compete with that or if its just about the writing anymore."

Evie drank her coffee black which was a sign she was stressed. "It's never just about the job, Felicity and you know it. But if you shushed him and caused him to fire his driver, and he still met with you, that means something."

"He wants to torture me slowly by making me feel like I have a shot just to hire the hot chick?"

"Maybe."

"You're not making me feel better, Evie."

"That's not my job. My job as your best friend is to tell you the truth. And here is a little truth bomb, we have less than one hundred dollars in our business checking account. I have less than fifty in my personal account. If you don't get this job then we can't buy more supplies to make coffees, teas, or pastries and then we won't pay our loan on time. Do you want to work for Isaac Keller for the next two years?"

There were only a few things Felicity wanted less than that and Evie knew it. She'd never understood why Evie remained friends with Isaac. He was awful and whenever he came around, Felicity would find an excuse to leave.

But Evie Mae was right and they'd both signed that contract with Isaac Keller. She had no choice but to go back for the interview and earn that job. Until then, she was going to film a fifteen minute video, called A Day in the Life, of a Coffee Truck Barista. She just needed to give Evie the script she'd written up and get to it.

Seven-thirty the next morning, Felicity arrived back at 1 Canal Place. She'd parked in the garage and made her way toward the offices on the tenth floor. When she got there, the front door was unlocked but the receptionist hadn't arrived yet. So, she took a seat and pulled out her journal to write some notes.

"Early bird?" Hudson said as he stood in front of her.

He had on a gray suit with a green tie. Clearly, Hudson Frost had a strong sense of style and whoever tailored his clothes, knew what they were doing because they fit him perfectly. Felicity stood to greet him. "When I need to be, I guess."

"Me too, Miss Storey," he seemed to look at her harder than before and she had to look away. She wasn't shy but it felt a little unnerving.

"Why don't you come on back and sit in Ira's office. He'll be in soon and can make some coffee," he grinned. "Not that it will be as good as you're used to but it'll do in a rush."

She didn't miss how he sort of complimented her coffee again. She was proud of the coffee truck and had worked hard with Evie to make it happen.

It wasn't long when Ira Sutton walked in. He gave her a genuine smile and then crooked his head for her to follow him. "Making brownie points already, I see," Ira told her as he pulled out a standard coffee filter, prefilled with ground coffee and plopped it into the office machine. She made a mental note to get them a glass carafe, and kettle to show Ira how to make a simple pour-over.

"I really need this job, Ira, and didn't want to be late again.

And honestly, I live on the other side of the lake and never know how to gauge the bridge traffic."

He nodded, "Twenty-four miles of bridge is no joke." He handed over a mug of stout coffee for her to add-in whatever she wanted and while he made his own cup and what she assumed was a cup for Hudson Frost, he confided in her. "Your writing credentials were better than any other candidate but you didn't have much job experience. But all of us really enjoy your social media content and that will go a long way with the boss."

Felicity had spent all of high school and college continuing to write articles for the local paper and then online magazines. If she'd been born in another place and time, she would've loved a career as a hard news journalist with a side-hustle of crafting her novels under a pen name. Writing for those publications, although small, had kept her writing muscle sharp and gave her a strong bi-line when applying for this job so maybe, just maybe, it was more about the writing than she'd first thought?

Suddenly, it registered what he'd just said. "Wait a minute, you and Mr. Frost have watched my social media?"

Ira grinned. "You betcha."

Felicity thought back to everything she'd posted for Espresso to Geaux and how she'd grown the audience to well over fifty thousand in just a few months.

"And he liked the Coffee Truck videos?"

"Who wouldn't. They were smart and creative but you and that cute friend of yours are authentic and most everyone in the main office are rooting for you. We had seven people take the morning off the day you opened so they could join in the launch fun. Between you and me, though, I think its the other videos that got to Hudson. The ones with your rescue dog."

"Winston?" Felicity couldn't help the giant smile on her face. He'd been the best thing that had happened to her last year after her break-up.

"The talking husky," Ira laughed. "He's brilliant. And the way you saved him was admirable."

"He honestly saved me," she whispered more to herself than to Ira.

Thankfully, Ira didn't ask her to elaborate.

"Well, Hudson is partial to him. He's also a big donor to all the local shelters, so you won points there."

The videos of Winston were on her personal Instagram and Tik Tok pages. They were both public but the idea of Hudson Frost, CEO, watching her there felt personal.

Ira led her back into his inner sanctum, taking a moment to run coffee in to Hudson and then closing the door between their offices as he returned.

He pulled a chair for Felicity beside him as he explained the manufacturing company ins and outs then how they set aside twenty-five percent of their profits for their philanthropic efforts. Hudson's father who started the company had instituted it in honor of his wife. Hudson's mother believed it was their duty as humans to leave the world better than they found it.

It was the driving force for her to finally retire a few years ago at the same time as her husband, Harry Frost. He appointed their son as CEO. They wanted to travel internationally to see first hand what some of their efforts had accomplished and where they could help more.

Taking notes so she could figure out how to create a company vibe for social media, Felicity had her head down and didn't notice when Sierra Colson arrived.

"You two look cozy," Sierra sneered. "What's up, Ira?"

"You made it just in time," Ira said locking eyes with her.

"Always do." Sierra grinned with the confidence of a woman who knew her worth.

Did they know each other before the interview process?

Felicity hadn't picked up on that yesterday but then again she was a little flustered from the fender bender.

"I'll let Hudson know you're both ready. We--," before he could finish his sentence, Sierra stepped forward with her stare focused on Felicity.

"I'm Sierra Colson. And you are-"

Not intimidated by you and your perfectness at all, Felicity wanted to say. Evie Mae would have pushed her to do it too. But they honestly believed in building other women up and admiring them for admitting what they may need to make themselves feel better. Clearly attention was what Sierra Colson needed.

"Hi, I'm Felicity Storey."

"You're training for an assistant position?" Sierra pointedly asked.

"No, Sierra. She's here for the ghostwriter spot, just like you," Ira answered.

Sierra nodded. "Storey. That's cute."

She didn't say it necessarily mean, and honestly, the fact that Felicity was a writer and her last name was Storey, was cute. So she decided to take it as a compliment. "Thank you."

Hudson Frost must have heard them or maybe Ira texted him because he opened his door and stepped into the office with that same CEO air he usually entered a room with, at least to Felicity.

"Good morning, Hudson," Sierra's voice seemed a little sweeter when she saw him.

"Morning, Sierra," Hudson responded but Felicity didn't detect any change in his voice. *That was good, wasn't it?*

"Ira. Can I speak to you in my office for a minute?" Hudson asked and Ira was already heading his direction. Those two always seemed in sinc and Felicity wasn't sure but they seemed like friends more than boss and employee.

"You ladies get to know each other. We'll be a few minutes,"

Ira said as he followed Hudson back inside and shut the door behind him.

Once they were left alone, Sierra seemed to set her sights on Felicity. "So tell me what I need to know about you, my little competition."

Chapter Five

Cutting her eyes at Sierra, Felicity sat up taller in her chair. She'd given the tall woman a lot of grace for the last five minutes but Sierra was going to make her step down to her level.

Noticing the way Felicity was staring back at her, Sierra shook her head. "Oh, I'm just kidding, seriously," Sierra dismissed the negative vibes Felicity was sending her way as she sat down in one of the chairs across from Ira's desk.

"How do you know Ira?" Felicity went straight to what she wanted to know.

"He didn't tell you?" she asked pausing for dramatic affect. "I know the whole crew around here."

It was worse than Felicity had thought. She was competing with someone who had both feet in the door.

"I work with the head of warehousing and wanted to make a change. Our company promotes from within, primarily, before going outside to find candidates."

I and *our*, she wanted Felicity to feel intimidated but she had no idea the strong stock that made her. Felicity not smiling asked, "So you're a writer?"

"I dabble, but how hard can it be? I mean, I have a bachelors degree in history and had to write all the time for my major. I can certainly handle email correspondences and social media. Besides, I am somewhat of an influencer with my fashion blog."

Okay, it was official, Felicity really didn't like Sierra. And, any job that Sierra was being considered for most likely wouldn't be the one for Felicity. They were worlds apart. The writing was the whole reason Felicity wanted to be there. Well, that and the money. But building the company's social media presence and image was exciting to her and clearly that wasn't important to Sierra.

The woman also couldn't read the room as Felicity sat back in her chair wishing she'd stop talking or that Ira or even Hudson would come back and interrupt.

Strawberry not Shortcake went on and on, blah, blah, blah, until she said something that got Felicity's attention.

"And of course, getting to travel with Hudson Frost sounds exactly like the job where I could excel. I'm sure you've noticed how handsome the CEO for our company is, and wow, is he rich."

Was she for real? "This isn't a dating app," Felicity said.

"Speak for yourself." Sierra flipped her super shiny strawberry blonde tresses over her shoulder. "It would be a hell of a bonus to get to spend more time with him and if things grow into more, well then, I am here for it."

Felicity couldn't believe this woman was admitting she wanted to land the boss. Of course, Evie Mae Shepard would say you have to manifest your own destiny and put into the universe what you want in order to make it happen. But this was taking it a bit too far. Wasn't it? Besides, Felicity was a strong, fierce, independent woman and making her own way was important to her.

Her father, or as she liked to call him, her sperm donor, had taught her that men don't stay. If she hadn't learned the lesson well enough her ex-boyfriend put the exclamation point on it.

Hadn't anyone told Sierra that standing on her own two feet was important to her well being? Felicity's mother had certainly told her that enough.

Sierra was irritating to say the least but Felicity was starting to feel bad for her. Didn't she have a good girl friend? A best friend that would tell her how important it was to follow her dreams and make it on her own, first? Sure, if you found the right person then it could work but wouldn't you want to be a strong partner?

As Sierra explained how she was looking for a man to take care of her like her father had her mother, it was obvious that they would never see eye to eye on the subject. So, Felicity sat there looking over her notes as Strawberry filled the air with how she wanted to decorate her mansion and dress her children.

Thirty-seven and a half minutes later, the door to Hudson's office finally opened. Sierra who had been completely absorbed in her own words jumped to her feet faster than anything Felicity had seen before. She had to hand it to her, Sierra was a woman on a mission. Felicity could only hope that if she didn't get the job, hopefully Sierra could close the relationship deal quickly and the ghostwriter spot would open up again.

Ira walked out first and ignored Sierra who wasn't looking at him anyway. But the way he rolled his eyes like he was irritated and then grimaced at Felicity didn't get her hopes up that things were going to go her way.

Hudson told them both to come into his office as he held the door, but never made eye contact with Felicity who was studying his face. Suddenly, she wanted to leave. Why make her go through the humiliation of sitting there with the beauty queen as he told Felicity she didn't get the job?

Oh, yeah, right, the car accident. Perhaps he was worried she would sue the company? She'd heard of people doing stuff like that but she wasn't looking for something for nothing.

Before he closed the door, she shook her head and walked right past him and didn't stop until she hit the hallway.

That was when Ira caught up to her and stopped her. "What's wrong?"

"What do you mean? He's going to hire Strawberry not Shortcake in there and I can't witness that nonsense. Did you know she wants four kids? She's already looking at H names so they can have the same initials as their dad. As in, Hudson." Felicity was ready to explode.

When Ira began laughing she turned and stormed off. The elevator opened when she heard her name.

"Felicity Storey!"

She turned to see Hudson Frost. Was he angry? *Whatever.* She wasn't hanging around for anymore nonsense. She had a coffee business that she needed to save and some social media algorithms to figure out. She could drum up the business they needed. *Couldn't she?*

She stepped into the elevator but before the doors closed, Hudson stepped inside with her. He was staring her down when he hit the emergency stop button and Felicity froze.

"This thing could plummet to the ground! What are you thinking?" She could feel herself hyperventilating.

When she sat down on the floor, Hudson knelt in front of her. "It's safe, I promise."

She couldn't breathe and little white flecks started swimming around in her eyes. The next thing she knew, the doors were opening and he was carrying her out the front doors of the building.

Two security guards met them at the concrete bench, near the sidewalk as she gripped Hudson's arm.

Was she in trouble?

One of the guards handed her a bottle of water and the other asked if he should call 911.

"Oh gosh, no. What happened?" Felicity closed her eyes and the last five minutes that had been a blur, came back to her.

She sat up on the bench and then punched Hudson's arm. "Why would you ever hit that emergency button?"

He laughed and shook his head. "You were running away and I wanted to talk to you."

"You couldn't have just ridden down in that metal death trap with me and talk?"

"That's where I know you from!" the female security guard blurted out. "You're Princess Parking."

Felicity gave the woman a slight nod.

"Girl, you had us laughing all day."

"Perfect," Felicity said under her breath but Hudson heard her.

"I think Miss Storey is fine now. Thank you both for coming to our rescue."

The security duo nodded. "Our pleasure, Mr. Frost," and "Anytime," they each said as they headed back inside the building.

Hudson fixed Felicity with a hard stare now that they were alone. At least as alone as they could be sitting on a public concrete bench.

"I apologize, Miss Storey. I didn't know you had a fear of elevators."

"Who said I have a fear of elevators? I'm fine with elevators. In fact, they don't bother me at all. As long as they are moving and not being stopped in the middle of floors nine and ten."

Hudson shook his head. She was one of the most infuriating people he'd ever met. It was a good thing she was cute. He shook his head. She wasn't cute, she was gorgeous, but he couldn't think that way, especially if he was going to hire her.

"Whatever you say, Miss Storey."

"And stop calling me, Miss Storey. My name is Felicity."

He wanted to argue that her name was also Storey but he didn't.

"Alright, Felicity. Want to tell me what happened up there?"

She shook her head. Sure she could tell him all about the wedding plans Sierra had plotted out for them, but it was against girl code.

"Have you changed your mind about the job? Do you not need the money for Espresso to Geaux?"

She didn't like the way he was looking at her. He was close enough for her to smell his scent which was a mix of sandalwood and whatever God had blessed him with naturally. It was lethal and a lady killer for sure. Drawing her in so he could crush her, no doubt.

Felicity shivered as the wind blew through them and she tried to stop thinking about how good he smelled.

"It's cold out here, Miss-- I mean, Felicity. Can we go back in and talk? Please? Give me another chance?"

Felicity nodded her head. When she popped up off the bench, he quickly sidled up next to her to make sure she was steady.

She nodded to let him know she was okay and then walked beside him back into the building. When he pressed the button to call the elevator, he looked at her.

"I told you, I'm fine with elevators," she said staring into his eyes and daring him to contradict her.

He grinned as he held the door for her to walk in first, then several more people stepped inside. As the doors slowly closed she leaned in closer and whispered, "Don't even think about pushing that button, Frost."

Chapter Six

F elicity and Sierra both stared back at Hudson Frost, neither one believing what he was saying. How on Earth could he want to hire them both?

They were as different as night and day. Would they split duties or have to work on things together like a team. A team of two people who didn't like each other.

Felicity shook her head. "I can't take a full time job for half the pay. Especially if I also have to travel and be away from home all the time."

"I'm not asking you to take a pay cut, Miss Storey. After talking to Ira, I realized that I might have underestimated the amount of work this position would require. But this ghost-writer spot is important to me and I want to make sure that I set the writer up in the best possible way to be successful. This will be a trial period of 30 days. If at the end of the thirty days, it doesn't work out, then we can rethink the position. I'll give severance pay to either of you if you choose to walk away or if it isn't what I need, but only after that thirty days so you'll have to stick around."

Sierra sat there watching Hudson as he talked about the duties and the possibility of letting one of them go. "Will we both travel? I mean, I was looking forward to the travel component of this position."

Hudson stared at her for a moment. "Yes, you both will travel."

Sierra huffed, clearly not liking his answer. Obviously, three's a crowd and having Felicity there was going to put a kink in Sierra's plans to seduce the boss.

Felicity looked away from Sierra when she felt Hudson staring at her. "So, when will we get started?"

"Personally, I would like you to start as soon as possible. I think Sierra has to give Rob in the warehouse some notice, but I have a trip to Brownsville Vermont scheduled in a few weeks. I'm hosting a small conference there for the philanthropic side of our company and have some donors that I would like to pitch some programs to in the area.

"We'll need to get everything set up and usually Ira takes care of a lot of it himself. However, I need you two to pitch in and help fill his spot because he can't travel this year that close to Christmas. But I also need some media out to all the attendees to get everyone pumped up about the event. Maybe put together some itinerary notes, or perhaps think of a creative way to handle those in a social media blitz?"

Hudson was pacing back and forth as he seemed to be brainstorming ideas for this conference.

He didn't seem like the type of person to do things last minute and it made Felicity curious about the entire event.

Hudson stopped to make sure they were both still with him. He was staring at Felicity specifically and she nodded to let him know she understood this was serious. "Ira has the details. But make no mistake, this isn't going to be an easy job. There will be long days and I expect you both to pitch in where you're needed.

But I think it will test your skills. It will also be an indicator of how you work together and perform under pressure."

"Cool as a cucumber, Hudson," Sierra said using that sugary sweet voice she seemed to save for him.

Felicity watched him to see if he noticed but if he had, he hid it well.

"We will work closely together but I also expect you both to take initiative when it comes to this upcoming project. I am booked most of the morning but Ira has your new hire packets with your pay and benefits details. You will need to sign nondisclosure agreements since you will handle sensitive information. Are there any questions?"

Felicity stood and Sierra quickly followed.

"Thank you for the opportunity, Mr. Frost," Felicity said but before she turned around to head toward the door, Sierra patted the top of her head.

"You're just so cute," Sierra said and when she looked at Hudson that time, he did seem irritated.

"You're welcome, Felicity," he said and as she headed out the door to meet with Ira, she heard him tell Sierra to stay there for a minute.

Then he walked over and closed his door.

Ira stood as soon as he saw Felicity exit Hudson's office without Sierra. "How are you?" he asked.

"Good. Surprised, I guess."

"I tried to give you a signal when I came out of there."

Felicity smiled. She really did like Ira. "Sorry, Ira. You probably need to know that I am not a signal girl. I also don't take hints very well either. I totally misread that situation and thought you were saying that Sierra got the job instead of me."

He pretended to write something down, saying, "Note to self, Felicity can't take a hint. Be blunt."

She laughed and shook her head. "Anyway, I don't know

what is going on in there but I'm certain she is thrilled to be alone with him."

"He's not interested in dating her. She's made passes at him before. Office Christmas Party 2021. He turned her down flat. But we have a policy that if a job can be filled from within the company, the employee has to be interviewed and given a shot. His father did it, and Hudson agreed that it was one of the things that has kept employee morale high."

"It's a great opportunity for me. And I'm excited to get started, so where is this paperwork?"

Ira handed her the new hire packet and told her she could take her time filling it out. He got her set up at the desk opposite him and that was when Sierra walked out of Hudson's office. She avoided their eyes as she walked out the door without a word to Ira or Felicity.

Hudson stepped into the room and told them that Sierra needed a moment and would be right back. Then he closed his door.

Ira made exaggerated big eyes at Felicity but neither of them said a word about what might have happened.

Once Sierra returned, Ira gave her some papers so she could review the change in position and salary increase.

He also handed Felicity the details sheet regarding her salary and benefits and she quickly looked up at him.

"Is something wrong, Felicity?" Ira asked.

Sierra looked over to make sure Felicity wasn't making more than her.

"It's the same amount, Sierra," he said dryly.

"Are you certain this is right?" Felicity asked. "I mean-" Sierra interrupted before she could finished her thought.

"I thought it would be more too, since we are working with the head boss but I guess they really did split the salary between us." Sierra rolled her eyes as she signed her name to her salary changes and promotion.

Felicity shook her head. That wasn't what she meant at all. She'd never dreamed the position would pay $70,000 plus potential bonuses and benefits. It was generous and she couldn't wait to tell Evie. They wouldn't have to worry about the loan to Baby Shark anymore. She could cover it.

"You alright?" Ira asked studying Felicity's face.

"Yes. Great," she said, stopping short of singing the answer back to him. She'd do anything this job required for that kind of money but they didn't need to know that.

"Alright. Hudson asked me to go over the NDA because it is nonnegotiable. He's quite serious about his privacy. The fact that you two will have access to his emails and company information makes this a legal matter if you discuss any of it. I repeat, if you discuss anything with anyone except for him or each other without his expressed permission."

The nondisclosure agreement was two pages long and must have been drafted by an attorney. Felicity signed it without hesitation and when she looked up, she saw Sierra signing it too.

"Alright the legal stuff is done so let's discuss the conference."

"Why all the way in Vermont?" Sierra asked. "It's going to be miserably cold and we'll miss the company Christmas party."

"Nope. The party is this Saturday, Sierra. You would know that if you looked at company emails."

"I've never seen snow. Do you think it'll be snowing?" Felicity couldn't hide her excitement.

"It's actually snowing there now," Ira showed her pictures.

Felicity put her hand over her heart. "I wish Winston could see snow."

"Your boyfriend?" Sierra asked.

Ira and Felicity both laughed.

"The love of my life," Felicity answered and Ira laughed again.

They spent the next hour and a half going over the conference details that Ira had already worked out. Hudson invited thirty of their best clients and past donors to attend. Reservations had already been made for all the attendees along with two assistants which were now Sierra and Felicity at the largest hotel in town. It was beautiful and had a wonderful view of the ski slopes. The conference would last two and a half days, although most would arrive the day before and leave on Sunday after the morning events.

Ira handed them each a basic itenerary that he'd scheduled and was preapproved by Hudson. "You can see the first day will start with a breakfast in the main dining room of the hotel. Hudson will need a speech that includes a thank you for coming and continuing to be a part of the Giving Campaign. He likes to discuss the history of the giving program which usually includes the total dollar amount donated by the members since its inception."

Felicity read ahead on the information sheet Ira had handed them. "Whoa, it's been going on for thirty years and they've donated more than seventy-five million dollars?"

Ira smiled at her. He knew from her social media that she had a giving heart, mostly for animals. She had tears in her eyes as she whispered, "What incredible people his parents are for starting something like this when she was just a teacher and his father had barely turned a profit."

"You'll get to meet them at the Christmas party," Ira told her and watched as she grinned and did a little wiggle in her chair at the thought she would get to meet them.

Sierra just watched Felicity and shook her head.

"After the history, Hudson announces which cause won the Spotlight Award."

Felicity highlighted that section. "It's awarded to the charity that has made the most progress or is doing the best job after receiving their financial gift." Then she gasped, "They then get a twenty-five percent bonus for Christmas." She looked up at Ira and shook her head. She had chill bumps on her arms. "That is so incredible."

"You alright?" Ira asked, wishing Hudson could see her. He would regret questioning whether or not she would stick around after a few months if he'd known how the charity side of the job would bind her to the company.

"Great, Ira. I'm just so impressed, you know?" Felicity smiled so much her face must hurt and Ira couldn't help but feel it too. He'd liked her for the job when he saw she'd gone to college at his alma mater. But after watching her videos on-line, he was certain she was a perfect fit for this position.

Sierra seemed impatient as she rolled her eyes at Felicity. "We have a lot to get through. Why don't you two sing your Kum ba yah song after we are done?"

Ira ignored Sierra. He figured she wouldn't make it to the end of the thirty day trial period and it would be great to finally be rid of her for good. He only wished he could tell Felicity that as she looked hurt over her callous behavior.

"You two will need to put together the slide show that goes along with that announcement. It should highlight all of their triumphs and amazing people."

Both Sierra and Felicity wrote that information down and when he saw them finish he added, "It'll be followed by an update on all the other groups that received donations. It's very important to Hudson that none of them are left out. A couple of years ago it happened and many questioned the administration of those funds might need to go to someone else." Ira didn't tell them that was the year Hudson had been made CEO. He'd been twenty-six and many had questioned his ability to handle something so important. Sure he'd worked for his father since he was a kid and knew their business inside and out. He'd also worked for the company since he'd graduated college as he worked on his MBA at night. But the Giving Program had grown into its own over the past twenty years and many felt like it was too important for someone so young to oversee.

"These updates sometimes include personal letters from people who have benefited directly from their generosity. In the past it has been a highlight of the event but it can make everyone emotional," Ira said pausing to make sure they were taking notes on that too.

"Finally there is a short discussion period before they receive a gourmet box lunch and then break for several hours. Before they leave out, they receive a folder with names of organizations with detailed descriptions to consider for next years endowments."

"So they don't help the same groups the next year?" Felicity asked.

"Sometimes. But there are a lot of great causes."

Felicity nodded as she made some notes. She looked so serious and Ira appreciated it especially since Sierra was currently on her phone.

The group will break until the next morning. While we don't have a set event Friday night, many break out into small groups.

Saturday morning, they can choose from several events. There is snow skiing, snow mobile riding, snow shoe hiking, and a spa treatment offered. They are free for lunch and then we get back together at dinner time. I've already booked several carriages pulled by reindeer to take the group to dinner at the private house where Hudson is staying."

Sierra's head popped up. "He won't be staying at the hotel with us?"

Ira shook his head but didn't answer her. "This dinner will be a culinary experience prepared by a local chef using locally sourced ingredients. It's a special night and his request to us is to use everything we can to show off the town and area. Over the dinner, Hudson has something to pitch that isn't in the folder or on their radar. It's important to him personally which is why it won't come from the usual fund. They would have to be willing to step outside their normal boundaries and donate a bit more. Then the dinner is concluded with hot buttered rum and dessert. But prepare yourselves for it to run very late."

Felicity looked excited. "Ooh, Mysterious."

"So what's the secret?" Sierra asked him flatly.

"Not my secret to tell," Ira answered.

Felicity raised her hand and Ira laughed. "How will we get everyone back to the hotel? I can't imagine late at night after drinks and dessert that anyone would like to ride in a carriage."

"I said the same thing," Ira explained. "But this is a super small town and the only thing I can figure out is that we could possibly rent a passenger van and a driver. But that hasn't been booked yet and needs to be done as soon as possible."

Ira went on to explain that Hudson would host breakfast the next morning at his house too and they had to book the chef and put together the menu. Keeping in mind that Hudson expects it to be a lighthearted event with pictures and reports of what their charitable contributions have accomplished over the last ten years. It should be a fun, feel good time. The entire conference is a great time and should feel more like they are old friends hanging out together and less like a formal conference. But it takes a lot of work to pull off successfully."

Ira single handedly organized the event last year and if he could help it, he would do it again this time. It should be exciting with the new venue but it was also going to have its limitations with the snow and cold. However, he did have confidence in Felicity.

"As a side note, this is the first time the Giving Project has gotten together this late in the month and that was due to some scheduling issues.

"Hudson wants social media to be used to create excitement for this event. Something out of the box." He looked at Felicity because he knew she would be the one to pull that off.

"This seems to be more of an administrative assistant's duties. How come you aren't going to be there, Ira?" Sierra asked as she looked at her nail polish and smoothed out a cuticle.

"None of your business, Sierra."

Sierra stood to stretch her stilt like legs. "Whatever."

Felicity reached over and touched Ira's hand to get his attention. He seemed to be having a stare off with Sierra. "Do you have a list of the places you have already reserved and who our contact person is for each one?"

Ira grinned. "It's all in this master book," he said handing over a two inch thick soft bound book to Felicity. I also have everything from the book in google docs. I'll email it over to you two this week.

Hudson rang Ira over the phone and told him to send the two ladies in to his office.

"But my hand written notes are in there and that makes it one of a kind," he added speaking specifically to Felicity.

She understood how important it was to him and held it tightly against her chest. Then Felicity nodded at Ira before standing up to follow Sierra who was always first into Hudson's office.

She honestly didn't care what Sierra's agenda really was because she was personally more excited about the job. Felicity's brain was also whirling with several social media ideas for the event and couldn't wait to tell someone.

She only hoped Hudson liked them too.

Chapter Seven

Hudson was serious when he met with Felicity and Sierra. He gave them more direction on the conference but also added in the email and additional ghostwriting duties.

It didn't feel like the right time for Felicity to share her ideas.

Surprisingly, Sierra was more reserved than before when they'd met with him and the vibe in the room felt off. Perhaps it was Felicity's own nerves making her feel antsy because making that much money for the first time in her life felt significant.

Not to mention the conference in Vermont affected where millions of dollars would be donated and could change the lives for tons of people and animals. She felt the enormity of her responsibility weighing on her by the end of the day.

Hudson had Ira order them lunch and they didn't finish until six. But the day had flown by for Felicity, and she only hoped she could live up to Hudson's expectations.

As she headed out of the building to her car, she couldn't wait to get home. She needed to take Winston on his long walk but also work out her nerves. She could be a ghostwriter in her sleep but handling Hudson Frost's speeches and social media for this event was going to separate her from a novice to a professional.

Her mind raced as she pulled up to the garage auto attendant and scanned her parking tag. It didn't work. Felicity tried it again, and then again, but no matter how she turned the ticket, it wouldn't give her a pay screen.

There was a phone number for her to call if there was a problem but when she dialed it, there was a fast busy signal.

She laid her head on the steering wheel wishing there could just be a person working there to help her.

Suddenly, when she looked up there were headlights from a large vehicle behind her. Felicity couldn't see the driver but there wasn't any room for her to move out of the way either. She stepped out of her car to tell them the reader wasn't working when she saw the back door open, and Hudson stepped out.

"You seem to have a lot of trouble with the whole coming and going side of things," he said.

"I'll have you know this isn't my fault either." Felicity looked as confident as ever as she held her head up high.

He held his hand out and she handed him her ticket. When he turned around to walk over to the automatic reader, she couldn't help but admire him.

Wouldn't Sierra hate to know that Felicity got to spend two minutes more with the boss than her. Felicity was completely distracted when the arm of the garage went up.

Hudson turned around and his smile was even bigger than before.

"I swear, I tried turning it around and then upside down," she didn't know how she got herself into these things but he certainly had a knack of showing up out of nowhere.

Before she got too flustered, he laughed and then showed her the key fob in his hand. "Remind Ira to get you one of these so you don't have to worry with the tickets."

When he winked at her and then headed back to his vehicle, she watched him go a little too long. She had no idea that he was funny. Humor wasn't something you could fake and had always been one of her favorite qualities in a person.

She hurriedly jumped into her car and then headed toward the bridge and home. She had so much to think about- the job, the difference she could make for her and Evie's business, the conference in Vermont, seeing snow, and leaving her sweet dog for the first time overnight since she'd rescued him.

Sure, Evie would take care of him while she was out, but Evie was working impossibly long days and he needed more attention. Of course, Winston's behavior was all Felicity's doing. They had a codependent relationship from the moment she'd brought him home.

Perhaps Hudson would believe he was a service dog and that she needed to bring him in to work with her?

It was dark when Felicity walked up to the pool house behind Evie's parents' home where they lived. Before she made it to the double French doors, Winston perked up. Had he been lying there all day waiting for her?

As she unlocked the door, he howled his greeting and then jumped up on his hind legs to lay his front paws on her shoulders. It was his way of hugging her, and it melted her stress away as well as her heart each and every time he did it.

"Is there a Winnie-dog in here?" she asked as he leaned in. "I missed you too, buddy."

She headed to her bedroom as he followed, hot on her heels. Give me just a second man and we'll go walking. Two minutes later, she wrestled his harness on and they were out the door.

Mr. Shepard was walking into the main house as she passed him. "Hey kiddo. Did you get the job?"

"Yes, sir. Started today too." Winston pulled on the leash harder as he tried to reach the mailbox.

"Great job," he said giving her a thumbs up.

They waved to each other as the black and white husky pulled her harder. Three miles later, he seemed satisfied, and they headed back home.

She needed to study her notes but also, she couldn't stand being home, knowing that Evie was working at the Coffee truck.

Packing items for Winston in a bag she loaded him into the car, and they headed to Espresso to Geaux.

There was a good crowd when they arrived, and Winston happily chewed his extra-large bone as he sat outside the back door.

But when Felicity opened it, there was Mitch steaming some milk as Evie worked the window. "What have we here? Have I already been replaced?"

Mitch laughed.

"I was desperate and had to call in back up. The good news is that I have hired my little cousin to work part time and now only need to hear whether or not you got that job."

Felicity shrugged. "I got the job," she said. "And it's enough to handle the loan but I'm not so sure we can afford to hire someone."

Mitch nodded. "You can afford her. According to our aunt, Katie has been running with an older crowd and they aren't seeing eye to eye. So, she's been offered up to work for free coffee and pastries. When Evie promised Kate that she would pay her more than coffee and desserts, she was thrilled. So, coffee and a pastry plus some cash on the side so her mother won't ground her for life."

"Win, win," Evie said as she handed over the next order.

They couldn't do that forever, but at least for now they

seemed to have a short-term solution for their long-term problem.

Mitch made Felicity a hot tea with steamed cream, and she sat outside with Winnie going over her notes from that day. She wanted to brainstorm ideas for social media, but she would need more research on the company before she had a clearer picture.

When it was time to close, she joined Evie and Mitch. The three of them made short work of the chores and were out of there in fifteen minutes.

"We need to bake cookies and muffins. We're out of both," Evie said and while they baked for the next three hours at home, Felicity told her the good news about her salary and the amazing job she would get to do helping people and animals in need.

"So, it's your dream job?" Evie smiled knowing the answer.

"I absolutely couldn't have imagined a better job, Evie. I mean, I still want to write novels but if I must work for someone, this is so awesome. And I love Ira."

"Love?"

Felicity shook her head. "You know what I mean."

It went without saying, Felicity's college boyfriend had ripped her heart out. Then stomped on it for good measure. Evie got an up close and personal view of the damage he'd done to her best friend and no matter how hard she'd tried, Felicity refused to go out on a single date since they broke up over a year ago.

"Well, I had an interesting visitor first thing this morning." Evie hadn't let on that anything was wrong. She'd always been emotionally strong in a way that was envious. Of course, she'd grown up with two great parents who still adored each other and a great older brother who also looked out for her, which gave Evie such a strong sense of self. But if Felicity didn't know better, she looked a little rattled as she left that statement hanging in the air.

"Who?"

"Sharknado blew through and insisted on coming inside the truck while I waited on customers." Evie pulled the last batch of cookies out of the oven while Felicity bagged the cooled one individually.

"I thought we decided that you weren't going to be alone with him again?"

Evie cut her eyes at Felicity. "I wasn't sure how this whole job thing was going to work out for you, and I figured I needed to be nice to him in the event we actually couldn't make the next payment on time."

"Oh, Evie, I'm sorry. I should have texted you as soon as I knew."

Evie shook her head. "It's not your fault. I let him hang out for an hour. He spent at least fifty-seven minutes of it telling me how I could persuade him to extend our deadline."

"He's such a sleaze."

"Yup, and I may have hinted that I would go out with him just to cover our bases."

"Oh no, Evie."

"I know but it still freaks me out a bit that we could've worked this hard for nothing. I can't give this business up to him. I just can't."

"And we aren't going to lose it. I promise." Felicity hugged her friend and felt the stress as it surrounded them.

But still she kept a strong stance. "Look you don't have to be nice to him. Your brother will drop everything to come and help if he's needed. Plus, your little cousin is going to start working there and that will give you some breathing room. When I'm not traveling for work, I'll bake pastries or work the closing shift so you can get a break. We've got this."

Evie locked onto her stare. "And you're sure this job is going to work out? I mean, he did say it was a trial period. Didn't he?"

There was no way Felicity was going to admit that had her

nervous too. "That was just his way of making us feel better with all the extra work we're going to have to do. I promise, this is an amazing opportunity but also in my wheelhouse. I've got this."

Neither one of them wanted to think about how long they would have to endure this crazy schedule in order to pay the exorbitant interest that Isaac Keller was charging them. It might even be criminal, but neither wanted to involve their parents and disappoint them. It was a huge mistake to sign a contract without having someone else look it over. But here they were, living the dream, owning a business and paying out the nose for it.

They finished wrapping up all the baked goods and cleaning the tiny kitchen before going to bed in the early hours of the morning. Each falling into a fitful sleep with the burdens they carried and the worry of how long they could keep this impossible schedule.

A lot of entrepreneurs started out this way, didn't they? Felicity thought as she tossed and turned. Owning a small business looked glamorous but being the chief coffee maker, baker, window washer, food truck cleaner, and supply ordering monger was more like it.

"Just living the dream," she whispered as she finally drifted off to sleep.

Chapter Eight

The next morning, Felicity helped Evie load baked goods and Winston into her car. They'd decided from the beginning that he was the perfect mascot for the business and knowing that Felicity would be gone for a minimum of ten hours a day, he needed more attention and care.

Still, it was difficult leaving him for such long periods of time. But Evie loved him like a second dog mom and at least Felicity wouldn't have to worry about him being alone.

After she saw them off, she spent fifteen minutes digging into storage boxes to find the kettle and carafe that she and Evie had used in their apartment in college.

They'd upgraded since they moved into the pool house but the old set up was still better than the office coffee machine and stale coffee Ira made each morning.

When she got in, just like the day before, Hudson was the only one already in the office. He nodded at her but then curiously watched as she unpacked her bag.

"It's only the second day, Miss Storey. You already hate our coffee?"

"When you know better, you do better, Mr. Frost," she said not hiding the sass behind her comment.

He grinned and continued watching as she ground coffee beans and began pouring the perfect temperature of water over them.

Felicity enjoyed the ritual almost as much as she enjoyed the taste of the coffee itself. When she poured him a cup, Hudson Frost seemed to like it too.

"Thank you, Felicity," he said before heading back into his office.

Ira asked her to marry him when he walked in, and she handed him a cup of the fresh brew. "I can't go back now, Felicity," he said making her laugh.

Sierra told her that she wasn't a coffee drinker and behind her back Ira made an ugly face. But Felicity had come across a lot of people that preferred tea.

Laughing to herself that she didn't understand people that didn't drink coffee, but she had come across them. What did they do, get an appropriate amount of sleep or something?

Ira told them that Hudson had meetings for most of the morning, but they were to each study his emails until they got the hang of his style. Then brainstorm together to come up with ideas for how to move forward with social media for the company.

"I'm sorry, Ira, I don't have a computer," Felicity said.

Sierra had taken the seat at the desk opposite Ira and pulled out her I-pad. Felicity frowned feeling like she should have brought her own computer to the office. It was four years old and had been a gift from her mother for college, but it still could get the job done. As she watched Sierra make herself at home, she not only looked like a third wheel but felt like one too.

Ira held up his hand as he answered the phone. "Great," was all he said and then hung up.

He smiled at Felicity and crooked his finger for her to walk over to his desk. "Go see Ed, in the I.T. department. He'll hook you up."

Before Felicity could ask him where the I.T. department was, two large men walked into the room carrying a desk and a third walked behind them with a chair.

Ira directed them on how to rearrange the office, asking Felicity and Sierra for their input as well.

"Thanks, Ira. It's great," Felicity said and Sierra simply answered, "Yes, great."

Ira decided to walk Felicity over to Ed's office and she took the opportunity to ask, "I kind of figured Sierra and I would have a cubicle in the big room. Are we not going to be in your way?"

He grinned at her, "We are actually out of space out there. The law office next door is moving, and we have plans to take over that space at the beginning of the year."

"Well, I appreciate you sharing your space."

Ira held the door open for her and when she stepped inside, there were two men that looked like tech experts with glasses and Star Wars' figurines on their desks.

Ira leaned in and admitted, "Honestly, I'm supposed to spy on you and Sierra."

"Ouch," Felicity said and Ira laughed which caused the older tech to finally look up.

It took thirty minutes for Ed to outfit Felicity with a brand-new company laptop and when she told him how nice his desktop computer looked, he assured her he could get her set up with one in her office too.

"I couldn't ask you to do that, Ed. But thank you."

Ed was in his late forties. He was kind and straight forward. She liked that.

"On the contrary, Felicity, all you have to do is ask. I was told to get you whatever tech you needed. I already have a desktop mac in the box waiting for you. I was told you probably would need it and a camera for still pictures and video. So, I took the liberty of ordering it along with a ring light. The mic hasn't come in yet, but it might get here this afternoon."

Felicity wanted to hug his neck. This was better than Christmas. By the time Ed put all her new items on his metal cart so he could wheel them into her office and set them up, her face hurt from smiling so much.

Sierra ignored all the new items as she typed away at her desk, but Felicity asked Ed if he had ordered one for her too. "She and I are partners and she'll need the same set up or at least a log in so she can use the desktop too."

"No problem," Ed said smiling at Felicity. He'd already had run-ins with Sierra from the warehouse and so he didn't address her directly. But he really liked Felicity. When she offered to make him a cup of coffee, he grinned at her and asked if she had cream and sugar.

"Absolutely. Just the way I take it too, Ed." Felicity beamed as she made another carafe of coffee and waited for him to finish setting up her desktop computer.

"I'll be back in ten minutes with the other computer," he told Felicity and she winked at Sierra who was trying to hide her smile.

After reading through Hudson's emails for thirty minutes, Felicity wrote a few notes and then asked Sierra if she wanted to brainstorm social media ideas.

Ed was back and setting up Sierra's new computer, so she moved her chair over to Felicity's desk. Felicity told her that she would like to make a feel good video about the founder of the company. "I think his business plan, the way he treated his employees, and the exemplary customer service will be impressive. But then we can highlight philanthropy and how Mrs. Frost was the wind beneath his wings when it came to giving twenty-five percent of their annual earnings to charity. Perhaps putting a banner at the top of the page with her words, 'Leaving the world a better place than we found it' could really be the anchor to our company image." Felicity looked at Sierra whose face was unreadable. "So? What do you think?"

It was obvious that Felicity was excited about this idea and had put a lot of thought into it overnight. But Sierra didn't act too excited and perhaps she had another idea. Or maybe, she just didn't gush over anything?

"I guess if that's the way you want to go," Sierra said looking down at her notebook.

"Well? What's your idea?"

Sierra looked up and grinned. "Well, I have a lot of followers on my Instagram page. You may not know this, but people online are really into style and glam. I think we could do something showing the building and our offices while they are decorated for Christmas with elusive titles. Building the suspense of who we are and what we do. You know like those old brand ads where you would see a sexy person wearing cool sunglasses and a watch but at the end it would just be the Gucci symbol or Coach?"

Felicity couldn't imagine that idea being the right path for a manufacturing company with heady philanthropic goals but perhaps she was wrong.

Sierra was excited and kept talking, "So I think we need to spend some money on a marketing firm to help us with a cool brand using the name Frost Manufacturing. It would be the way we are known and coming up with hot ads would get us attention from women and men."

Felicity couldn't think of any guys she knew that liked that sort of advertisement. Sure, cool and funny ads like those played during the Superbowl but not perfume or watch ads. Still, she didn't want to insert her opinion when this was the most Sierra had talked to her in two days.

"Well, I'm not sure that is the vibe for us-" Felicity was cut off by an enthusiastic Sierra.

"You've only been here a minute and I've worked for the company for a year and a half. Hudson is young and has style. A young, cool vibe is definitely the way to go."

Felicity, still trying to be diplomatic, nodded. "I think you should run with that idea and put together your bullet points, maybe some videos with examples. We can pitch these ideas to Mr. Frost this afternoon and let him decide."

Sierra stood up and smoothed down her sweater dress. She looked stunning in it and her suede boots. It was obvious that Sierra put a lot of effort into her style. Felicity was wearing another outfit of Evie's and the black pantsuit was flattering, hitting her in all the right places but also understated.

Leaning down, Sierra locked eyes with Felicity. "Ed and I don't get along very well, and I appreciate you asking him to set up a new computer for me too. It was sweet of you."

"Of course, you're welcome." Perhaps Sierra wasn't as bad as Felicity first thought? Only time would tell. But for the rest of the morning and early afternoon, they each worked on their ideas so they could present them to the CEO.

Ira left at noon for lunch and then Sierra took off around one. Felicity had brought a sandwich from home along with some of the broken cookies she'd helped bake the night before.

She met seven other employees in the break room and when she shared the extra cookies, they all pledged to drive across the lake to check out Espresso to Geaux that weekend.

A couple of the women had recognized her from the YouTube channel she'd set up during the summer and another asked her how Winston was doing.

Felicity hadn't made a video with her dog in a couple of weeks and promised to do it as soon as possible.

She repeated everyone's name in her head ten times so she

wouldn't forget them if they ran into each other the next day or even in the hallway around the office. "Betty, Charline, Kathryn, Janice Loretta, Jeri, and John," she mumbled as they left her in the break room and went back to work.

As she put the other half of her sandwich back into the plastic bag and closed the Ziploc holding the rest of the broken cookies, Hudson walked by and saw her. Instead of continuing on his way, he turned around and walked into the break room to see her. "Miss Storey," he said and looked at her leftover lunch.

"Did I interrupt your lunch?"

She shook her head. "I'm finished."

He crooked his right eyebrow and she wondered if he practiced that serious look in the mirror. "You aren't going to finish that sandwich? It's going to be a long afternoon."

Shrugging as she looked down at her plain turkey sandwich with mayo on white bread, she looked back up at him with a twinkle in her eyes. "If you're asking for the other half, it's yours but I get at least one of the left-over ginger sugar cookies."

He laughed. "Those are your homemade ginger cookies that you make for the coffee truck?"

"I made them myself last night."

"Got any more of that coffee left?"

"If your nice, I'll make another carafe."

He put his hand over his heart like she'd hurt him. "I'm always nice," he said, and she could see the devilish gleam in his dark eyes.

"Uh-huh," she said as she stood up and quickly packed the sandwich back into her brown bag. She handed him the one with cookies. "You better not eat them all," she said as he held the door for her to walk out first.

Ira and Sierra were back when Felicity and Hudson walked into the office together. When Felicity told him she would make coffee and then join him and Sierra in his office, Sierra didn't waste a second hustling in there to have him alone for a few minutes.

Ira walked over to watch Felicity as she made the third carafe of coffee that day. She explained to him how her best friend and business partner Evie discovered the coffee roasting company. They'd spent a couple of months trying different beans and finally settled on a blend that was made just for their business. She ground the coffee beans and let him smell them.

"I don't do drugs, sweetheart, but if I did it would taste like your coffee."

Felicity put her hand over her mouth to stifle her laughter. Ira was so easy to like, and she wondered if he was single. Evie might just be his soul mate and she was going to have to introduce them one day.

She handed Ira a cup of coffee as she poured one for Hudson and one for herself. He leaned in and kissed her cheek. "Thanks, doll. Listen, I wanted to tell you that I really think you are on to something with your ideas for the branding of the company. Hudson is close to his folks and I think highlighting how his father started the company and how his mother was the inspiration for philanthropy is exactly what Hudson wants. You go in there and sell it."

Felicity nodded, feeling happier about her idea than before. Truth be told, she loved writing but if it hadn't been her thing, she could see herself working as a social media marketer.

She tucked her laptop under her arm as she picked up both cups of coffee and Ira opened the door into Hudson's office for her.

Sierra was talking super-fast and as Felicity handed Hudson his coffee, she heard her say, "And the banner would read your mother's words, *Leaving the world a better place than we found it.*"

Felicity quickly turned to look up on the large screen in

Hudson's office where Sierra was projecting her proposal, originally Felicity's proposal that she'd shared with Sierra earlier. Felicity's mouth hung open as she saw the slides flashing across the screen. Before she could say anything, Hudson began to praise Sierra for her incredible idea. That was when Felicity accidentally dropped her entire hot cup of coffee which hit the corner of Hudson's desk and splashed all over her clothes, her new laptop, and the floor.

"I'm so sorry," she said and couldn't believe her eyes watered before she turned and practically ran out of there.

Chapter Nine

F elicity hit the door to the restroom with some force as she swiped at a stray tear that dared slip down her cheek.

It wasn't like she hadn't met mean girls before and had always stood up to them. Usually, they respected her for it, but this was a corporate setting. How could she go into their boss's office and confront her without looking unprofessional herself?

Felicity had gone out of her way to be nice to Sierra, offering her coffee and then making sure Ed set up a brand-new desk top computer for her. How was she supposed to work with someone like that, forget about being partners.

As she paced back and forth in the restroom, one of the ladies from lunch walked in and saw her.

"Are you alright, Felicity?" Betty asked.

Felicity stopped pacing and looked at her. "Yes. Sorry."

Betty handed her a napkin and pointed to a bit of smeared mascara at the corner of Felicity's left eye. Looking in the mirror, she cleaned up her face and then blotted the coffee that had splashed on her clothes.

After drying her computer, she gave Betty a determined look before thanking her and heading back into Hudson's office.

The memory of seeing her hard work up on the screen and the shock of how brazenly Sierra had betrayed her was instantly erased when she saw Ira cleaning up the mess she'd made. Felicity had thought she wore most of the coffee, but she'd been wrong. It was everywhere.

She dropped to her knees and took a fistful of napkins from Ira. "I'm sorry, Ira. It was an accident," she said as she cleaned the bottom of Hudson's desk.

"The cleaning crew will get the majority of it," he said. "But Sierra was in tears because her shoes were ruined. Apparently, they were some expensive Italian brand that her parents bought her for her birthday. Hudson helped her and they went to go see if the cleaning crew had something to clean suede."

"Was he really mad?"

"You could say that, but he seemed to really like Sierra's presentation and was trying to defuse the mayhem by complimenting her.

"She was in tears, of course, and said you were jealous of her. Then implied this," he motioned around the carpet, desk, and chairs where the coffee looked like it exploded instead of simply slipping out of her hand. "I guess she didn't imply, she actually said you dumped it on her on purpose."

"That isn't true," Felicity tried not to grit her teeth. She needed to calm down or she'd never be able to explain herself properly. It had always been a problem for her, and she couldn't just explode, speak gibberish, and then storm out like she'd done when she was younger. Her mouth got her into a lot of situations that Evie had to usually smooth over for her. But Evie wasn't here, and Felicity needed to be professional. She also needed this job and she'd done nothing wrong except for share her ideas with the she-devil. So, she tried to use humor until she could sort out her next step. "I didn't mean to spill the coffee, Ira. You know, I'd never waste it on someone like her."

Ira nodded, but before they could laugh about it, Hudson cleared his throat. He'd heard the comment and didn't find it funny.

"I need to speak to you, Miss Storey."

"Good luck," Ira whispered and left her alone with Hudson. She was still on her knees when she looked up to see his flat expression.

Before standing up, she gathered all the used napkins. He watched her purposely take longer and then reached his hand out to help her stand as he also took the wet napkins and threw them in the garbage can next to his desk.

Felicity watched Hudson as he sat in his massive leather chair. It fit him perfectly and she'd never thought about how muscular he was until that moment. He looked huge. *Maybe it was the anger?*

She stood there staring at him and he stared back for what seemed like forever. Finally, he spoke, "Have a seat, Felicity."

She sat instantly and then scolded herself for being so obedient. She had every reason to be angry herself but explaining that would also make it seem like she poured the coffee out on purpose.

"Did you know the shoes Miss Colson wore today are worth three thousand dollars?"

What?

"Apparently they're an Italian leather brand and when she wore them the first time, it was her first viral video. They were special."

Were?

"I've given Miss Colson the rest of the afternoon off so she can pull herself together and also see if they can be repaired."

Felicity nodded.

"I told her that we would pay for the repair or replacement whichever was needed."

She couldn't read his face. He had that irreverent CEO look and it felt like the end for Felicity at Frost Manufacturing.

"I don't have three thousand dollars, Mr. Frost. And if you fire me, there is no way that I can pay her back, but it was an honest to goodness accident-"

He held his hand up for her to stop. The truth of what had caused her to drop the coffee cup was right there on the tip of her tongue, but he hadn't given her the chance to explain.

"I'm not going to fire you, Miss Storey, yet."

She closed her eyes. Thank goodness.

"This accident as you call it has taken up over an hour of my time already. Do you know how much I usually get done in an hour?"

Felicity shook her head.

"Of course, you don't. Because we haven't had a chance to spend a regular day working because of one thing or another."

She remembered how she walked out the day before and now, of course, he thought she poured the coffee on Sierra on purpose and then walked out again.

"I'm sorry, Mr. Frost, but I truly can explain," this was her chance, she could just spit it out and then-.

Hudson shook his head, and she could see he was frustrated at her, the situation, perhaps something else. But whatever she said or did next could be the end of her employment, so she stopped talking.

"What would you like for me to do for the rest of the afternoon, Mr. Frost?"

Finally, she said something that didn't cause him to frown.

"I presume you and Sierra talked about her ideas for social media?"

She clenched her jaw and didn't miss how he stared at her.

He was clenching his jaw too before he continued, "I like her ideas and want to move forward with it. Spend the afternoon working on that plan and in the morning, you can show them to Sierra. I would like you two to have something put together for me when I get back, I'll be out tomorrow."

"Yes, sir," Felicity said and quickly turned and walked out of his office.

I presume you and Sierra talked about her ideas for social media? If he only knew the shallow ideas that Sierra had, then he wouldn't make her pay for the two-faced reptile of a woman's shoes.

Who in the hell wore three-thousand-dollar shoes? The woman used to work in the warehouse. What the hell? And she also got the afternoon off! Felicity was screaming in her head as she sat at her desk.

Ira stared at her for a few minutes, but she didn't look up. She was afraid she'd spill the entire story to him and maybe even cry. She hated crying.

So, she pulled up the outline of her presentation that she'd worked on earlier and added pictures and examples to it. It was a great idea and she could pull it off better than Strawberry not shortcake. She would use her time to slam dunk the next presentation and see if Sierra could keep up with her after that.

At the end of the day, Ira walked over to Felicity's desk. "Don't beat yourself up over today. Okay? If you ask, I know Hudson would pay for Sierra's shoes and let you make payments out of your paycheck to pay him back."

Felicity shook her head. She couldn't talk about it. She needed every penny she made to cover the loan payments and help cover supply costs for Espresso to Geaux. How was she going to tell Evie that she'd screwed up? Poor Evie left earlier than Felicity and had to do all the work at the coffee truck herself. It was a lot harder than sitting at a computer and working on social media marketing and answering emails.

But Ira wasn't finished, "I have to say though, I'm surprised he liked Sierra's presentation. She'll be insufferable for the next month."

Felicity remembered the disappointed look on Hudson's face when he walked back into the office and heard her remark about not wasting coffee on Sierra. Felicity had always preferred someone to yell at her than be disappointed. Letting someone down was the worst thing she could do in her book. Well, that and steal another person's work. But there was nothing she could do about it now.

She nodded at Ira and then thanked him for always being so nice to her. He winked at her and then left for the day.

It was seven when Felicity pulled out the other half of her sandwich and took a couple of bites. She'd sent a text to Evie to let her know she would be in late and to make sure Winston was okay.

Evie reassured her that everything was under control there and to keep up the hard work. Of course, she didn't know what a terrible mess everything was at the office and if Felicity could help it, she wouldn't find out. What a jerk friend she would be to complain when Evie was balancing the entirety of their business as well as taking care of Felicity's dog.

Rubbing her eyes, Felicity began editing her power point presentation when she heard Hudson's door open for the first time in hours.

She kept her head down as he walked by and only looked up when she thought he was gone. He was standing in the doorway leaning against the door jamb studying her.

"I don't expect you to work all night, Miss Storey."

"Yes, sir. I thought I should stay and finish this since well, you know, today and yesterday." She avoided looking at him as she spoke and then went back to typing. But he didn't leave.

"The building locks up at seven and there is only a night guard at the front desk. You won't have anyone to walk you out to your car."

"I'll be fine, Mr. Frost."

Still, he stood there. When she finally looked at him again, he smiled. "You may be fine, but I won't be able to leave if I know you're here alone. Come on. I'll walk you out to your car." He raised that powerful eyebrow at her until she nodded.

It only took her a couple of minutes to gather her things and she threw the stale sandwich in the outside trashcan. She'd felt terrible all afternoon about what had happened and hadn't thought about food. Now that Hudson didn't seem so angry, all she could think about was how hungry she was and how she wished she'd eaten her whole sandwich at lunch.

As they neared her car, she thanked him for walking with her. Truth be told, it was kind of spooky in the garage at night. There were only a couple of cars still left and not a soul in sight.

"Not a problem," he said and then looked thoughtful. "For what it's worth, Miss Storey, I don't think you poured that coffee on Miss Colson today."

She looked down at her feet. If she could just go back in time, she wouldn't have even poured herself a cup of afternoon coffee. "Thank you. I swear, I didn't mean for that to happen."

He watched her like he was measuring his words. "I know Sierra can be difficult to work with and she has a hard time making friends in the office. But she's done a good job for the company and really wants to do this ghostwriting role well. She put a lot into her idea for today and I hope you'll try to get along with her."

What Sierra wants is Hudson Frost and she's pretending to do a good job while Felicity does all the hard work, but she didn't tell him that. Instead, she nodded her head and agreed. "Yes, sir. I'll try harder tomorrow."

"Thank you, Miss Storey." He tipped his head at her as she unlocked her car and then walked away.

The entire way across the bridge she reconsidered her revenge on Sierra and instead decided she had to try harder to get along.

She drove straight to the coffee truck and hugged her favorite dog in the whole wide world. Then she helped get everything cleaned up so Evie could get out of there faster.

Once they got home, Evie stopped and stared at her. "You've been quiet all night, want to tell me what's wrong?"

Felicity stared at her best friend. Evie had always known her better than anyone. Could she possibly keep a secret from her?

Chapter Ten

E vie Mae Shepard looked at Felicity expectantly. Felicity was a worrier and usually needed to talk things out or she would make herself sick. Even as a kid, she worried over tests or whether she was helping her mother enough.

Miss Storey, Felicity's mother, usually held at least two jobs in order to make ends meet and Felicity was a latch key kid from the time she was twelve. She'd get home, clean the house, and start dinner while doing her homework.

She seemed to carry the worry of the world on her shoulders some days. When they were in college, Felicity worked full time on top of carrying a full load of classes. Evie couldn't remember a time when her friend slept more than four or five hours.

It was the reason Evie didn't want to tell her about the job opportunity and if she'd had any other choice on how to handle their financial situation then she would have certainly chosen something else instead. But here they were, both working like crazy to make ends meet. Evie hadn't even brought up the fact that Isaac Keller came back to the coffee truck again that morning. He wasn't going to leave her alone unless she went out with him, but Felicity didn't need to know that.

"Everything is going great at the coffee truck. In fact, our numbers are looking a lot better than I predicted," Evie said trying to ease Felicity's mind.

What had happened that day was right there at the back of Felicity's throat, but she couldn't let the words out. Evie had no idea how many things were wrong, the mean girl at work, the way she'd lost her boss's confidence, the mess she created and Ira had to clean up, and how much her heart hurt because she missed her dog.

Winston must have sensed her feelings because he came and stood next to her, bobbing his head into her hand. She smiled and bent down to kiss him.

"I'm just tired and missing this sweet guy here," she said running both hands down his sides. "I think I'll take him out on a walk," she said keeping a smile on her face. It wasn't completely fake because she was happy to be home with Winnie and to know things were going well with the business while she was away.

Evie handed Felicity the large silver flashlight her brother had given them. It was supposed to be brighter than regular flashlights, but he also told them it could be used as a weapon if they needed to hit someone with it.

"Thanks. We won't be long. Make a list of the baked goods we need, and I'll get on them as soon as we get back."

Evie nodded and got to work on the list. She knew that Felicity wasn't telling her everything but figured she would tell her when she was ready. That was usually how it worked.

The only time it hadn't was when Felicity's rat boyfriend cheated on her. Evie had never really liked Troy Brooks, but he and Felicity had met their sophomore year at ULL. He'd come into the coffee shop where they worked and bought coffee and pastries everyday just so he could talk with her. It took him months to get her to go out with him and it took Evie a long time to forgive herself for talking Felicity into giving him a chance.

It was four months after that when Felicity admitted she thought she was in love with him. Evie had dated a couple of guys during that time and one of them was in the same Fraternity as Troy. He'd told Evie that Troy was a player and to warn her friend.

Felicity had already slept with him and then worried herself to death over the news. Evie again tried to smooth it over by saying maybe he'd changed. He did seem to care about Felicity and sent her flowers and took her on dates and not the regular college dates to the library and Taco Bell but nice dinners or the movies.

Right after their one-year anniversary it all went to hell and Evie was there when Felicity walked in the door and fell apart.

Watching her best friend, who'd always been so self-reliant and strong, question her worth and walk around like a hollow version of herself had almost been more than Evie could take. She'd called her own parents to come and help. But it was Mitch who took Felicity to meet the people from Craig's list selling their ten-month-old Siberian Husky. He didn't trust an ad that sounded too good to be true. And was surprised when the dog was real, and they weren't sex traders looking for a naive college girl.

Winston was in bad shape though, and it took three baths to get the fleas, mites, and ticks off him. While Felicity was at work, Mitchel took the feral looking dog to the vet and had him vaccinated and treated for the various things he had wrong with him.

The sweet dog really needed someone and so did Felicity. It was a match made in heaven or at least in Lafayette where they went to school.

The unconditional love Winston showed to Felicity brought

her back to her old self. But she guarded her heart even more now than ever before. She didn't trust anyone.

But Felicity Storey was the best person Evie knew outside of her family. She had integrity and a fire in her belly that burned twenty-four hours a day to help her family, which included Evie's family, and to help animals.

Finally, half an hour later, Felicity and Winston came bounding in the door. Winnie howled his usual greeting when he saw Evie and then almost knocked her over when he jumped to give her a hug. "Win, get down," Felicity said knowing it was useless. She and Evie had let him do it from the beginning and it was going to be near impossible to teach him differently.

The friends stayed up again until the early hours of the morning baking muffins and cookies together. Packaging them just so for the coffee truck and taking the broken or misshaped ones for Felicity's office.

It would be difficult to do this alone but together the two friends felt like nothing was too much for them to handle.

They each got up extra early the next morning. After Felicity helped Evie get the morning brew going and set out all the pastries at Espresso to Geaux, she walked Winston before heading across the lake to work.

She felt better, stronger, and more in control of her destiny today. Evie's father had told them both that when someone showed you who they are that was a gift. After all, knowing where you stood was important. Knowing whether or not you could count on someone was also vitally important. So, she chose to look at what Sierra did as a gift. An rotten, low down gift, but still she could work with that. And it had made her focus so much harder on fine tuning the social media component. Felicity had spent the extra time at the office getting it together too. Evil Strawberry not shortcake would have to just try to keep up because Felicity was going to kill that next presentation.

Once in the office, Felicity set up the coffee carafe and thermos on the end of her desk along with the imperfect desserts she brought. She'd made a few friends the day before and along with her and Ira, the thermos would come in handy.

When Ira walked in, there were seven people in the office standing around Felicity's desk drinking coffee.

She handed him a warm cup and he winked at her before stepping into the middle of their conversation. "Hey Love, you aren't going to be able to afford to work here if you keep giving us your gourmet coffee and treats."

Everyone realized that she had given them all what would have easily cost five or six dollars or more at any coffee shop in the city. Ira passed around an empty coffee cup after putting some cash in it. The crowd happily donated money and thanked her again for sharing it with them.

Each promised to come back the next morning and Felicity shook her head. "I can't believe you did that, Ira? It was my treat and now it looks like I'm opening a coffee shop in here. If anyone finds out, then I'm going to get into trouble."

"And why is that?" he asked rolling his eyes.

"You can't run a business without a license, my friend. There are licenses, inspections, and taxes.

Ira smirked before drinking more coffee. "You have shoes you need to buy, Cinderella. I'm just looking out for you."

Felicity laughed at him and then counted the money. There was thirty-seven dollars in the coffee cup. At this rate, she would have those shoes paid off in eighty-one days. Shaking her head, she grabbed a pecan muffin and her coffee so she could get to work.

Sierra didn't show up until eight and Felicity didn't feel the need to speak to her. Hudson wouldn't be there all day to run interference so she could ignore her without any issues.

But Sierra wasn't someone who liked to sit quietly and do her work. She needed drama to get through her day. She sat her purse and things down at her desk and then walked over to stand in front of Felicity. But Felicity didn't look up.

"Ahem."

Felicity couldn't believe she actually said, *ahem*, instead of clearing her throat. It wasn't a word.

Ira spoke up. "What do want, Sierra?"

"I would like Felicity Storey to act like an adult," she said with a twinge in her voice.

Felicity wanted to throw her coffee on Sierra today but again, she wouldn't waste her good coffee beans.

"You can pretend like you didn't do anything wrong, but you're not a victim, Sierra Colson. And you know that I know that better than anyone. What goes around comes around."

Sierra's eyes filled with fake tears.

"You can stop performing because Mr. Frost won't be in today," Felicity said. She'd never met someone that could turn them on like a switch to a light.

Sierra's tears magically dried up. "Here's what you owe me for my Italian leather shoes." She said handing over a receipt that said $3500 on it. "Inflation. And next time, watch what you're doing." She didn't even try to hide the meanness in her voice.

The coffee donations weren't going to help. It would now take ninety-five days. The woman was awful. "Oh, don't worry, Sierra, next time it will be on purpose," Felicity stood up and took a sip from her coffee cup.

Sierra gasped loudly, "Are you threatening me? I'll go to HR and report you."

"Why do I have a feeling that you've done that many times before?"

Sierra's nose went into the air, and she turned around and stomped over to her desk. After a few minutes, when she saw

Ira's head down while he was working and then Felicity's too, she asked what was going on.

Ira shrugged his shoulders, "Work."

Felicity shrugged too, "Work, you should try it sometime."

Sierra stomped out of the room dramatically and Ira locked eyes with Felicity, "Good job."

She smiled because she would have all day to work on the rest of her social media campaign and write more follow up ideas for the various platforms, she thought they could use. But things weren't going to stay that good because the boss would be back and when he returned, she had no doubt that Sierra was going to play the victim again. After all, he'd taught her that he would come to her rescue by the way he handled things yesterday.

It was crazy to think that anyone in the world would believe Felicity was a bully. Felicity had only ever tried to help others. She didn't even know how to be a villain. She suddenly felt the urge to laugh like a wicked bad character in a Disney movie but figured Sierra would walk back in and film her. So, she did it inside her head instead. *"Mwahahahaha."*

Chapter Eleven

H udson Frost arrived at the office early every day. It was a practice he'd learned from his father and still believed was important. He didn't want his employees, many of whom were much older than him, to ever believe he wasn't pulling his weight.

However, this morning when he got there, he heard what sounded like a crowd already inside. Checking his watch, he confirmed it was only seven-twenty in the morning. Most employees didn't need to get there until eight or eight-thirty.

As he walked around the corner to his private office, he could see a small crowd gathered there and a line out the door.

The group parted when they saw him, and he was reminded for the third time in so many days why the woman standing behind what looked like a coffee cart was going to be the ruin of him.

"Miss Storey," he said firmly, and the room instantly became quiet.

"Good morning," she said giving him that saucy smile he

tried to ignore. She quickly poured him a cup and scooted around the cart to put it in his hands.

"Sorry, for the crowd. I didn't know there would be this many. I promise to be done in five minutes or less."

He drank some of the delicious brew which helped him keep his temper in check. "I need to see you in my office when you're done."

She looked him in the eyes when she said, "Yes, sir," and it got to him. He didn't know why, but she always did.

He shook his head as he went into his private office and shut the door.

A few minutes later she knocked lightly before walking in with that glass carafe to refill his cup and a pistachio muffin that looked a little lopsided.

"Peace offering," she said sweetly, and he wanted to growl at her.

"Have a seat, please."

She nodded as she sat on the edge of the chair closest to the door.

"Do you want to tell me what is going on out there, Miss Storey?"

From the look on her face, she didn't. But she took a deep breath and said, "Hold on just a minute and I'll show you." She smiled before she popped out of the chair and hustled back into her office area. He could hear her talking to someone, was it Ed from the I.T. department?

Ed was laughing at something she said and then thanked her. Was she making him coffee? What the hell was going on?

When she walked back in, she was holding a coffee can in her hands.

"Miss Storey, are you running a coffee service out of my office?"

She looked like he'd stolen her thunder and he felt half bad for saying that before allowing her to explain.

"Yes, sir. I mean, not exactly but you see-" she handed him a receipt for thirty-five hundred dollars. "Sierra said the shoes have gone up in price and well, I really need the money from my paycheck to go to Espresso to Geaux for now. I just don't have money to spare for a crazy expensive pair of Italian shoes. So yesterday, a few of my lunch friends showed up for coffee. You know they really don't care for that stale coffee in the kitchen. I had extra so I shared it with them. Ira told me that I wouldn't be able to afford to keep handing it out for free and then, everyone donated some cash."

She smiled nervously as she continued. "I swear I didn't tell anyone else, but this morning just so happened to bring in extra for just us, you know. But everyone from the office must have been talking about it and before I knew it, there was a crowd waiting for me to make more and more coffee."

She handed him the can of cash and he looked at it and then her. She smiled sheepishly, "There's two hundred dollars in there. I only took out what I needed for the supplies, but you see, I'll be able to pay back the shoe money this way and still be able to pay my business loan. That is, if you'll let me?"

Hudson stared without saying a word. He knew he shouldn't approve of this, but she was working her ass off to be all the things she needed to be and his father had always rewarded hard work. He'd been the recipient of so much grace himself with his entrepreneurial ideas. As a kid, he even stocked the coke machine in the lunchroom for extra money. However, Felicity Storey wasn't a kid, and this was a huge distraction.

"Miss Storey, I can't have forty people coming into my office for coffee and day-old pastries every day."

"Those are fresh. I made them last night."

He looked at her as he took a bite of the muffin she'd given him. It was freaking delicious. "After work, you went home and baked these?"

She nodded her head. "Just about every night. But last night I had to go work at the coffee truck for a few hours first. But it's all good. My friend, Evie, wasn't feeling well, so I sent her home. She said she felt better this morning, so I helped her with the early shift and got here in plenty of time to make coffee. I swear it won't interfere with my duties for you and I could set up the cart in the break room. With your permission."

"You'll be at your desk by eight sharp every morning?"

"Absolutely."

The hopeful look she gave him made him smile but he kept a stern voice. "If you're late one time-"

"I won't be. I promise," she said, and he nodded.

Before she left, he called her name, "Miss Storey."

And when, she turned around, her face was practically glowing. "Yes?"

He held up a ten-dollar-bill and gave it to her. "Thanks again for the coffee," he said and when she tried to refuse it, he shoved it into her can of cash and made her take it all with her.

She made another seventy-five dollars before she ran out of coffee and was back at her desk with ten minutes to spare.

Ira looked disappointed when he walked in and didn't see any coffee. But she'd put a pumpkin muffin, albeit a wonky shaped one, back for him along with a large thermal cup full of coffee.

"You truly are the most amazing human being, Felicity Storey," he said, and she laughed at his caffeine addicted sweet talk.

The day started off so wonderfully that Felicity refused to let Sierra taint it. Of course, it was difficult not to notice evil Strawberry not shortcake as she strutted in wearing a skin tight red dress that looked more like cocktail attire than office appropriate. But who was Felicity to say what she should wear? If the tall woman wanted to wear four-inch stiletto shoes then she should get to wear them.

Hudson met with Ira for an hour and Felicity went over her notes and presentation making sure to not let Sierra see a single thing. And it wasn't for lack of trying as Sierra kept looking over or leaning back in her chair.

Finally, Ira came out and told them Hudson was ready for them. Sierra sprinted to the door to make sure she got to walk in first. She really was ridiculous.

When Felicity brought in her laptop, Sierra put her hand over her heart. "Oh, thank goodness, I thought you had another cup of coffee."

"Funny," Felicity said lowering her eyes at the demon partner she was forced to work with.

Sierra looked shocked at Felicity's comment. It was all she could do to not ask Sierra if she'd been a childhood theater kid with all the over acting.

Hudson finally spoke. "Alright, I would like to see what you two have come up with. Did you finish your presentation yesterday for me? Who is going to give it?"

"I'll present my work," Felicity said locking eyes with Hudson.

"That's not fair, because she got an extra half day," Sierra pouted. And she had that perfect bottom lip jutted out just enough that Felicity almost felt sorry for her. Almost.

Hudson shook his head. "This isn't what I asked from the two of you. I expected to be wowed today and approve the go ahead for this new branding and image. We needed to charge forward and also get on the conference media. I planned to hand off my email correspondence to one of you and have the other work with me on my speech."

Felicity stood up and stepped closer to his desk. She knew he wouldn't like the fact that they hadn't worked together but was confident he would like her work. "If I may," she said opening her computer and projecting her presentation onto the huge television screen in his office.

The first clip was a brand-new logo for the company. Felicity had talked to her new friend Betty in the marketing department. Over their brown bag lunches in the break room, Betty admitted she'd dabbled in new logos for a while for the company but had kept the mockups to herself. She was proud to show them to Felicity and together they chose the one on the screen.

Sierra tried to stay relevant by adding, "The logo is okay but adding a little bling would make it stand out. What if we did it in gold?"

Felicity shook her head but didn't speak to Sierra. She'd had her chance to be friends and while she could forgive her, Felicity wouldn't forget how she'd taken credit for Felicity's work.

"Moving on," Felicity said since Hudson didn't make a comment. Instead, he was sitting back in his chair with his arms crossed.

The next video had clips of Hudson's father, speaking to a large group of employees with his shirt sleeves rolled up, sitting on the ground with a tool in his hand, and working on some piece of equipment while others looked on, dressed in a fine suit and speaking to other professionals and then finally in the throes of building a home with Habitat for Humanity.

Hudson's face was stoic, but his lips turned up slightly and she knew he was trying to hold back his approval and smile. But she had him.

The third video was of Hudson's mother who was teaching a class of sixth graders. The kids were following her lead by helping unload boxes of groceries for Second Harvest Food Bank in New Orleans. Then she too was helping nail boards into a home next to her husband for Habitat for Humanity, and then finally there was a clip of her saying, "This is a town we are passing through and our duty is to leave it better than we found it."

The final video showed twenty-five of the various charities that their charity group had helped over the years and there were captions showing the start date and how they continue their philanthropic work still today. At the end, it gave a rounded number of how much had been donated, a new website where people could donate money for the causes or volunteer, and then a banner that read, *Leaving the World Better Than We Found It.*

When she finished the presentation, Felicity wanted to burst with pride. She'd spent every minute possible perfecting her work but also finding the right photos with Ira's help and then added the uplifting background music that morning.

Sierra was biting her bottom lip staring at Hudson. And Hudson hadn't said a word during the entire presentation.

"We can change out the photos if you don't like them or add in different music. I'm open to whatever suggestions you have, of course." Felicity had shown the rough draft to Ira who said it was magnificent. But perhaps she'd missed the mark?

Hudson stared back at Sierra and Felicity wished she knew what he was thinking. Heck, maybe those two really did have something going on outside of work and Felicity had missed it.

She closed the presentation and then the lid to her laptop. "Don't you have anything to say, Mr. Frost? I mean, if you don't like it, then just say so. I can take it."

He finally looked up at her and shook his head. "It was incredible, Felicity. No changes necessary. Where do you propose we use the videos?"

Felicity didn't think he would stand up and clap after the presentation, but his lackluster reaction had her head spinning. He had said it was incredible but his voice had no inflection in it and she questioned whether he meant it. She suddenly had to remind herself that he said yes to using them and now wanted her advice on where to post them.

"Well, Betty said she could make the changes to the website, using the new logo and then we discussed having the pictures scroll automatically across the screen. But I think the usual suspects would be a great place to start, like Instagram and Facebook but also maybe a YouTube channel. I can have them up in a couple of hours if you want to set an ad budget. But you know, Betty would love to get her hands on this too. She said things are a bit stale in the marketing department and she's been curious about those platforms for years. I could give her a crash course in a couple of hours and then she could maintain those accounts."

"I'm an influencer on Insta and I could set those up and maintain them too," Sierra said.

Hudson nodded at Felicity. "Take them to Betty and get her rolling. I would like them to be up by the end of the day. Once you train her, then I would like you back here so we can go over the conference media. I'll email the budget to Betty."

He looked at Sierra who sat there feeling left out. "Sierra and I will work on emails until you get back."

Instantly, Sierra perked up.

Felicity saw her sit up in her seat and cross those long legs at the ankle to show off her heels. She was an expert show-off and to have Hudson all to herself for a couple of hours was exactly what she wanted.

"Yes, sir," Felicity said. Hudson grinned at her but had that judgy eyebrow thing going on again. *What was that about?* He certainly didn't look at the two women the same and Felicity was annoyed by it.

As she headed down the hallway to see sweet Betty, she couldn't get Hudson Frost out of her head. Sure, he tried to be fair. In fact, he seemed to work hard at scolding them both that morning for not working together. But whenever they spoke outside of the projects and tasks, like the parking garage or over coffee, Felicity felt more like they could be friends.

But then *I'm too sexy for this job*, Sierra Colson, walked in and Felicity instantly felt invisible. Sure, the strawberry blonde was beautiful. Like model gorgeous and Felicity could never pull off a red dress like Sierra had worn. But she fancied herself as the fun girl-next-door type and didn't men like that too?

She shook her head before she walked into Betty's office. What was wrong with her? Was she jealous of Sierra and the possibility that she would in fact, land her dream guy, Hudson Frost?

What did she care? It wasn't like Felicity wanted to date him. She'd sworn off men a year ago and only had room in her life for one male and he was covered in fur.

Besides, who got a crush on their boss anyway? Especially a boss who Felicity wasn't sure even liked her as an employee. She needed to stay focused because keeping this job was the most important thing.

Chapter Twelve

I t took a little longer than Felicity had predicted to get Betty up to speed with the social media platforms. Who knew that Betty didn't have a personal account on any of them and would need to start from the ground up? Felicity promised to come back and help her again as soon as time allowed.

They spent three hours going over the basics and then revisiting them so Betty could take thorough notes. But it was clear that Felicity would have to load everything herself and oversee it for the time being.

She just didn't think it was something she should share with her boss at the moment. So, she decided to omit that detail when she saw him unless he directly asked.

Finally returning to Hudson's office, she felt her stomach rumble when the scent of garlic hit her. "Betty has what she needs?" Hudson asked the minute she walked into the room.

"A good start," Felicity replied as she noticed Sierra eating the last slice of a gorgeous pizza.

"We had lunch," Sierra said with a cheesy grin.

When Hudson realized the box was empty, he looked over at

Sierra and then back at Felicity. "I thought we'd ordered enough." He stood up and seemed a bit flustered. Had she ever seen him that way? Perhaps she'd interrupted something?

"It's okay. I brought my lunch," Felicity said and walked out of there before she acted ridiculous. It didn't matter if they had pizza together while she was working. She was doing the job she was hired for, and she'd offered to train Betty. But still, she couldn't help feeling left out?

She smiled at Ira who was also eating pizza and it made her feel a bit better. Hudson hadn't just eaten lunch with Sierra as the she-devil would have liked it to seem. Yet, no matter how hard Felicity tried not to feel out of place, she still felt like an interloper. And she worried that after the trial period, she would be let go.

Pulling her bag out of the refrigerator, she had a seat at a table alone. It was past everyone's normal lunch time and so she wouldn't have anyone to talk to while she ate.

She sent a text to Evie to see how things were going at Espresso to Geaux. Evie's teenage cousin, Kate, was going to start that afternoon and it made Felicity happy that Evie had someone. But if she was being honest, it also made her feel a little left out there too. Knowing her mother was at work, she sent a quick heart emoji so she knew her daughter was thinking about her.

Then she pulled up recent pictures and videos she'd taken of Winston. He really was her emotional support animal and she smiled at him howling over a butterfly that had landed on his nose and then flew away.

Felicity laughed for several minutes over her wonderful dog as she peeled back the bread on her chicken salad sandwich so she could pile her potato chips on top.

While she ate, she posted the video on her Instagram page and instantly Hudson Frost liked it before two hundred more people quickly viewed and did the same. As usual, the comments blew up because her beloved dog was a super star.

She'd known it from the second Winston looked at her and the instant love she felt made the rest of the world easier to take.

When she returned to her office, Sierra was typing away at her computer and Ira was on the phone. Hudson's door was open, and she peeked in, "I'm back whenever you need me," she said and he looked at his watch.

"You already ate?"

She leaned against the door jamb. "I'm a multitasker."

He grinned. "That was some video. He just let that butterfly land on his nose?"

"Winston is one of a kind."

"He's a great dog."

"I dare say, the best, but I might be biased."

Hudson laughed. "I'll have to meet him someday."

"He'd be a great office mascot. You just give me the word and I'll bring him in to bolster the troops."

Hudson laughed again. "I think your coffee is already doing that, but we'll see."

She laughed because that was the most diplomatic answer he could have given. But then she had hope that she could talk him into it someday. And no doubt that he would fall for her seventy-pound husky dog.

They both kept smiling at each other for a beat too long, until Sierra walked in. "I'm done with those emails if you would like to take a look?" she said making sure to stand between Felicity's sight line to Hudson.

Before Felicity could walk back to her desk, Hudson told her to grab her computer so they could all three get to work on the conference.

Ira joined them too and the rest of the afternoon flew as they sorted most of the details, finalizing travel dates and more.

As usual, Sierra logged off her computer and headed out the door at five sharp. Ira had an appointment and left an hour earlier than usual.

When Hudson walked out with his briefcase in hand at five-thirty he stopped at Felicity's desk. "You're going to make me look bad if you keep working this many hours, Miss Storey."

"And how is that a poor reflection on you, Mr. Frost?"

When they were alone, he really enjoyed her quick comebacks. It showed confidence and a wit that he hadn't seen in a while.

"The staff will think I am overworking you," he said giving her a stern look.

"Or maybe they will think that this job is so much fun that I can't stay away?"

He laughed and shook his head. "Come on, coffee girl. I'll walk you to your car. I'm sure you have some cookies to bake."

"You know it. And a dog to walk," she said as she quickly packed up her computer and grabbed her cloth bag, she used for coffee supplies.

As they neared her car, he silently watched her unlock the trunk and place her items inside. When she turned around it caught her off guard.

"What?" she asked, locked onto his stare. His dark eyes seemed to always hold a little mischief.

"Friday would be a good day to give our mascot a trial run. Don't you think?"

"This Friday? As in tomorrow?" She couldn't believe what he was saying. "You're sure?"

"Yeah. I'm always sure about everything, Miss Storey."

The smile on her face couldn't be knocked off if someone tried. "He's a great dog but you know, he's really vocal and there isn't a lot I can do about that."

Hudson Frost gave her a half grin and she was hit instantly

with how incredibly sexy he was. "I look forward to it, Miss Storey," he said, and she hugged him before she thought better of it and then quickly got into her car.

This was the best job ever.

As she drove to the coffee truck, she thought about all the things she would need at the office for Winnie. Mentally making a list and knowing that everyone would love him.

She considered how much fun it would be to bring him with her every day and how this could be the beginning of a wonderful career at Frost Manufacturing.

Once she settled into the job even more, and things finally leveled off with Espresso to Geaux, then she could use her nights and weekends to start back on her novel.

Things truly were going in the right direction for the first time in a long time. And she couldn't help but remember when they'd gone astray.

The day Troy Brooks had walked into the small college coffee shop where she'd worked, she hadn't even noticed him. He was an average looking guy with brown hair and eyes. Dressed like all the other college students in a sweatshirt with the college logo on it and some jeans. Perhaps he had on expensive shoes and an expensive backpack, but she hadn't noticed at the time.

He flirted but almost all the boys did back then with either her or Evie. It helped keep their tips high, but neither girl took it seriously.

They kept each other grounded that way and laughed at how they were all missing their mama's attention.

But Troy Brooks wouldn't take no for an answer, and he'd pursued her with an interest she hadn't encountered before. He came in all the time and eventually she agreed to go to dinner with him.

They had fun that night, but he talked an awful lot about himself. She didn't think they had any similar interests. And,

Felicity wasn't particularly impressed but he asked her for another date that same night. Looking back, she understood now that he was someone who liked the chase.

Felicity challenged him at every turn. She was comfortable in her own skin and self-reliant in a way a lot of young people weren't. It was all her mother's fault. Her amazing mother had shown Felicity that a single woman could take care of herself and a kid. The two of them had a wonderful life and although they spent a lot of it working, they made the most of the time they had together. Her mother would always say it was quality of time and not quantity.

Thankful that she was thinking about her mother and not her ex as she neared the end of the bridge that led to Maisonville, Felicity called her mom.

They laughed and talked about each other's week until Felicity pulled into the parking lot where the coffee truck was semi-permanently parked.

"Come have coffee with me this weekend mom. Your grand dog would love to see you."

Asha Storey laughed whenever Felicity called Winston her grand dog. Growing up, Asha's family never felt familial about animals but Felicity had shown her another way. She did love that dog and he seemed to understand them when they spoke.

Asha Storey agreed to see her Saturday and they got off the phone just in time for Felicity to see the rowdy crowd of teenagers swarming the coffee truck.

She got out of the car but as she headed toward the crowd, she heard Evie. "Back the hell up," she said in that mean Evie voice that got people's attention. She was short like Felicity, but she had her mom's temper.

"We don't have to serve you, and if you're rude, we absolutely won't," Evie said as Felicity walked up to stand beside her.

"What's going on?"

"These used to be Kate's friends," Evie said as she lowered her eyes at the crowd. Most of them towered over her and Felicity but that didn't deter either of them from standing their ground.

Felicity played good cop. "If you stand in line and wait your turn, then she'll make you the best coffee you've ever had. I sure wouldn't want to miss out on a cafe mocha or a chocolate cream cheese muffin."

The teens rolled their eyes, a couple walked away, but the majority pulled themselves together. Kate seemed embarrassed and Felicity wasn't sure if it was over her cousin yelling at the crowd or the fact that her old running buddies swarmed the place without warning.

Winston stood point by the back door and none of the teens dared to come near him. The breed wasn't known to be watch dogs, but Winston had defied all the norms from the beginning. And Felicity wasn't going to call his bluff in front of the unruly crowd. Let them be afraid of what her dog might do if they stepped out of line again.

It took a while to get all the orders filled, since Kate was still training, but together the three of them whipped up coffee drinks and desserts like professionals and the kids seemed happy to sit out back on the patio together.

All the while Winston kept an eye out.

"I'm sorry, Evie. I didn't know they were all coming."

"Well, you probably shouldn't have put it on your story if you didn't want them to come," Evie Mae said as she cleaned the blender. "But I for one, hope they come every single day if they're going to buy coffee drinks and dessert."

She winked at her cousin. "We might have to extend the back patio, but it would be worth it."

Kate threw her arms around Evie and hugged her tightly. It was then that Evie and Felicity realized that Kate's mother, Evie's aunt, was overreacting to normal teenager behavior.

Kate was a hard worker and quick learner. So, Evie Mae was able to step away from the window and chat with Felicity.

"Sharknado showed up again today," Evie said. "He isn't going to take no for an answer, and I don't think he's intimidated by my brother."

"Does he know that Mitch is in the National Guard?" Felicity shook her head. "Maybe we can set up target practice in the parking lot and let Mitch show him what a sure shot he is?"

"You know my brother would go to jail for me and I can't let that happen. Please don't tell Mitch."

"Okay, I won't. But what are you going to do, Evie?"

"I was thinking of getting someone to be my pretend boyfriend. Someone big and scary."

Felicity looked around the back patio at the young high school jocks. "Well, you probably have a few local choices."

Evie made a gagging face. "Seriously, that's gross. They're babies and he would call my bluff in a second."

Felicity nodded, "I might have someone that would volunteer to help." Ira wasn't as big as Hudson but still he was at least six feet tall and worked out. Felicity had rarely seen him without a smile on his face, unless he was making a funny face behind Sierra's back. But he could pull off menacing if he had to and Baby Shark needed a stronger *no* than Evie was giving him.

She promised to talk to him at work the next day and then told Evie her exciting news.

"Really? And he watches your Winston videos too?"

Felicity hugged her best friend because she couldn't contain her excitement. "Can you believe he likes dogs too? It's everything I ever wanted in a boss. I mean job. It's like my worlds are merging and it's going to be a great big happy-fest in my office."

Instantly, Evie got quiet, and Felicity stopped to look at her. "What?"

"You like him?"

91

"Who?"

"Your boss."

Felicity rolled her eyes. "No. I mean, yes, but not like-like. Sure, he's handsome and sort of funny and smart but not my type at all."

"Why because he's rich?"

Felicity didn't need to tell Evie that she wouldn't date another spoiled rich kid again. "Because I only have room in my life for one boy and his love is unconditional."

Evie nodded her head. She hadn't seen Felicity show interest in another man since Troy Brooks. But if she wanted to deny it then she would let it go for now.

However, if Hudson Frost knew what was good for him, he would make friends with Felicity's dog.

Chapter Thirteen

W inston looked dapper in his red Christmas themed bandanna as he and Felicity headed inside 1 Canal Place.

It wasn't until she tried to get him into the elevator that he hesitated for a moment. "I know buddy. I don't like it much either. But there is no way we can walk up twelve flights of stairs with this heavy bag of treats, coffee, and dog toys.

When the doors closed, Winston howled for the entire ride up to her floor. As soon as the metal doors opened, Ed, Betty, and Charline were standing there.

"We heard Winston on the way up," Betty said as she laughed. Felicity shook her head and hoped Winnie wouldn't talk all day.

Ed took the heavy bag from her hands and Charline held the squishy dog bed Felicity had rolled up under her arm, while Betty held the door open for them.

"I know your hands are full and I'm almost ashamed to ask, but just shameless enough-" Betty said when Felicity answered her unfinished question.

"Of course, I have coffee and treats for everyone." Felicity pointed to the bag that Ed held in his hands, and she heard the collective sigh.

Standing at the door of her office were twenty more people. "I'm sorry, but I promised Mr. Frost that we would do this in the break room, so he isn't disturbed.

"If someone could give me a hand with the metal cart and Ed if you could carry those supplies for me then Winston and I'll be there in two minutes."

Everyone jumped in to help where they could and then the group headed toward the break room.

Hudson was there when the crowd dissipated. "So, this is the infamous Winston, aka Winnebago, Winnie Pooh, Winnifred, Winnie, Pooh Dog and sometimes just Win?"

The look on Felicity's face was nothing short of overwhelmed surprise. He really had been watching her social media. And paying close attention.

She took a deep breath to pull herself together. Winston sat straight up as if meeting the boss was important to him too. Felicity answered, "Yes, this is the best dog of all dogs, Winston the great meet Hudson Frost."

She looked at Winston and told him to shake and he held out his paw toward Hudson. The man's entire face warmed and his eyes shone when he smiled at the friendly dog.

But without warning, Hudson went to his knee in front of Winnie before she could warn him and the seventy-pound fur monster put both paws on Hudson's shoulders, hugged him, and then promptly licked him in the face.

"Oh my gosh, Winston. Sit, no sir, sit, sit." Felicity was beside herself as she stared with horror at Hudson.

But to her surprise, the man reached both arms around her dog and hugged him back as he laughed.

Felicity didn't say a word as she stood there speechless.

Hudson stood but kept petting Winston's head and giving him praises for being such a good dog.

"Um, you have Husky hair all over you," she whispered looking at Hudson's beautiful dark suit.

He shrugged as he took off his jacket. "I'll get some tape and get that off. So, are we getting any coffee around here this morning or is the superstar distracting us from our caffeine addiction?"

Felicity felt like she'd stepped into one of those sappy Hallmark Movies as she tried to reign in her emotion and answer him. "Everyone's waiting for me in the break room. You're welcome to join us or I can bring you a cup."

"You have your hands full. Why don't I come with and then I can keep Winston entertained while you take care of your fan club?"

Felicity wasn't sure she was actually awake anymore, until Winston jerked on his leash and sent her stumbling. She tried to recover her embarrassment by laughing and slightly jerking the leash back. "He heard there were T-R-E-A-T-S and got a little excited," she said but felt her face flush.

This might not have been her best idea, but she was super happy for her new friends to meet her dog. She wondered if parents felt that way about their children? Did Frost Manufacturing have a family day for its employees so they could all hang out and meet each other's kids, parents, significant others or pets? She would have to suggest that one day.

The crowd for coffee was even larger than the days before and Felicity laughed when Ed and Betty stepped up to help take orders.

She'd had the forethought to bring twice as much as yesterday and baked a few extra items just for the office crowd. Still, she ran out of everything by eight.

Quickly gathering up the mess, she stacked everything onto

her cart and decided to finish cleaning at lunchtime. She didn't want to be late. Rushing out the door with coffee and treats in one hand, Felicity planned to grab Winston and get to her desk before Hudson could see she was late. Ed had her dog last, and his office was on the way.

But when she stepped into the hallway, a tennis ball went sailing by her head and she stepped out of the way just in time to avoid being run over by her own dog. "Sorry," Hudson yelled down the corridor as he came jogging her way. His smile was genuine, and she marveled at how it made him even more handsome.

"We were just getting rid of some of that energy. You know, mascots probably need a good bit of exercise before the workday," he said to her before whistling for Winston to bring him back the ball.

Felicity marveled at their behavior and could plainly see that Winston and Hudson were already good friends. The little traitor really liked hanging with men, who seemed to always have random balls around to throw for him. *What was up with that?*

Ed stopped in the hallway to talk to Hudson for a moment and she called Winston to follow her. He'd long lost his leash, thanks to Hudson. She'd leashed trained Winston the first month she had him and by month three he would walk beside her without it. No doubt her boss saw that video too.

Ira met her at the door with a hug and a kiss on her cheek for the coffee and muffins. She made a mental note to talk to him about Evie that afternoon when Sierra wasn't around.

It was the first day all week that Sierra was sitting at her desk before Felicity, but she could see her watching the interaction with Ira.

Two seconds later when Winston walked in the door, Sierra let out a scream that would have woken the dead.

Winston howled back and Felicity knelt beside him, while Ira stepped in front of her.

Thirty seconds later, Hudson came running into the office and everyone was staring at Sierra who had a horrific look on her face as she stood on top of her desk.

A woman with all that reddish-blond hair and heels that made her almost six feet tall standing on a desk was a sight to behold. Winston was certainly afraid of her, and it made Felicity wonder if she shouldn't be more suspicious of Sierra too. After all, her dog was a great judge of character.

Winston whimpered and then howled again which got Hudson's attention. "Calm down, boy. It's okay."

Winston nuzzled Hudson's hand and then everyone turned back to the woman on the desk again.

"Is that a wolf?" she asked, and Felicity stood up to face her.

"Do you think someone could domesticate a wolf, Sierra? Seriously?"

"It's a Siberian Husky," Ira said. "He's sweet, look," Ira held out his hand and Winston reached his paw up to shake it.

Sierra kept shaking her head as if Winston was going to attack her any second. It was the most ridiculous behavior Felicity had seen from Sierra yet and that was saying something.

Hudson stepped forward and told Sierra to get down off the desk before she fell. He reached a hand up to help her and Sierra practically fell into his arms.

If Felicity had to guess, it seemed like a ploy to get him to hold her, and the whole act was ridiculous. Everyone loved Winston. Everywhere she went with him, people would tell her what a wonderful dog he was or how beautiful he was and when he talked to them or did any little trick, they would praise his behavior.

It only made sense that the one person that wouldn't like Winnie would be Sierra Colson.

She was mumbling something intimately to Hudson as he tried to disentangle her arms from around his neck and give them some space.

However, Sierra looked petrified of the dog and wouldn't stop hanging on Hudson. Felicity had never wanted to tell Winston to get someone so much in her life.

But still she knew there were people in the world that had bad experiences with dogs and truly had a fear. Was Sierra really one of them?

"I'm sorry, I can take him home." Felicity offered.

Ira tried to be the diplomat as he stepped toward Sierra and tried to talk some calm into the situation. "Are you just afraid of dogs or allergic?"

"Afraid," she whispered like a child and Felicity wanted to scream, "Woman-up, Sierra!"

"And I think allergic," she said and of course, that changed everything.

Felicity backed out of the office with Winston by her side and stood out in the hallway while Ira and Hudson got the details of Sierra's supposed allergy.

She could hear them asking questions and suggesting this or that solution. It didn't surprise Felicity when Sierra suggested she work alongside Hudson in his private office away from Felicity and her mongrel.

Felicity was happy that she'd worn gray slacks and a sweater that morning as she kicked off her low heels and sat on the floor next to her perfect dog. "Don't listen to that slander, Win. She's the mongrel around here and don't you forget it," Felicity told him as she kissed the top of his head.

When she sat back up, Hudson was watching her. He always seemed to be around whenever she said something ugly about that woman.

His face was serious though, and Felicity felt like she knew what was coming next. So much for an office mascot. She would need to carry Winston home and that would make her miss a solid two hours of work.

He reached his hand out to help her up off the floor, but Felicity sat like that all the time. She could stand from a seated position or drop into crisscross apple sauce at the drop of a hat. She looked into his eyes as she stood without any help and slid back into her shoes. Yep, she was sitting on the floor, barefoot next to her dog like the unprofessional heathen that she was.

"Miss Storey."

"Mr. Frost."

The spark in his eyes got to her and she laughed. "I understand. I'll take him home."

"I have another solution. If it's alright with you?"

This was his company. Why was he asking her permission to do something? She really needed to pinch herself but honestly, if she was dreaming, she didn't want to wake up.

"Winston could hang out in my office today. Sierra can work in the outer office, so she won't be near him on the off chance that she might be allergic."

Felicity reached out to touch his forearm and he stopped talking to look at her. She'd just meant to tell him something, but the feel of his warm muscular arm made her stomach feel all fluttery.

She quickly removed her hand, but her eyes were staring into his. Why did she suddenly feel out of breath. When his lips parted and he exhaled, she swore time had suddenly stood still for a second.

"Were you going to say something?" he asked, and she swore his voice was deeper than usual.

She nodded but didn't say anything.

"Yes?" he asked, trying to laugh at her reaction but his eyes were smoldering between brown and black.

Felicity had to close her eyes to break the spell. "I just wanted to say that if she is allergic to dogs then usually people are most allergic to a Husky."

"She'll be fine," he said and then crouched down to talk to Winston. "Come on, boy. Let's go have a T-R-E-A-T in my office."

Felicity laughed when Winston made a noise as if to say sure. Still, Hudson didn't put the leash back on Winnie and they walked right through the office and into his private space without another look back at Sierra.

The rest of the morning, Felicity sent out flash videos to their conference guests while Ira finalized catering, airport shuttles, and gifts to be delivered to each room for the conference guests.

It was a busy morning, but Hudson seemed happier than usual and took Winston out for two bathroom breaks.

Felicity dashed down the hallway to see how Betty was doing with their social media ads and gave her a few pointers on how to respond to comments left for them online.

When she returned, Sierra had gone to lunch, but Ira, Hudson, and Winston were piled in Hudson's office eating together. "I guess you boys don't need anything?" she asked. Hudson and Ira both stood up when she walked into the room.

Had she noticed their manners before? It made her face heat, and she focused her attention on Winston so she wouldn't give herself away. "What have you got there, baby?" she asked, and Ira coughed.

"I was talking to my dog," she said rolling her eyes.

"I'm glad you cleared that up because I was about to take Winston out and let you and Hudson have the room."

"Ira Sutton!" Felicity scolded him by saying his name. Hudson didn't say a word.

Ira ate the last bite on his plate and walked over to her. "I'm actually going to let you have the room anyway. I'm done," Ira grinned at her and when he walked past her, he waggled his eyebrows.

What was he doing? He was such a prankster that he probably thought that was funny, but it was only her first week and she didn't want Hudson to think she talked about him in that way.

Before she could have a complete panic attack Hudson walked around his desk to replenish the water in Winston's bowl.

"I actually owe you lunch since we didn't save you any the other day," he said not looking her way.

"You don't owe me anything. I always bring my lunch with me, so it's fine."

He stood to his full height and shook his head. "Winston disagrees, Miss Storey. You can't live on cold turkey sandwiches alone."

"Today I have chicken salad, Mr. Frost."

He stood in her space and smiled. "Didn't you have that yesterday? And put potato chips on it?"

"How did you know that?"

"I know everything that happens around here."

"Stalker."

He grinned. She had no idea how much he'd like to stalk her. With her permission, of course.

They stood like that for a couple of minutes, sort of like a standoff but it felt a bit more intimate. Finally, Hudson stepped back as Winston stood up and licked his hand.

One steak bone and Winston was already dedicated to the man. Felicity shook her head at Winnie, but her smile gave her away. She liked that Hudson liked Winston and vice versa.

"You're welcome to eat your sandwich in here, Felicity. But if you're interested, I have hot Mexican food, including chips, salsa, guacamole and queso."

"You had me at chips," she said, and he smirked.

"Come have a seat, would you like a bottle of water?" He opened the small refrigerator in his office to show her bottled tea, soft drinks, and water.

"Peach tea is the bomb diggity," she said, and he grinned at her again.

Pulling open the containers of food, he practically had a buffet of items from the restaurant. "Are you feeding the whole office today?"

"Maybe," he nodded. "I honestly didn't know what you liked, and Ira and I usually eat enchiladas or fajitas."

"I like enchiladas and fajitas," she said looking at all the food. It looked like he ordered one of everything. She quickly looked up to see him watching her. "Thank you, for this. It was really thoughtful," she sounded out of breath again and stopped talking. What was wrong with her? She wasn't like Sierra, and she certainly wasn't trying to date her boss. But he was handsome and sweet to her dog.

They stood a bit too close and when Sierra cleared her throat from the doorway, Felicity jumped. It wasn't like they'd been caught doing something but still she felt guilty about her thoughts.

"I'm back," Sierra said. "And I'm finished with the emails, if you want to give me something else to do." She was flashing her super glossy red nails and it was obvious she wanted someone to compliment her.

"Your nails look great, Sierra," Felicity said still trying to be a better woman when it came to Strawberry not shortcake.

Sierra beamed and stepped a foot inside the office so she could show Felicity and Hudson the rhinestones on the tips of her red nails. "I got these for the party tomorrow. I'm so excited for Christmas."

Hudson nodded and then turned back toward Felicity. "You got an invitation for the party tomorrow, right?"

Felicity nodded but she hadn't realized it was formal. "Where is it again?"

"The aquarium," Sierra answered taking another step into the office. Winston stood up between Hudson and Felicity, but mostly leaned his body against Felicity. Sierra's behavior earlier put him on edge, and he didn't like her.

Felicity reached down to pet him reassuringly. Hudson did the same. When Sierra tried to come a little closer, he held up his hand. "Sierra, you said you might be allergic to him. You can't come in here now since his hair is all over the place. You're allergic, right?"

She shrugged but it was too late to take it back or Hudson would know she was lying.

Felicity had a feeling he already did but that was a conversation for another day.

Chapter Fourteen

Saturday morning felt luxurious for Felicity. Sure, she had to be up by five in the morning but she could wear leggings and a big sweater to work at the coffee truck.

Quickly scrubbing her face and throwing her hair into a messy bun on top of her head made her happy.

However, when she and Winston walked into the kitchen of what could honestly be described as their tiny home, there was no sound from Evie.

Had she left already?

Felicity saw the cookies they'd baked last night still on the counter and went to knock on her door. When she quietly opened it, Evie Mae was still sound asleep.

Through the years, Felicity had always been the one to run on fumes instead of rest, but Evie was no slacker. And she wanted the business to succeed more than anyone.

It was a tell that her best friend was wiped out and Felicity understood. It had to be exhausting to run the daily operations of their business practically alone.

So, she gathered up their supplies and headed out to Espresso to Geaux with her furry buddy. Felicity could do it for most of the day and still make it to her Christmas party.

Daydreaming about what Hudson would look like and excited to meet the company founder, his father and his mother, would be the highlight of her week. Not to mention the fact that she and Hudson had a fun rapport that bordered flirting. Yet, it was safe for her to remain aloof.

He was handsome and smart, but that humor is what got to her. However, she meant it when she said she wouldn't date anyone for a very long time and guys that came from family money were completely off the table.

As she began brewing the morning coffee and setting out all her supplies, she tried not to think about Troy Brooks. But she couldn't help it. He was the one who had supposedly fallen for her first, but when she fell for him, it was completely and unconditional.

It was just over a year ago at Thanksgiving, Felicity joined Troy and his family for the holiday. She'd met them a couple of times but never been to their home or spent more than the equivalent of a dinner with his family. If you want to know what someone is truly like, then spend the holidays together.

The house was a magnificent Acadian style home and the interior had been professionally decorated. Felicity had seen nice homes before and she complimented Troy's mother on her beautiful decor but didn't act out of place. After all, money didn't define your character, your behavior did, and Felicity's mother had proven that to her. Especially when Asha Storey brought her along to help clean office buildings late at night for extra money. Her mother always held her head up high when she greeted business owners still at the office or the janitors who took out the trash. She would remind a young Felicity that they were all just people with the same flaws and insecurities.

And that lesson had stuck with her as caterers set up the meal that day and then servers waited on the family and their friends. But at the end of the meal when a server brought out dessert before his mother or father told them to, they showed their true colors.

Mrs. Brooks went into the kitchen and yelled at the server until she cried and then belittled the caterer for hiring inadequate staff.

The entire dining room could hear her, and Felicity was embarrassed to be there.

Then at the end, Mr. Brooks, who had millions of dollars, refused to pay the caterer in full for the event. He told the owner that the service was subpar and that she needed to go back and refigure what it was actually worth, and he would write her a check for that amount on Monday. Then he added that it had better be significantly less than the original quote.

Those poor people had spent the holiday away from their families to ensure the Brooks family had a wonderful meal. They got there early and left late without being paid. The caterer left there in tears and unable to pay her staff in full until Mr. Brooks paid her on Monday. Would it even cover her costs?

When Felicity brought that up to Troy, he sneered and said, "I guess she'll try to be better next time."

Then the next evening, Felicity heard Troy and his father talking in the study. Mr. Brooks made an off-color comment about Troy slumming with her.

It was offensive and hurtful but what made it worse was that Troy laughed at his father's comment and never once tried to defend her honor.

They hardly spoke on the way back to school and she barely saw him that next week. They had finals and a rigorous schedule, so she tried to not think too hard about it.

If she could go back now, she would have broken up with

him then. But she'd ridiculously thought he loved her. And unfortunately there weren't any do-overs in this life.

Winston howled at the back door and pulled her out of her misery. Evie must not have seen the note she left for her telling her to stay in bed for an extra few hours. Did she forget her keys too?

The doorknob wiggled again and when she opened it, laughing at her best friend, she was surprised to see Isaac Keller standing there annoyed.

"What are you doing here," Keller said.

Felicity shook her head. "Sorry, we aren't open yet. You'll have to go around front and wait until I pull up the metal shutters," she said flatly as she closed and locked the door.

She laughed when she heard him curse. Winston growled and Baby Shark must have gotten the message as he stormed around toward the front and waited.

Thankfully there weren't any other customers yet. It had rained the night before and the wind and cold had rolled in afterward. Her sweet hometown got a slower start on mornings like this, and she loved that about it.

Waiting the full two minutes until it was the exact time to open, Felicity casually slid open the metal window cover.

Why would that jerk be here every single morning? Has Evie Mae had to deal with him every day?

"Where's Evie?" Isaac demanded as he looked around.

Felicity stared back at him. She wasn't going to answer questions about her best friend.

"Would you like to order a coffee or a pastry this morning?"

He rolled his eyes, "Give me a mocha latte and one of those pecan cookies."

"Please and thank you are the magic words, Keller," Felicity couldn't believe he was even more unlikeable than when they were in college.

He didn't say either one but kept glaring at her. She made his drink and told him the total before handing it over.

"Evie doesn't charge me," he said.

"Or maybe you just don't pay her. But I'm not Evie and you aren't getting this coffee for free."

"I'm the owner of this coffee truck, Felicity Storey. And you better show me some respect."

"No, Evie and I are the owners. You are merely the lender of our business loan. You get respect when you earn it, Baby Shark."

His entire face turned red as he clenched his teeth and warned her not to call him that again.

"Get a sense of humor, Isaac. And why don't you stay away from here until you do."

Felicity saw Mitchel Shepard pull up in his giant truck and as he walked over to the window. Isaac leaned in closer to her. "I can't wait until you work for me. We'll see how respectful you are then."

"Not going to happen, Sharknado," Felicity said with a smile on her face.

Mitch stood beside Isaac Keller and felt the tension between them. "Everything alright this morning?"

Isaac pushed off on the counter and stormed away without another word and Felicity laughed. "What a jerk."

"Want to tell me why he's hanging around so much?" Mitch asked.

"Partly because he wants to date Evie."

Mitch looked at her like those were fighting words. "And the other part?"

Felicity grinned. "Trust me, you do not want to know."

"You see, that's the problem. I do want to know and if you and Evie don't tell me then I'm going to have to beat it out of him."

Did Mitch think that was a threat? "Go ahead. His beatings are way overdue."

Mitch stared at her for a long time, but Felicity was like a steal trap when it came to discussing her problems. She'd been like a little sister to him forever but wouldn't dare let him fight her battles. Sure, Evie called him to come help Felicity when she wanted to meet someone from Craig's list about a dog, but it took a month before he pieced together what had happened with her boyfriend.

Something told him the situation with that Keller kid was going to be bad and he didn't know how, but he was going to get to the bottom of it.

"What can I make you this morning?" Felicity asked, trying to keep Mitch from plotting his next vigilante move on her behalf.

"Just a coffee. Black," he said as he looked over their baked goods. "Surprise me."

Felicity smiled at him. Mitch Shepard was a great guy and secretly loved sweets. She handed over a large coffee and a brown sugar and cinnamon muffin.

He knew she wouldn't charge him, so he shoved fifteen dollars into her tip jar and strode off, waving in the air. "Thanks, shorty," he said as he got into his truck and drove off.

The rest of the morning was busy but much less eventful. Felicity's mom stopped by and brought with her a couple of old dresses she could try on for the Christmas party that evening.

Evie rolled in at eleven, bringing in more baked goods and hugged Felicity's mom before she left.

"Your mom is so cute, and you look just like her."

"Thanks," Felicity said as she handed Evie a peppermint mocha that someone had ordered and then remembered they weren't supposed to have sugar.

Evie Mae smiled as she sipped the perfect holiday drink.

"You were supposed to be resting and not baking," Felicity said as she pulled out the warm cookies. Evie hadn't bagged them yet because they were too warm, but Felicity was certain customers were going to snatch them up as soon as she told them they were still hot.

"I don't know what came over me, but I didn't hear my alarm or anything."

"It's called fatigue," Felicity said and then waited on the next three customers, selling five cookies to them along with drinks.

Then they discussed Isaac Keller and how he was borderline harassing Evie to go out with him.

"I'm telling, Mitch," Felicity said matter-of-factly.

"You can't do that because you know he'll punch his lights out and then Keller Shark will press charges."

"You can't just let him run all over you, Evie."

"I just don't want to lose the business and you know how his family is and how he-"

"Yes, I know he wants to be a big baller by threatening us about taking this food truck. But Evie Mae, we aren't going to let that happen."

Evie shrugged and then had a seat in the corner where customers couldn't see her. Felicity had always admired how tough Evie was and understood it came from being so adored as a child. Her family had a love for each other that was powerful.

But this thing with Isaac Keller had her rattled. "He's been coming here every morning right before I open. Just barges in and sits here eating free baked goods and demanding I make him coffee. I don't know why I let him get away with it, but there was something about the way he kept saying we would be working for him soon or how much he can't wait to own a food truck coffee business. I told him we were doing great and would absolutely have our payments to him on time. But he had that look, you know, that evil little weasel look he would get when we were in school and he knew something we didn't"

Felicity waited on five more customers before Evie could continue. "Evie, just tell me what it is, and we'll figure it out."

"You already know that he's charging us outrageous interests on the loan that started accruing the day we signed the papers. But he also has a clause in there that in January of each calendar year that we don't pay off the loan in its entirety, he reserves the right to twenty-five percent of the business."

"What? We aren't going to just give him twenty-five percent of this when we're paying the loan and putting all the sweat equity into it."

"It says he has to pay for the shares but as long as we aren't profitable, the business isn't worth much."

"And who is going to evaluate the business' worth? Some crooked friend of his?"

There wasn't much room, but Felicity paced back and forth two steps and then turned around two steps. How had they signed such a bogus contract.

He knew he had them in a rough place and told them the offer was only good for that moment. It seemed too good to be true. Someone giving them a shot at owning their own business. But they'd hastily read over it and signed the papers.

Mr. Keller was there too and took advantage of them on purpose. "Maybe we should tell your parents? They could get a lawyer to look over it and see if there is anything we can do?"

Evie shook her head. "They're so proud of us for graduating college and starting this business. The whole town is happy for us, and I just can't stand to see them disappointed. I knew better. I have a degree in business and know contracts should be examined by an attorney. I talked you into this Felicity and I am so sorry."

"I'm a big girl. It's not your fault, Evie Mae. I wanted to do it too." Felicity hugged her friend and held on tight. She'd always been there for Felicity, and she owed it to Evie to figure a way out of this disaster.

Even if they had to let Baby Shark have the business, neither of them should have to work for him.

There had to be a way out of this mess.

Chapter Fifteen

The rest of the afternoon was lighthearted. Felicity tried on the dresses her mother brought. Slipping them on over her clothes and making Evie laugh at her furry sweater peeking out of the arm holes and causing lumps under the tight-fitting bodices. But they both agreed on a green dress that was stunning and vintage.

"Without the sweater, of course," Evie added and they both laughed again.

"Strawberry not shortcake is wearing red, and I know whatever her dress looks like, it will be stunning on her."

Evie listened to Felicity talk about Sierra and how she planned to marry the elusive Hudson Frost. But if she didn't know better, she would say that Felicity had a crush on him too.

"She is not your competition."

"Believe me, Evie, there is no way to compete with her. She's all that and a bag of chips."

Evie laughed because Felicity always said funny comments she'd picked up as a kid from her mother.

"I'm just saying that if he liked her then why didn't he already date her? She's been there a year, right?"

"Yes, but why would he give her the job near him if he wasn't interested?"

"That makes zero sense. She could have the skills he needed in a ghostwriter like you. You know, Hudson Frost could just be interested in his assistant, Ira."

Felicity rolled her eyes.

"Sounds silly doesn't it," Evie smiled wickedly. She could twist and turn a story around to fit a situation like no one Felicity had ever known.

"You aren't there and haven't seen what I've seen. She's all pouty and standing on the desk scared of a dog, kind of helpless. She's got that *look-at-me* thing down to a science."

"So, what you're saying is that you want him to pay attention to you? You have a crush on someone for the first time in a year."

Felicity stopped talking and looked at Evie. Finally, she shook her head and looked serious. "No. That isn't what I'm saying. I just don't think she should date him."

"Right. Totally," Evie helped the new stream of customers, mostly teenagers who were afternoon regulars during the week that came back on the weekends with their folks.

She sat on one of the extra barstools afterward and looked a bit flushed. "I think you need to slow down on that caffeine," Felicity said.

"I'm good. Just still tired. Glad we don't open until eight tomorrow."

Felicity watched Evie for a couple seconds more before she gathered her things to go home and get ready. "You sure you're going to be okay? Maybe I should call Kate or even Mitch?"

Evie shook her head. "Don't be silly. Mitch has some car show thing he's going to at Miss Lynn's diner. And Kate actually has a date."

"Your teenage niece has a better social life than we do."

"You know it."

Felicity hugged Evie goodbye and told her she would stop back in to drop Winston off with her before heading to the party.

It took Felicity two hours to shower and get ready for the fancy event. She wore what Evie called party makeup with a little glitter on her eyelids and black eyeliner and mascara.

The wavy curls in her long hair looked fancy even to her and when she slipped into the vintage emerald green dress that cinched at her waist, she felt beautiful for the first time in a very long time.

She envisioned walking into the aquarium downtown and everyone turning around to see who was there in the stunning green dress. After all, most of the ladies at lunch had either a red or gold dress and she wasn't one to follow the crowd.

Twirling in front of the mirror she laughed at herself for being silly. But she honestly couldn't wait until Hudson saw her in that dress.

She kissed Winston on the top of his head as she grabbed his leash. Then they headed out the door so she wouldn't be late.

As she pulled up to the coffee truck, she was a bit concerned at the long line that didn't seem to be moving.

"Come on, Win. Let's help Evie get caught up," she said as she held the door for him to hop out with her.

Inside the coffee truck, the heater was blasting like a furnace, and she could see Evie shivering.

"Hey," Felicity said and when Evie turned around her cheeks were beet red.

Felicity threw her things down and rushed over to her, feeling her head.

"You look so beautiful," Evie said and her voice was weak.

"Thanks. You're on fire."

"Not me, you. You're hot-hot-hot and I bet your boss will want to kiss you at midnight in that dress."

Felicity laughed at Evie because there was no way she was going to remember that comment in the morning.

She sent a text to Evie's mom, who got there in less than five minutes. "Wow, you look fancy," Kristy Shepard said when she saw Felicity waiting on customers at the window in her green dress.

"It was just a work thing. Winston and I found her like this, and I didn't want her to drive."

Kristy Shepard helped her daughter down the steps and into her car. Felicity should have known when her friend overslept that morning something bigger was going on. She slipped on an apron and got to work, taking care of their night customers, and trying not to think about the party she was missing.

Sierra probably loved having all of Hudson's attention. No doubt she was stunning in her red sequins gown she'd talked about all week.

It was close to eleven when Felicity closed the window for good and began cleaning the coffee machine, utensils, and wiped down everything. She organized the counter and refrigerator so in the morning she could slide in at seven-thirty and be ready to go quickly.

Winston was sound asleep on the floor next to her when she wrapped up the garbage and flipped off the lights so they could go home.

She needed to bake muffins and at least two dozen cookies before she could go to sleep.

"Come on, sleepy head," she said as she nudged him out the door. But when he stepped down, he quickly lifted his nose to breathe in the cold air. He was so stinking cute.

"You like the cold, don't you, buddy?" she said, and he looked at her and then took off around the building.

She still had the garbage bag in her hands along with the plasticware she used to bring baked goods back and forth. "Winston! You can't run off man, I'm too tired to chase you," she said whining a bit when she stopped and stared.

He didn't run off because of the cold. Winston ran to Hudson who was standing there in a black tuxedo. The green tie he wore was loosened and the top buttons on his shirt undone, but he was gorgeous and if she didn't know better, angry.

"What are you doing here?" she asked locked onto his face.

"I could ask you the same thing," he quipped, and she could tell he was upset about something.

"I'd told my parents that you were going to be there tonight, and you weren't. I guess I needed to know why you didn't keep your word? Now I know. This business is your priority and always will be. Isn't it?"

Felicity didn't know what to say. She was a writer first. But the business was important to her too. More importantly, Espresso to Geaux was her best friend's dream and she had to do whatever she could to keep it going.

His eyes broke away from hers and he must have seen her green dress for the first time at that moment.

He walked over to her purposely and stood in her space. "I don't understand. You look stunning."

"This old thing," she said, and her eyes lit up. "Put on a green dress and everyone acts like it's a big deal."

Hudson stepped even closer, and she caught her breath. He looked like he was going to kiss her but when she inhaled, he stopped.

They both stood there in the freezing cold staring at each other. Because in that freezing air, they were on fire.

Winston barked for their attention and they both laughed as they stepped apart.

"I wanted to come to the party. Really, I did but when I came to drop Winnie off, Evie was sick with a high fever and we had a ton of customers. There wasn't anyone else that could run things and so I put on my apron and stayed."

He ran a hand over his mouth and chin. Remorse on his face. "I'm sorry. I know the coffee shop is important to you and I had no right to say what I said."

"I would have called if I'd had your number. I didn't realize until tonight that I don't have anyone's phone number from the company, not even Ira."

He pulled out his phone, "What's your number?" He plugged her number into his phone and then sent a text to her. "Now you have my number."

Felicity smiled as she added him to her contacts. "You better watch out. I'll text you while I'm baking in the middle of the night."

"I'm counting on it," he said before taking the trash bag and plastic containers from her hands. He walked over to the large trash receptacle and threw the heavy bag inside.

"Thanks," she said, and he nodded at her.

"I wanted you to meet the company founder and show him the social media videos you'd put together."

"I was very much looking forward to meeting your parents in person. They are kind of my heroes after I did all that research."

She couldn't read the look on Hudson's face after that and stood there as he seemed to study her again.

"Where's your coat?"

"I didn't want to keep up with it, so I left it at home."

"You're going to catch pneumonia out here," he said, and she smirked.

"Yes, sir, grandma."

He shook his head at her sass. Felicity Storey tried to take care of everyone. Who took care of her? He slipped off his jacket and put it around her. "It's late. Let me walk you to your car."

She nodded but didn't say anything until they walked around the building to her car door. She unlocked it and threw her things inside before clipping Winston into his buckle.

When she turned around Hudson was grinning.

"What?"

"That is a spectacular dress," he said making her roll her eyes. He leaned down closer to her face and her stomach contracted. He really was a gorgeous human.

His dark eyes were shiny as he looked at her. "You know, Felicity, it's okay to take a compliment. I don't hand them out freely and I wouldn't say it if it weren't true."

"Noted," she said when she really wanted to just say thank you. But she honestly had a hard time taking compliments and she wasn't sure when that had started but it certainly was where she was at presently. "You look pretty amazing yourself. And we kind of match with your green tie."

"We would've had people talking," he said and laughed.

She rarely didn't have something to say but he'd caught her off guard with that comment. Was he flirting with her? It had been so long, and she wasn't quite sure.

She handed him back his coat and grinned that saucy grin she liked to give people to diffuse a serious situation.

"Well, I'm off to spend the night with the Keebler Elves."

"The cookie company?"

"Bad joke."

"It's almost midnight and you're going home to bake?"

"Evie and I usually do it together but she's sick. I'll be fine."

"Want some help?"

Felicity stared at him. Was he being funny? "You know how to bake?"

"I used to do it with my mother, when I was a kid."

"Well then, follow me, sir." She couldn't believe she'd missed the party and Hudson Frost was here in her little town and going to bake cookies with her.

Evie believed you manifested the good that happened in your life and if you put good things out in the universe then they come back to you.

Felicity closed her eyes and thanked the universe for this opportunity and when she opened her eyes, Hudson was right behind her and waiting to follow her home.

Chapter Sixteen

F elicity excused herself to go change into leggings and a long sleeve t-shirt. When she returned, Hudson had removed his coat and rolled up the sleeves on his dress shirt.

Was he seriously going to get his hands dirty? She made them hot coco as she pulled out the ingredients to make the muffins first and preheated the oven.

"Are these trade secrets?" he teased as she used organic cocoa powder for the first batch of chocolate muffins and added a dash of cinnamon and sea salt.

"Are you planning on selling my recipes?" she asked, giving him a pointed stare.

He held his hands up in surrender, "Not me." His smile was genuine, and he seemed to really enjoy helping her in the kitchen.

They each talked about not having any siblings. Felicity explained that she'd met Evie in kindergarten, and it felt a lot like they were sisters.

He admitted that he'd had an older brother that passed away

when he was three and his brother was five. Although he remembered him, he couldn't remember much about the day of the accident. But he'd been told the story and it felt like a memory.

"We were at my grandparents' house in Vermont and Pierce fell into the river while out hiking with my father and grandfather. It was freezing but not frozen over and he was a good swimmer. My father went in after him and pulled him out, but he'd inhaled too much water. He didn't make it through the night."

"I'm so sorry. That must have been incredibly difficult for your family." Felicity stopped filling the next muffin pan with tin foil cups. Sitting next to him she reached over and squeezed his hand.

"We were crazy happy, and I remember my parents and brother laughing all the time. It took years for my parents to find that laughter again. But eventually, they turned that grief into a positive by helping others. People look at them and how successful they are but have no idea the pain they've been through or the work they put into building a business and life where they could help people."

Felicity had only known Hudson for a week, but he was always so serious. At least until he met Winston. Had the loss of his brother created that austere behavior?

"You and your family's generosity is pretty epic. I'm sorry, I didn't know about Pierce or your loss. Perhaps we should add a photo or tribute to him in our history synopsis?"

Hudson looked thoughtful before nodding. "I'll discuss it with my parents and see what they think. It was twenty-five years ago but we still talk about him. I guess you never get over grief you just manage to live with it." He looked at her and then shook his head. "I don't know why I unloaded all of that on you. I've never discussed it outside of my immediate family."

"Evie and I call it midnight confessions. Something about

baking in the middle of the night makes us talk about things we wouldn't normally say during the day. Maybe it's all that warm sugary goodness that loosens our secrets and our tongues."

He watched her run a finger through the chocolate mix left on the side of the bowl after she'd poured the bulk of it into the muffin pan. Then she handed it over to him.

Hudson hadn't licked the bowl since he was a kid, but he happily shared it with her. "You could probably sell it just like this. It's so good."

Felicity shook her head. The private side of Hudson Frost was incredibly sweet, and she wasn't sure if she could go back to looking at him the same way after spending a night baking together.

They talked and licked bowls and spoons of muffin mix and then cookie dough. And never ran out of things to say. It was one-thirty when she pulled the last batch of cookies out of the oven.

Hudson was wrapping the cooled baked goods in the Espresso to Geaux signature wrap and looked pleased with his work.

Felicity cleared her throat before she smiled slyly at him. "If things don't work out for you in the whole manufacturing business, you might have a future in running your own food truck."

"Ha ha," he said sarcastically, and she handed him a warm cookie.

"Sorry, I can only pay you in baked goods."

"Worth it," he said before he took a big bite.

He looked like a kid, eating that giant cookie and smiling. It was going to make it harder for her to kick him out, but she had to get up early and serve coffee to the public.

"I guess it's time for me to go," he said, and she smiled that he picked up on her thoughts.

"Sorry, I have to be at the coffee truck by seven-thirty. I open at eight tomorrow morning."

He admired her hard work but couldn't imagine how she could keep going seven days a week on what looked like four or five hours of sleep. "I guess Evie is going to be too sick to open?"

Felicity pulled out her phone and held up the text Evie's mom had sent her an hour ago. Kristy Shepard had taken her daughter to the all night pharmacy where they gave her a flu test and then strep. Evie had strep throat and would be out of commission for at least the next twenty-four hours. That would probably be the only amount of time her parents could keep her away from the business.

Hudson read the message and then hugged Felicity. "Try and get some rest," he said and then walked over to Winston who was stretched out on the floor in front of Felicity's bedroom and pet him on his belly. "See you later, boy."

Felicity walked Hudson to the door but before he walked out, he turned around to speak to her. "You don't need to walk me out, Miss Storey. Go to bed," he said.

She grinned and then pointed her finger at him, "Don't tell me what to do."

Hudson laughed and then walked down the driveway toward his car.

Felicity closed the door and went to bed wearing her clothes. She was too exhausted to change. But the extra time she'd spent baking with Hudson had been the cherry on the top of her week.

Winston jumped up on the bed with her and sidled up close. "He's a nice guy, isn't he Winnie?" she said and couldn't wipe the smile off her face.

Work on Monday was going to be hard because she would have to act like she didn't know he had such a sweet side.

The next thing she knew her alarm was blaring, and it was

seven the next morning. Felicity stared at her phone. Hadn't she just laid her head down?

She was having the hottest dream she'd ever had, starring Hudson Frost, and it was going to make pulling herself out from under those covers even harder.

"That's what she said," Felicity said out loud and laughed as she forced her feet on the floor.

Winston was ready to go and standing by the front door as she ran through her morning routine at breakneck speed.

She let him run around the yard for a second while she loaded her car. Mr. Shepard came out and helped her put the last of it inside the trunk and then buckled Winston inside for her too.

"You okay, kiddo?" he asked, and she knew he wanted to offer to help her. But she and Evie had agreed that they wouldn't allow either of their parents to work with them as they already put in twice as many hours as they should with their own businesses.

"Absolutely. I've got this!" she said, giving him a big smile. Amazed at herself for being able to pull it off without a cup of coffee in her system yet.

She slowly circled around the food truck and noticed a bit of trash that had blown around the building. Spending a couple of minutes cleaning it up, she let Winston explore the parking lot and every tree in it before they went inside to begin grinding fresh coffee beans and brewing the first coffee.

Just as she got started inside, she heard the rumble of a car. Was that freaking Isaac Keller again?

When she heard a knock on the back door, she was ready to give him what for and swung the door open with vigor.

But standing there with rumpled hair and a gorgeous grin on his face, was Hudson Frost. He was wearing gray sweatpants and a black sweater. *Holy hotness.*

"Morning," he said, and she couldn't help but notice his voice was deeper when he was tired.

"What are you doing here?"

"I slept over at my parents' lake house last night and figured you could use some help."

She looked confused and so he stepped inside, crowding her in the small doorway. She took a deep breath and wanted to melt at how good he smelled mixed with the scent of coffee brewing.

She really needed more sleep, or she might just say something that could get her called into the HR department at the office.

Would it count if they weren't at work?

"What do we do first?" he asked, and she wanted to tell him he had no idea what a loaded question that was but thankfully she didn't.

"I've already started the morning blend. It's my favorite. And I'm going to need a cup before I can open this window." She sat on the barstool and tried to pull herself together. Evie was right, she had it bad for her boss and he'd done nothing but act friendly toward her.

She needed to cool her jets.

"So, give me something to do, woman," he teased and before she said something inappropriate, a loud knock came from the back door.

"Expecting someone?"

She shook her head but figured it was Sharknado.

Hudson opened the back door and Isaac Keller scowled. "Who the hell are you?"

Hudson sort of towered over Baby Shark and when he laughed at him, she knew Isaac was going to lose it.

She scooted between the two men and tried to defuse the situation. "This is Hudson Frost. Hudson, this is a friend of Evie's, Isaac Keller."

Isaac glared at Felicity. "Where is she?"

"What do you need, Isaac?" Felicity suddenly wished Hudson wasn't there. Keller was rude and liked to show his power when he had an audience.

"It has to do with your loan payment."

Felicity shook her head at him, but Isaac Keller didn't care who was around. "We made the payment on time and in full. So, we shouldn't see you again until January 1st. Don't come back here unless you plan to buy a coffee. And stop knocking on our backdoor. You don't have backdoor privileges, Isaac."

"I've had it with your disrespect, Felicity."

Hudson tried to stay out of the conversation since it seemed personal but when he heard the guy sound like he was threatening Felicity, he stepped up behind her. He had her back.

"Or what, Mr. Keller?" Hudson asked and the menace in his voice even made Felicity look up at him.

His jaw was tensed but the fury in his eyes was formidable. Isaac stepped back out of the doorway and pointed a finger at Felicity.

Hudson reached around her and shut the door and locked it as she walked over to the coffee maker and began brewing another pot of some special blend.

He waited for her to get it started and then he asked, "Does that guy come here every day?"

"So far," she said avoiding looking at Hudson.

"What's the deal, Felicity? You owe him money?"

She put her hand on her hip and wanted to tell him she didn't want to talk about it, but he didn't look like he would take that as an answer. "Evie and I got a business loan from him, and he has been insufferable ever since. It's not a big deal. We can handle it."

Hudson had a lot more questions, but she was upset about that guy already and he didn't want to upset her more. "It's eight.

Want me to open this window?" he asked instead, and she grinned at him.

His smile faded when he saw the crowd waiting outside. Ten hours later when they closed, he didn't understand how she or Evie could ever run that place by themselves.

It was a madhouse.

Chapter Seventeen

Monday morning, as Felicity predicted, Evie came strutting into their small house. "I'm back!" she said with a huge grin.

She still looked flushed, but Felicity knew there was no talking her out of opening Espresso to Geaux and Felicity had to go to work across the lake. At least, her younger cousin Kate would be there that afternoon and take some of the pressure off her.

Felicity helped Evie load up the baked goods she'd prepared. With thoughts of Hudson and the day she'd spent with him on her mind, she baked three days' worth of items, but Evie didn't question her.

As she set up her own coffee cart in the break room at the office, she listened to all the buzz about the Christmas party.

Betty was the first to ask her where she was Saturday night, but everyone quieted down to hear her excuse and to tell her that she'd missed an amazing event.

Apparently, the company does a raffle and hands out tickets at the door. If your number is called you could win an amazing prize like a television, and hundred-dollar gift cards. At the end, someone wins the grand prize of a trip for two to either the owner's beach home or ski lodge.

Felicity wasn't surprised to hear how generous the Frost family was as she learned more about their family creed.

Hudson came through but he was as professional as usual and began discussing business with Ira who walked in for his morning coffee at the same time.

The morning routine felt comfortable as Felicity sat at her desk to log in to her computer for eight. She hadn't had time to count the money in her donation coffee can and so she slid it into her bottom desk drawer and as Sierra annoyed Ira, Felicity thumbed through it.

She'd had her biggest crowd yet, and there were two one-hundred-dollar bills in there. Her grand total for that morning was over four hundred dollars. That put her total for the coffee donations over a thousand dollars and she could potentially meet her goal in a third of the time she'd originally estimated.

Looking up to see if anyone was watching her, she relaxed when she heard Sierra still talking about the Christmas party on Saturday night.

Locking her drawer, she began going through her emails, stopping when she saw one addressed to her from Hudson's private email address.

Again, she looked up to see if Ira or Sierra were watching her. Sierra was apparently waiting for Felicity to pay attention.

"So, you missed an epic Christmas party. The aquarium was decked out for the event and there were people in body suits like the kind that covered their heads all the way down to their toes, so they looked like mannequins. They sat or stood on podiums and struck a pose for a few minutes and then subtly moved to another interesting position. So cool. Right Ira?"

Ira nodded. "It was nice. We missed you, Felicity."

Smiling at him she looked down to read her email, but Sierra wasn't done. "Oh, Ira, it deserves more praise than that. There was an open bar, and the band was incredible. I swear I didn't sit down once all night. You know Hudson is an incredible dancer." She beamed as if she were remembering some fond moments. "And that sequins red gown fit me like a glove. My Insta pages were on fire when I posted the pics."

"I wouldn't know," Felicity replied wanting to change the subject. Sierra humble bragged about her social media following all the time and now seemed to add Hudson to the mix.

"And I won a gift card in the raffle," Sierra said as she did a little dance in her chair. "When that party ended, I did not want to go home, and I could tell Hudson didn't either."

Was she seriously implying that Hudson went somewhere with her? Of course, Felicity knew better but she wasn't about to say where he'd been or what they'd been doing. She wouldn't want anyone to mistakenly believe they had something going on when they didn't. At that moment, she was happy just knowing the truth but what was Sierra thinking?

Ira cleared his throat as he stared at Sierra. "He didn't go home with me, Ira Sutton. Don't give me those judgey eyes. We just had a great time is all. And a woman knows these things."

Ira looked back down at his computer and Felicity went back to her email and saw that Ira had just emailed her too.

Don't listen to her, she is all talk and no substance, he wrote.

Felicity looked up to smile at Ira. It was funny having a private conversation without Sierra knowing it as she talked on and on.

When she finally opened her email from Hudson, he'd paid her a sweet compliment. "*The brew this morning was exceptional, Miss Storey. I appreciate all the extra effort you are making and how happy you have made the entire office. It's no small feat getting* in early every day so you can brew that secret blend and serve everyone before eight."

The smile on Felicity's face was making her cheeks hurt. Trying to reign in her facial expressions, she sent him an email too. "You are welcome, Mr. Frost. But you know I do have ulterior motives, at the moment. By the way, there were two Benjamins in my donation coffee can this morning. You wouldn't happen to know anything about that would you?"

Twenty seconds later a reply came through. "Benjamins? I don't think we have anyone that works here by that name."

Felicity had to stop herself from laughing. The smile on her face notwithstanding, Hudson Frost was not as funny as he thought he was. "I'll be watching tomorrow so I'll catch whoever is doing it. I don't need charity.

P.S. If you find out who did it, please let them know that I will get Sierra paid back on my own. But also, please tell them I said Thank you."

Sierra seemed annoyed that Felicity was ignoring her comments about the Christmas party. As Felicity typed and kept smiling at her computer, Sierra closed her desk drawer loudly, dropped her bag on the floor and partially battled with tangled cords but neither Felicity nor Ira paid her any attention.

When she'd finally had enough, she leaned over to try and read Felicity's email messages.

"Can I help you, Sierra?"

Sierra held her head up as she looked over at Felicity. "We're supposed to work on emails together. I was just trying to see who you were emailing and if I needed to be involved."

As if she needed Sierra to help her write an email. "I am in my company personal account, not Mr. Frost's emails."

"Well don't you think you should be handling his emails since it's after eight?"

Felicity wanted to throw a stapler at Sierra after she told her that she wasn't her boss or responsible for assigning tasks.

Sierra was smirking at Felicity and Felicity had turned her chair around to face Sierra. Before they got into an actual argument, Hudson opened his door and looked at them.

"Good morning, Hudson. I was telling Felicity how amazing the Christmas party was on Saturday. Oh, and how great the band was and the dancing." Sierra said with a sappy grin on her face.

Felicity wanted to lunge out of her chair at Sierra. It might be worth the visit to HR, too. The crazy red head kept trying to make small talk with Hudson but she sure wouldn't tell him that she'd been trying to eavesdrop on Felicity's emails. Or that she was trying to start an argument while Felicity was minding her own business.

"Have either of you had a chance to look over emails yet?" Hudson asked.

"I was just telling Felicity that she should probably be focused on those instead of her own email account," Sierra answered him as she crossed her arms and looked over at Felicity.

"I wasn't in my personal email account, it was my company email account, Sierra." Felicity didn't think that she got enough credit for not losing her temper when she'd only had one cup of coffee and had that woman to deal with first thing on a Monday.

Hudson smiled at them both and Felicity didn't know what to make of it. Had he heard Sierra trying to throw her under the bus? What about Sierra telling her to check emails when she herself was perfectly capable?

Felicity stood up with her hands on her hips. She was angry and this was ridiculous. Hudson's eyes got bigger, and she stopped herself from saying what she really wanted to say about Sierra. The woman was annoying, but she really hadn't done anything wrong.

Hearing her mother's voice in her head, "This isn't the hill you want to die on," Felicity calmed down. Her mother had a lot of little sayings and had helped her diffuse her temper in the past.

"Everything okay, Miss Storey?" Hudson asked and he looked concerned.

No, this wasn't something to make a big deal over and Sierra's ridiculous attempt at bossing Felicity around didn't have to be a big deal if she didn't make it one.

"No, sir. I mean, yes, sir, everything is fine. Is there something you need me to do first thing this morning?" Felicity looked at him directly.

"As a matter of fact, I could use your help looking over my speech. I'll send it to you. Knock on my door when you're done and we'll go over it together," he said and then before going back into his office, he looked at Sierra. "Please go through all of my unopened emails. Send the important ones to Ira and answer or sort the rest like we discussed last week. Thank you."

Felicity knew it was petty and just as likely to have been her who was assigned the duty of email. But she couldn't help the little spiteful part of her that wanted to dance in her chair because now Sierra had to do it.

Ira followed Hudson into his office and closed the door. He nodded when his boss and friend finally sat in his chair and looked over at him.

"I told you not to hire Sierra, but you are a man who loves to make life difficult."

Hudson shook his head. "You know I had no choice. The guys in the warehouse were all threatening to quit if I didn't get Sierra out of there. And her mother used to work with mine at the school and I had to give her a chance. She's not that bad and she does have a degree so she's trainable."

Hudson kept adding excuses, but it didn't make the situation any easier. He also really liked his other ghostwriter and that wasn't professional at all. Every single time she called him "*Mr.*

Frost" or said "Yes, sir" to him, he wanted to throw her up against the wall and kiss the smirk off her face. He was certain everyone could see how he felt and had to work like hell to keep things professional.

Ira certainly suspected something which was the reason he kept giving him a hard time. But when he sent Hudson a text that Sierra was stirring up trouble that morning and Felicity looked like she might quit again, he immediately stepped into the room and tried to stop it.

"Will we be ready for the conference, Ira?"

Ira Sutton had been friends with Hudson ever since he'd started with the company. He was overqualified to be an executive assistant and when Hudson pointed that out during the interview, Ira explained that was why he would be the best person to hire.

Ira had stepped in and helped Hudson when he'd become the CEO of Frost Manufacturing at the ripe age of twenty- five. While he had the knowledge and backing of his father, there were many who thought he was too young.

Ira had finished his MBA in the spring of that same year and helped Hudson keep the wolves at bay. Vowing to have his back no matter the situation. They'd instantly become close friends, but it took six months before Ira admitted he'd had to refuse other job opportunities because he needed to move home and take care of a family member.

It was because of that reason that he couldn't travel to the conference this time but it didn't make it any easier for him or his boss to accept.

"I don't think Sierra can handle this conference and while Felicity is smart and capable, she has only been here a week and this is a hell of a lot to put on her."

Ira shook his head. He knew Hudson was right, but they had no other choice. It had to be them.

Chapter Eighteen

When Ira stepped out of Hudson's office and walked back over to his desk both Sierra and Felicity watched him. They hadn't spoken a word to each other in that time and both were a bit worried about whether or not Hudson wanted to replace them for not getting along.

Sierra couldn't take the pressure and finally spoke up. "Everything okay, Ira?" When he looked over at her, she smiled sincerely. "I mean, is he mad at us for fussing with each other again?"

Felicity couldn't believe she and Sierra were on the same page for once. She watched Ira and when he saw her concern too, he let them both off the hook. "He's more concerned about the upcoming conference and whether or not it will run smoothly since I won't be there."

Felicity understood the pressure Hudson was under. She felt the pressure to succeed in her coffee business every single day. The burden was doubled now that she couldn't be there to help with day to day operations. "Ira, is there anything that we can do that we aren't doing."

Ira looked over the notes he'd made and the items he had circled in red. "To be honest, there are a few things that can't be done from here and if you two could fly in a couple of days earlier that would probably make the difference."

Felicity nodded in agreement. "It makes sense. Honestly, moving up my ride on the metal death trap a few days would be like ripping the bandage off quickly."

Ira and Hudson had discussed that if she didn't like elevators then she probably didn't like to fly. But watching her talk about it made him suspicious. "Have you ever been on an airplane, Felicity?"

"Not yet," she said grimacing at the idea.

Ira shook his head. She was funny and headstrong. Why wouldn't she have said something sooner? He knew why. She wouldn't want anyone to question her ability to do the job.

"Our travel is already booked for the fifteenth," Sierra pointed out.

Shaking her head, Felicity looked over the calendar. She'd been opposed to flying in the day before the event already but as time got closer, she worried how they could get it all done. There were gifts to put together for the attendees and final approvals to be made on food, reservations, and some decorating for the big dinner night, and it would be difficult to correct any problems discovered with only twenty-four hours lead time. She'd personally talked to the hotel manager who also seemed skeptical for them to handle final approvals online or by phone before they arrived.

"I think if you both fly on Tuesday there would be enough time to iron out the details," Ira said looking at his calendar and also flights.

"I'll go ask Hudson what he thinks," Sierra said but she'd already made her way over to Hudson's door. Before Ira could tell her that he'd already messaged Hudson, she'd knocked and walked inside, closing the door behind her.

Ira shook his head, but didn't comment about Sierra, always looking for an excuse to get Hudson alone. But everyone knew it was true. Felicity tried not to worry about handling her first big event for Hudson and the company as she began looking over Hudson's speech.

She was impressed from the very beginning because the speech Hudson wrote was great. He was heartfelt and genuine, and she was certain the audience would receive it and him well.

When Sierra returned, her face was lit up. It was common for her when she had something to brag about and this time she acted as if she'd really done something. "Hudson says that leaving on Tuesday sounded like a great idea to him," she said and then giggled.

When no one asked her what was funny, she offered it up anyway. "He knows I don't really like flying, so he offered the company plane."

Ira stared at her. Hudson knew Felicity was nervous about flying but Sierra had flown a hundred times with her family. Was everything out of her mouth a lie? And since when did he just give an employee the option of flying on his families personal plane?

Ira messaged Hudson who confirmed that he did offer the plane but didn't explain why. He had to be up to something, and Ira was going to figure it out if it took him all afternoon.

Felicity sent a quick email to Hudson that she'd finished his speech and asked if he was ready to deal with all the red slashes/marks... like a teacher does in school to printed work.

"Bring it," he said making her grin as she headed into his office.

Hudson looked at the printed copy she'd made and studied

the notes in the margin. "Wow, Felicity, I thought you were going to be harder on me than this."

"Believe me, I tried. But you actually did a great job."

He saw how hard that compliment was for her, "Why does it feel like paying me a compliment was difficult for you?"

She shrugged. The truth was that she was trying to be funny, but she was a bit resentful that he might have the same rapport with Sierra as he did her. She'd mistakenly thought for a moment that there was something more between them.

Hudson studied her as she avoided answering his question. "I've not seen you tongue tied before, Miss Storey, let me take a mental picture of this so I can remember the moment."

Felicity flattened her hands on his desk and peered down at him. "I'm never at a loss for words. I'm just trying to be polite."

Hudson stood up to meet her stare. "Trying? What did I do wrong?"

"I don't want to talk about it."

Hudson moved around his desk to stand beside her. When she stood up to her full height, which wasn't very tall, and put her hands on her hips, he wanted to tell her how damn cute he thought her angry face was, but he didn't figure it would win him any points at the moment.

"How can I fix it, if you won't tell me?"

His warm smile was disarming, and she didn't want to admit that a lot could be forgiven with a sweet gesture. He was already too smug, and she wouldn't give him any ammunition he could use against her later.

"Do you joke around with Sierra the same way you do with me?" There she said it.

Hudson was now at a loss for words. "Miss Storey, I would like to think that I conduct myself like a professional with all employees while at the office."

She cocked her hip and rolled her eyes. "You know that isn't an answer, don't you?"

He couldn't help but laugh at her. She clearly didn't like it as she turned around and walked away without another look back. But as she swished her hips in those tight dress pants, he sure enjoyed watching her go.

For most of the day, Felicity worked quietly and diligently on tasks for the upcoming conference. Every time she finished one item, she went back to Ira to get another. She was quickly going through his checklist and smoking Sierra in her dust.

At half past four, Hudson called for her and instead of going inside the room with him, she stood at the door and waited for him to speak. He didn't seem to pay attention to her attitude as he smiled at her. "Miss Storey, would it be too much trouble for you to make me a cup of coffee from your stash in the break room? It's going to be a long night for me, and it would truly help."

"In the afternoon, sometimes I like to add some organic cocoa powder for a bit of kick. Want to try it? With cream and sugar? I can foam some cream on top too." She always seemed to get swept up when it came to discussing coffee.

"I trust you," he said, and she looked at him like there was a double meaning but he didn't change his expression.

As she walked out of the office, Sierra followed closely behind her.

"Can I help you?" Felicity asked.

"He just wanted coffee?"

Felicity nodded as she pulled out the grinder and kettle. "Yup."

"I guess he really does like his coffee, huh?" Sierra looked deep in thought. "Maybe I should try and start drinking it? It would give us something else in common. Don't ya think?"

Why was Sierra asking her? As if she was going to help her get his attention. "Sierra, I don't think if someone is interested in you that they care whether you like coffee or not."

Sierra nodded. "Still, would you mind making me one too?"

Felicity made four cups of cafe mocha, handing one over to Sierra, and delivering one to Ira and then Hudson. As she sat at her desk and sipped on her cup, she noticed Sierra trying to drink without making a face.

"It's good," she lied as she faked a smile at Felicity.

"I've been drinking coffee with my mother since I was ten. It's an acquired taste, Sierra," Felicity tried not to laugh at her. The woman was nothing if not dedicated to her mission as she tried not to gag as she sipped the hot drink.

"Got it," Sierra said and turned her face to spit in the trashcan.

Felicity waited until five when Sierra left to corner Ira. "Alright, Ira, I need to ask you a personal question."

As usual, Ira was fun and flirty as he held his arms out and said, "Ask away, I'm an open book."

She didn't know how, but she knew that wasn't the truth. Still, she played along, "Are you dating anyone seriously?"

Ira gave her that devilish grin she'd come to know and really like, "Why Felicity Storey, I didn't know you were interested in me."

Hudson must have heard her question as he stepped out of his office and looked at them both. "Excuse me," he said and walked off down the hallway.

Felicity watched him walk away in what she could only describe as a huff. *Was he mad?*

She threw her notepad across the room at Ira. "Ewww, not me, Ira. Seriously." She rolled her eyes as she stood up and walked around her desk to pick up the notepad that didn't quite make it over to her intended target.

"My best friend, Evie-" she started to say, but he cut her off.

"Yes."

"I haven't even told you what is going on."

"Doesn't matter."

Felicity looked at him. "Evie has this guy who is bothering her."

"Yup. I'll do it. Whatever it is if it involves Evie," he said with a serious face.

"You've never met her," Felicity said and then thought about all the videos she'd posted online with her cute friend. "Ah, but you have watched everything I've posted. Haven't you?"

"At least a few times," he admitted while he packed up his desk for the day.

Felicity laughed. Ira seemed to have it bad for Evie and she really was awesome. "Cool beans. Then I'll talk to her today and maybe you could come over tomorrow after work or something? She'll be at Espresso to Geaux, but I could work while you two talk."

Ira stood up with his briefcase of paperwork he seemed to always take home with him, "It's a date."

Of course, Hudson walked in to hear that comment as Ira told them both good night. Hudson barely looked her way as he went into his office and closed the door behind him.

What was wrong with him?

As soon as Ira left, she knocked on Hudson's door. He didn't say come in and so she knocked a little louder.

"Yes?" Hudson called out.

When she walked into his office, he had a ton of paper work on his desk and looked annoyed at her. "I guess that coffee didn't help your mood any?"

"What is it, Felicity? I'm busy."

She mistakenly thought he was mad at her. Perhaps it really was about something to do with work. "Is there anything I can help you with before I go?"

"No. Run along on your date with Ira."

She looked at him. *Was he jealous? Was that her wishful thinking?* She mentally scolded herself. She didn't want to date anyone, especially her boss.

"Is there anything else, Miss Storey?"

She shook her head, turned to walk out, but then stopped and turned around to look at him. "Um, I was talking to Ira about my roommate, Evie. You know that guy that came to the coffee shop Sunday morning? He keeps harassing her and I figured if she had a guy around then maybe he would leave her alone."

Hudson was expressionless as she explained. What was all that moodiness about. He was such a grump.

She shrugged and left without another word. Why did she explain anything to him? It wasn't like she owed him anything except for a hard days work and she'd done that day in and day out. So what, he came over to her coffee truck after the Christmas party and then hung out with her while she baked. They'd had fun working together Sunday and perhaps she'd mistakenly thought they were friends or becoming friendly when it had just been a small gesture on his part.

Grabbing her things, she walked out of the office angry at him for making her feel anything. She was just trying to be a good person and wasn't that enough?

This was why, outside of her mom and Evie, she didn't want any other personal relationships except for her dog.

People were annoying.

Chapter Nineteen

Felicity took Winston on an extra-long walk after she changed her clothes. She needed to clear her head and it was the only sure-fire thing that worked these days.

Winnie dutifully checked out every mailbox in the neighborhood and happily sped up when the cool wind blew. He truly loved cold weather and Felicity vowed to take him to see snow one day.

After their walk, she loaded him up in her car and headed to Espresso to Geaux to help Evie. "How's it going," she asked as she stepped inside their food truck, home away from home.

"Good. Busy day," Evie said as she continued cleaning some wet coffee grounds she'd spilled earlier. "Had a rush of people and a small spill," she explained and Felicity grabbed the dustpan to help her get the mess cleaned up.

Two customers walked up, and Felicity took care of them as Evie had a seat. Once she handed over their coffee and hot chocolate, she turned to look at Evie. "What's wrong?"

"The usual. Just worried about making our numbers, Felicity."

"But you know my salary will cover the costs. You don't have to worry, Evie." Something more was going on with her best friend. She watched Evie avoid the conversation as she refilled sugar and cream dispensers and wiped the small counter that was already clean.

When she finally looked up at Felicity, she frowned. "Baby Shark keeps coming by every morning. I've looked through the paperwork to make sure I'm not missing anything because he just seems smug that we aren't going to keep up with the interest. He told me that if I go out with him then he could forgive some of the payments. Perhaps it wouldn't be so bad. Especially if he would take away that twenty-five percent ownership thing."

Felicity saw Evie shiver when she thought about dating Baby Shark. He was such a creep. "There is no way I would let you go out with him."

"You know I would do anything to save our business, Felicity. If I have to go out with Isaac Keller then I will but if there is a way to avoid it, I want that option." Evie had always been strong-willed and confident. But this situation was getting out of hand and she wasn't sure how or what to do about it.

"While you were sick, he came by, and I told him that he wasn't allowed in here and that he had to pay for any coffee or pastries like every other customer."

"Oh, Felicity. We don't want to make him mad at us."

"There is nothing in that contract that says we have to be friends with him. And I was thinking that maybe if he thinks you have a boyfriend then he would leave you alone?"

"Right. I'll just conjure one of those up with all of my free time."

"What would you say if I told you that I might have found you one already?"

"Felicity Storey, what have you done?"

"He is really funny and has a great personality."

"So, he's hideous."

"No. He's very handsome."

"Uh-huh, and that's why you aren't going out with him?"

"It isn't like that, Evie. I swear."

They had a bit of an end of the night rush of coffee drinkers and couldn't discuss it any further. But as they closed up, Felicity explained that she'd talked to Ira and he was willing to help out in any way possible. She told Evie about his quick wit and how he was smart. She kept selling the idea to her best friend until they got home and began baking.

"So, if he's so great, then why aren't you interested in dating him?"

"You know that I am not dating right now or any time in the near future."

"It's been a year, Felicity. Troy Brook's doesn't deserve to mess up your life for this long."

"He hasn't. In fact, I owe him a big thank you because I wouldn't have Winston if the low life hadn't cheated on me."

"My mom said she ran into him the other day and he didn't look so good. As usual, she said you definitely came out ahead because you are too good for him."

Felicity laughed at her best friend. Evie and her mother had spent a ton of time trying to make her feel better about the devastating break up, but it didn't matter. She would never forget how he'd treated her or the words he'd said to break her heart. But that was in the past and she could at least pretend to be over it. "I don't want to hear about anyone running into him unless it was with their car."

Evie laughed at her best friend and was relieved that she could at least say negative things about Troy Brooks because he was a horrible human being. The way he'd treated Felicity was unforgivable and it didn't matter how much money his family had because being rich didn't automatically give you class.

Felicity pulled out the last batch of muffins and sat them down to cool while Evie wrapped cookies. "So, I mentioned to Ira about coming over tomorrow after work to meet you. I figured I could work the window and you two could sit and have a coffee together or go to Miss Lynn's Diner and have something to eat?"

"I'll meet him. But I can't guarantee that we'll even like each other. I'm definitely not going to dinner with a stranger either."

Felicity laughed. Evie couldn't stand up to Isaac Keller because they owed him money, but she could handle anyone else.

Later as Felicity laid in bed and thought about everything they had going on, she wondered what it would be like to just have a quiet life. She was exhausted and at this point would take just a day or two off from the hustle and bustle of her daily life.

She stared out her small bedroom window and could see the sliver of a moon shining. Finally closing her eyes, she thought about flying for the first time and everything she would have to do once she landed in Vermont.

The worry of traveling by plane and then about being separated from Winston for the first time stayed with her while she slept and when her alarm went off, she glared at it.

Had she even slept at all? Dragging herself from her warm covers, Felicity rushed through her shower and got ready for work. When she made it to the kitchen, Evie had already loaded her car and was back to grab Winston.

"Who's the best boy in the whole world?" Felicity said to Winnie the wonder dog and kissed his head. He nuzzled her back and then yawned.

Evie laughed and then Felicity hugged her too. "Remember, lock the back door and Shark Boy doesn't get any free coffee! I'll be by after work to introduce you to your new fake boyfriend. We've got this."

"I'm glad you're so chipper this morning. I could've used at least four more hours of sleep," Evie said, zipping her coat all the way up and giving Winston's leash a light tug.

Felicity wasn't sure she'd even had an hour of sleep and didn't know how she would actually make it to the end of the day, but Evie didn't need to worry about her. If she were being honest with herself and she currently wasn't, she was concerned over pulling all of this off too. She'd been running on no sleep ever since they'd bought the food truck and started the whole own-your-own-business-and-manifest-your-own-destiny plan. She hadn't even told Evie about ruining Sierra's expensive shoes and how she was getting to work extra early to sell coffee just to pay those off. Otherwise, she really couldn't pay their debt to Baby Shark.

No need to make Evie worry extra, she had this under control. She reminded herself that she could handle this, she could handle anything as she drove across the long bridge into the city. Finally, making it into her office, she stowed her coat at her desk before heading to the break room to make coffee. Hudson's light was on, but when he didn't say anything, she quietly slipped out.

Ed and John were the first two customers that morning and neither were very chatty. Felicity was thankful to have a few minutes to drink her coffee before the real crowd showed up. But as she sat back in a chair, Hudson came in and looked at her curiously. "Miss Storey? Everything okay?" he asked.

She jumped up to make him a cup of coffee. Of course, everything was fine, so she was sitting down for a minute was that a crime? "Yes, sir. Would you like something to eat this morning with your coffee?" she asked as she handed him his warm drink.

He still looked puzzled and then leaned forward, "I think your shirt is on backwards."

It took Felicity a minute to realize what he was saying and then she looked down at her blouse. Not only was it on backward but it was also wrong side out with the tag hanging loose. She really did need to get more rest. "I'll be right back," she said and ran to the restroom to flip her shirt around before the rest of the office came in for their coffee.

Hudson was still standing there when she returned. "Still baking cookies all night long?"

"Evie and I do it together, so it doesn't take too long." She didn't want to admit that she was running on fumes. Felicity didn't need her boss to question her ability to do a good job for him.

Still, he looked concerned anyway and she put on a big smile and greeted Betty and Charline. Hudson seemed convinced she was okay as he left her in the break room.

Ira was the only one she hadn't seen that morning and when she got to her desk, he wasn't there either. *Was he sick?* It wasn't like him to be late and so she sent him an email hoping he would still be able to go meet Evie after work.

Sierra came in and went straight to Hudson's office. "She closed the door behind her, and Felicity wondered what that was all about."

When she came back out, she smiled curtly at Felicity and then left. After an hour of sitting in the office alone, Felicity had sorted all the email messages for Hudson and cleared the final two items she had on her list for the conference.

She wasn't quite sure what to do next and had never been left there alone. It was important for her to stay busy or exhaustion would slam into her. Stifling a yawn, she wondered where the heck everyone else was.

"You're wiped out, aren't you?" Hudson asked as he stood in the doorway to his office.

He'd surprised her and she'd jumped when he spoke.

"Just need to finish my coffee is all," she lied.

Hudson didn't miss how she never asked for or acted like she needed anything. In her world, she was invincible, just ask her.

Ira will be in after lunch and Sierra took a personal day. If you need anything or have any questions then let me know, Miss Storey."

"Yes, sir, Mr. Frost." She hadn't forgotten how angry he'd been toward her yesterday. It didn't make sense, but he seemed fine now. Still, she wondered if he was angry because he thought she was going on a date with Ira? There hadn't been anything in her new hire paperwork that said she couldn't date anyone in the office, and she was pretty sure Ed and Betty had a thing. She refused to ask him about it, so instead she got busy with more conference details and pretended that Hudson standing there didn't intimidate her a bit.

Relieved that he didn't ask her anything else before heading back into his private office, Felicity sent a text to Evie to check on her. "Shark Boy came by again, but I did as you suggested and kept the back door locked. He was so angry when he had to stand in line, and I couldn't help but give him his coffee. Baby steps."

Felicity was irritated that Evie was letting that jerk push her around. The coffee truck was important to her too, but she wasn't about to let Keller Shark manhandle her.

She was up and pacing as she tried to think about what else they could do about him and still she came back to the idea of having Ira pretend to be Evie's boyfriend.

As she sat back down at her desk and tried to reel in her temper, she heard her phone make an odd noise. Then Hudson's voice came over the base speaker, "Miss Storey, can I see you in my office?"

Chapter Twenty

Felicity didn't know why she felt nervous when Hudson called her into his office. Maybe she felt guilty for thinking about the coffee shop more than her busy work at Frost Manufacturing that day? Perhaps the sleep deprivation was making her irrational? She hadn't done anything wrong even if the day before he acted angry with her. Felicity needed to pull herself together. Hudson didn't know if she was worried about the coffee business or that she was slower than usual. And she'd made it clear that she wasn't interested in Ira or going out with him, not that it should matter to Hudson.

"Yes, sir," she said as she walked into his private office and had a seat across from him.

"I saw that you've already gone through all of my emails. Ira said he'd left you and Sierra a list of items, have you completed those as well."

Felicity wasn't sure why she felt like she was sitting in the principal's office, but she answered him honestly, "Yes. Yes, sir."

"I have written two more speeches for the conference and could use your input if you have the time?"

Felicity nodded and then mentally scolded herself for acting paranoid. She was doing a good job for Hudson and needed to stop being so hard on herself. "Sure."

She stood up thinking that he would email the speeches to her but instead, he stood and pulled a chair over next to him. She sat down and watched as he took his seat and moved in even closer. Well, at least he didn't seem mad at her any longer. She leaned in and smelled his cologne, trying not to close her eyes and inhale deeper.

He smelled incredible, like sandalwood and something. When she looked up from his computer screen, he was looking at her and she knew she'd been caught. "What?" she said putting him on the spot.

"You just didn't look like you were here with me. Did you read it already?"

Felicity wasn't about to admit that she was distracted by how great he smelled. "Um, not all of it. I'm a slow reader, give me a minute?" she said as she kept her eyes on the computer screen.

He leaned back in his office chair and when she finished reading the first speech, she turned to look at him. He seemed to be closer than before and his eyes were dilated. "Distracted, Mr. Frost?"

He laughed. She was giving him a hard time and he shouldn't like that so much, but he did.

"Laser focused, Miss Storey," he said locked onto her stare and she squinted her eyes at him. "The speech is good, but you repeated yourself in paragraph three and then five. We need to delete one of those."

He looked surprised and pulled his chair in closer to look. She watched as he deleted the repeated passage and then pulled up his second speech for her to read.

"Mind if I make a couple of changes?" she asked, and he held out his hand showing her it was all hers.

She spent ten minutes moving things around and adding or deleting a few words here and there. When she was finished, he read it again and nodded.

"You're really good at this," he said and leaned back in his chair looking like he had more on his mind. After a brief pause, he asked, "This seems to come naturally to you. Have you always wanted to be a writer?"

Felicity finally broke their staring game. "Much to my mother's disappointment, yes. I think I wrote my first story in first grade. She had to suffer through all of my tales and wasn't too happy when she found out that I was going to study it in college."

"You two are close?"

"Of course. She's an incredible person, but we're different as night and day. She was born in New York to Ukrainian Immigrants. Neither of my grandparents spoke English so she had to translate for them their entire lives. She has a crazy strong work ethic, and she couldn't imagine how I would find a job with that type of degree."

"And look at you now."

Felicity grinned. "Yes, but she doesn't understand it. The food truck she understood."

Hudson knew what it was like to want to impress your parents and always feel like you were falling a bit short. But he didn't offer up that information.

Instead, he ordered them lunch and once it arrived, he and Felicity sat at the small table and chair set in his office. He seemed so casual as he opened the containers and offered for her to pick what she wanted first.

The whole office was swirling with the scent of oregano, basil, and garlic. Felicity was certain eating pasta with red sauce and a large meatball would put her in a carbohydrate coma. Yet, without hesitation, she piled it onto her plate as if she didn't have a care in the world.

Hudson followed her lead and then opened another bag with a warm baguette of French bread. Felicity was starving and took several bites before she realized he was watching her. "You like spaghetti?"

"I love pasta. You?" she asked as she twisted her fork in the noodles and then took a good bite.

"Yes," he smiled watching her dip bread into the red sauce and take another bite.

"So, what do you think about the job so far, Felicity? Feel like you're getting the hang of it or more like it isn't for you?"

She stopped eating and locked onto him. He sat his fork down when he saw her serious expression. "Is this a goodbye lunch? Did you do all of this so you could fire me?"

"What?"

"Am I getting the hang of it? And do you feel like this isn't for you, sounds like the beginning of you wanting to fire me," she said as she pushed her plate away. "Oh my gosh, is that why no one else is here this morning? They didn't want to be around when I got fired?"

"Miss Storey," he said and then softened his voice, "Felicity?" When she looked at him, he continued, "I think you're doing an incredible job, I merely wanted to know how you felt about it while we were alone. Please eat," he said as he pushed her plate closer to her.

She picked up her fork but didn't take a bite before she explained, "I love writing and honestly, it feels really important to help edit speeches and go over our media for the conference. I want to do a good job and hope you can see how dedicated I am to do it right."

Hudson smiled. "I see you, Miss Storey."

She wasn't sure why that gave her chill bumps, but it did. He was just her boss giving her feedback, wasn't he?

He seemed to relax even more and after finishing his spaghetti, he leaned back in his chair and smiled slyly at her. "Tell me something I don't know about you?"

Felicity smiled and shook her head. "You first." She challenged him.

Hudson shook his head. She enjoyed questioning him. No one ever did that. It was refreshing and a bit intimidating. "I love my job."

Felicity rolled her eyes. "You can do better than that."

"I love my job, but I want to do better work with the charity effort and this conference than I've done in the past."

"Duly noted, Mr. Frost," she said, and he liked the way her eyes shined when she looked at him.

"I taught myself to read when I was three and told my mother that I was born to be a writer because I could see a story in everything." When she looked up to see Hudson's face, he was smiling at her.

"Go on," he said.

"My grandparents spoke Russian because where they were from in the Ukraine was still under the USSR umbrella. My mother was the first member of her family to be born in the United States and she speaks Russian and English very well and is great with numbers. But she had to drop out of college because her parents got sick. So, she has always made it her mission to make me her success story." Felicity shrugged.

"What did she want you to do instead of writing?"

Felicity shook her head, but he kept smiling at her until she answered him. "Accounting."

"Accounting?" he confirmed and then whistled.

"She has worked two jobs as far back as I can remember and

when I told her I was going to college so I could be a writer one day, she didn't support that decision. She told me that she didn't know anyone that could make a living off writing. The most successful person she knew was an accountant, so she wanted me to go into accounting."

"Do you like bookkeeping or numbers?" he asked remembering how she handled her money from the mornings in a coffee can.

"I'm without a doubt, the worst student in the history of students who ever studied math. I would never have made it through accounting, but she didn't want to hear it. She had my best interest at heart but-"

"But you studied writing anyway."

Felicity nodded. She wasn't sure why she was telling him all of this and tried to stop giving him so much personal information. But he kept prodding her.

"How did the whole coffee truck thing happen?"

Felicity took a drink from her bottle of water. "As my mother predicted, I didn't get a great job after I graduated from college. I mean, I wanted to write novels but couldn't make her understand that it would take time to build that career. And Evie and I worked at a coffee shop while we went to school. We were good at it and Evie wanted to open her own business for about as long as I wanted to be a writer. So, we put together our business plan and borrowed some money to get started. Asha Filatova Storey was one hundred percent behind the idea of opening a food truck that specialized in coffee and pastries. It was nice to be on the same side with her for a change and to see her really proud of me."

Hudson locked onto her stare. "I get it. I know what it's like to want to impress your parents or make them proud of you. It has been my struggle for my entire life."

"Your father started this company though. And you worked here as a kid too, right?"

"Exactly. He had high expectations and I put a lot of pressure on myself to not make any mistakes."

Felicity pointed around the room. "From where I'm sitting, you seem to have everything under control."

"Believe me, it's a lot better on this side of the learning curve but when my father first put me in the CEO spot, I was wound tight. I was so worried about making a mistake that I couldn't make a decision without talking to him. He wanted me to know that I had all his support and so he left the country with my mother so that I would have to handle it on my own."

"Wow," Felicity said. "He must have a ton of confidence in you."

"He has a lot of love for me but I'm not so sure he believed I could do this in the beginning."

Felicity knew how hard it was to want something so badly but not know how to get it. "Maybe you were the one who wasn't certain?"

Hudson raised that judgmental eyebrow he probably practiced in the mirror. "I knew I could it, Miss Storey."

Felicity wasn't so sure he was telling her the truth about that but she liked his swagger. It seemed to be part of his personality and she liked confidence in a person. She also was built that way and would often tell Evie, *fake it until you make it.*

"Well, I can't imagine that kind of pressure." She'd learned through all her company research that his father had started the company from nothing and grew it into the successful manufacturing business it was today. The philanthropy side-hustle was almost as big as Frost Manufacturing. "I'm just co-owner in a food truck with an identity crisis of wanting to be a coffee shop. I'm pretty sure everyone who knows us has given Evie and I 50/50 odds on whether we'll make it a success or fail the first year. It's not so hard to deal with those types of expectations. Half the people you know are going to be right and the other half, well, better luck next time." Felicity mindlessly put away the leftover food and cleaned up their trash as she talked. Hudson watched her curiously and when she realized he was just watching her, she instantly stopped talking.

"What does your father do?"

Felicity crossed her arms in front of her body, and he remembered that stance from the day he met her when his driver ran into her car. "I don't talk about him."

"It was just that you said you couldn't imagine running a company that your father built, and I realized you had talked about your mom but not your dad."

"Yeah, still not going to discuss him. Ever." She looked determined but also a bit mad and he made a mental note not to bring up her family unless she specifically did it herself.

"What you and Evie have done with that food truck is incredible. You make great coffee, muffins, and cookies."

"And donuts but that's hard to do when there is only one of us running the window."

"Do you honestly think your business only has a 50/50 chance, Felicity?"

As tired as she was at that moment, she believed it was probably more like eighty to twenty. She wasn't so sure she or Evie Mae could keep up the pace they'd kept for the past six months. If she gave into the exhaustion she worried everything would crash and burn. But Felicity shrugged it off as if it wasn't a big deal before she lied. "Nah, I'm just kidding. Things are going fine. Some days are harder than others."

"Perhaps getting some sleep would help?" he said as he bumped his shoulder into hers.

She laughed and flippantly told him, "It's all good, I'll sleep when I'm dead, Mr. Frost."

Hudson watched as Felicity kept up her brave face but there was no mistaking how seriously she took the success of her coffee business. And failing wasn't an option she would take lightly. Still, it was hard to watch a young entrepreneur with a great idea and not a lot of business experience to keep it going.

Would she let him help her if he offered?

Chapter Twenty-One

Wednesday morning Felicity managed almost four full hours of sleep and woke up to a smiling Winston, ready for his early morning walk. Bundled up in black joggers and a black sweatshirt, she found Evie's parka by the door and slipped it on as she and Winston made quick work of their two-block walk.

When she stepped back into their small apartment, Evie laughed. "You look like a cat burglar with the black hoodie and all."

Felicity nodded. Ever since the annoying daylight savings time change, she woke up in the dark and got home after dark. It felt like they were in Alaska having one of those month-long polar nights she saw in a movie once, sans the vampires.

"As if I could sneak anywhere with this loud thing," she said and as if on cue Winston threw his ears back and howled.

"Who is the smartest boy in the world?" Felicity said lovingly to Winston. Then Evie chimed in, "Winston."

They worked together loading Evie's car with all the fresh baked goods, along with Winston. It gave Felicity a full twenty minutes to get ready for work. This time making sure her clothes were on properly.

In the break room at work, Felicity hummed *We Wish You a Merry Christmas* as she set out the extra baked goods and brewed coffee. She'd remembered to bring in some extra garland Evie's mom had left over from her Christmas decorations and strung it around the coffee cart along with some twinkling lights.

She was feeling festive and happy since she was getting closer to having Sierra's fancy shoes paid off. The first person to walk into the break room was Ira.

"I'm sorry to have left you in the lurch yesterday." He'd sent a text to Hudson that he needed to take the whole day off before he sent one to Felicity asking if he could meet Evie that weekend instead.

"I didn't mean to put you on the spot the other day and if you would rather not-"

"Trust me, Felicity, I would much rather go meet Evie." He didn't explain what was going on in his personal life and Felicity could see by the serious look on his face that he didn't want to discuss it.

"No worries. Come over this weekend or in a few weeks when you have the time," she said before handing him a peppermint mocha coffee and a chocolate muffin.

"Death by chocolate," he laughed.

"It would be a great way to go," she said, and Hudson walked in.

"What would be a great way to go?" he asked.

Ira winked at her and then left them alone.

Shaking her head at Hudson, she let him in on the secret, "Death by chocolate, of course."

"I don't get it."

"What's not to get? Decadent dark chocolate or smooth milky chocolate. "Yes, please, I'll have another," she said as she made him a cup of espresso and looked up to see him shaking his head at her.

"What?" she asked as she stared back at him.

"You're just funny, Miss Storey. That's all." She saw the devilish gleam in his eyes. "Am I to assume that you had a proper night's rest, finally?"

The break room began to fill up with more employees needing caffeine, but she leaned over and conspiratorially told him, "Yes. Almost a full four hours, uninterrupted."

He shook his head at her as she enthusiastically waited on others. She was something else and he liked her more than just about anyone new he'd met in a long time.

When Felicity got to her desk, Sierra was waiting for her. "You won't believe the amazing dress and coat that I picked up yesterday for the conference."

Felicity tried to act interested as she logged on to her computer and went through some of Hudson's emails. "Great. Can't wait to see them."

Sierra sat on the edge of Felicity's desk and talked for thirty minutes about the cashmere coat and how she posted it on her social media accounts.

Making a note to post a Winston video and a day in the life at Espresso to Geaux that week, she nodded at Sierra. Felicity didn't say anything else but Sierra didn't seem to notice as she talked on and on about herself and how she was going to stun everyone with her incredible outfits.

"Have you even started to pack, Felicity?" Sierra asked and finally stopped talking as she waited on Felicity to answer her.

Had Sierra taken the whole day off just to shop for their three-day conference? "No. I probably won't put things together until Monday night. We fly out Tuesday morning, right?"

Sierra looked like someone had slapped her. "I don't think you understand how important this conference is, Felicity. You are a representative of this company but also Hudson and the Frost name. You have to look the part."

Felicity shook her head. It was going to be the first time she'd really been anywhere. She'd never been on a plane or really seen it snow. She was excited to see the snow, even if it would be from the window inside the hotel or Hudson's house where the main dinner event would be held. She needed to make sure she was warm first, cute second, and honestly, she would borrow most of the clothes from Evie who'd been skiing several times and had winter attire.

The most important thing for them to worry about over the next three days would be putting together the video presentations and sending out a few teaser clips for the attendees. But they couldn't do that without getting actual footage.

"Have you set up the interviews so we can get video today, Sierra?" It was the most important task Ira had given her and Sierra hadn't mentioned it.

"They weren't available. Besides you know it's going to rain all day today and tomorrow. I heard we were under a severe weather watch." The excuses rolled off her tongue almost as easily as she talked about her wardrobe.

"You said they weren't available last week too."

"We can use stock footage from their websites or get them to forward pics. It's not a big deal."

Felicity stood up and looked at Sierra. "You talk about social media all the time, so I assume you realize this is a big deal. Like the biggest deal because we want original footage. How are we supposed to get the attendees excited without great content? And how are we supposed to get content without doing it in person?"

"Did you hear the part about the rain or severe weather? I swear you don't listen to me." Sierra threw her hands up in the air and walked off down the hallway as Ira came back from a meeting with Hudson.

"What's up?" he asked seeing Sierra strut out of the office.

"We're running out of time." Felicity explained that they still didn't have fresh video footage from the charity recipients, or the upcoming groups being considered. She would have to edit all the footage after they got the raw clips and that took a lot more time than most people realized.

Ira didn't want to make a big deal about it, but he'd only given Sierra the one task for the conference, call and set up the appointments. She could've done that all in an afternoon. Felicity on the other hand, had taken care of everything else.

"Would you want to call and set them up, Felicity?" he asked, feeling guilty that she'd practically done it all on her own and then would also have to go out and take the videos.

"If you want something done right, Ira, you have to do it yourself." she said and winked at him. "Yes, please."

He sent her the email he'd sent Sierra with the details but then walked over to Sierra's desk to find the printout he'd made for her. She had doodled all over the page, but it hadn't looked like she'd called more than a few on the list.

Handing the sheet over to Felicity, he headed down the hallway to find Sierra. She was in the break room with a diet coke and her cell phone. He'd already felt guilty for not being able to go to the conference and handing the tasks off to Sierra and Felicity had taken a piece out of him. Like he wasn't doing his job or able to fulfill his duties due to his personal life.

Sierra finally looked up to see Ira standing there glaring at her. "What's up, Ira?" she said in that tone he didn't like and that was all it took for him to lose his temper.

"How the hell can you sit in here looking at social media and drinking a diet coke while Felicity is in there doing your job?"

Sierra rolled her eyes. "We have the same job, or haven't you noticed? We must help each other. It's the nature of our positions as Hudson's ghostwriters. We don't get credit for what we do and signed an NDA so what's the big deal?"

"The big deal is that she's doing circles around you and I for one can attest to the fact that she handled every single thing associated with the conference. Are you okay with Hudson knowing that, Sierra?"

"You wouldn't snitch."

"Hudson doesn't like disagreements going on within the company but I think he would find it interesting that Felicity is doing everything on her own without your help."

"Well, we all have secrets, don't we, Ira. And if you don't want yours told to everyone in the company then you should keep your mouth shut about me."

Ira and Sierra hadn't gotten along in the past, but she happily kept his secret for her own gain. When she wanted to interview for the ghostwriter position, he threatened to tell Hudson about her behavior, but she waved her little truth bomb around until he stepped back and let her wiggle her way into the position. She'd also used her mother's friendship with Hudson's mother because she was shameless when it came to getting things she didn't deserve.

He'd tried to get Hudson to only look at Felicity, she was fresh and had mad skills when it came to writing. Exactly what Hudson was looking for, but his mother had a lot of pull with him and he'd known Sierra had to be moved out of the warehouse division.

It wasn't fair to Felicity or him but what could he do? He'd wanted to keep his private life private.

"While you're sitting in here, you'd better hope that Felicity doesn't tell Hudson everything. She may not realize that she's done all of your work, but he sure will."

Sierra jumped up and scowled at Ira. She couldn't take a

chance that Felicity inadvertently gave Hudson the ammunition he needed to finally let her go. She'd worked for Frost manufacturing for over a year in hopes that Hudson would finally notice her. When her mother explained that he was all about the company and work then they'd schemed to get Sierra closer to him. She certainly wouldn't let some young girl fresh out of college walk in there and take her opportunity to date one of the most eligible bachelors in the City of New Orleans. Now that the mayor was off the market, there were fewer men available in her age range. And she could feel her biological clock ticking. She wanted to get married and build the beautiful house of her dreams before they had two kids and a summer home at the beach. She would post it all on her Instagram page for the world to watch and was sure she could grow her following to a million with him by her side.

Outside of her office, she bent down to adjust one of her heels. No one needed to know she'd been running. But as she neared the door, she could hear Hudson laughing at something Felicity said and was worried she was already too late.

Chapter Twenty-Two

Hudson stood beside Felicity, watching something on her computer screen when Sierra walked into the office. She was angry that they looked so cozy and comfortable with one another. When had that happened? Sure, he'd scolded her that first day for patting Felicity's head, but was it more?

She saw her worksheet on Felicity's desk as she wrote notes in the margin. "What are you doing with my worksheets, Felicity? Have you been going through my desk? My Things?"

"What? No?"

Sierra looked at Hudson with her most helpless pout and Felicity had never wanted to strike another human being as much as she wanted to hit Sierra in her collagen injected lips.

Sierra walked over to Felicity's desk and snatched the documents from her hands. Felicity stood and shook her head. "Look Sierra, you haven't finished the list and I was afraid we couldn't get everything done if we didn't get out to these clients and film some of their responses."

Sierra looked indignant as she continued to perform in front of Hudson. "I told you that I was going to finish that as soon as I got back. Rob needed me in the warehouse, and I can't be in both places at once."

Felicity knew for a fact that Rob was out for the rest of the week because his son had to have his tonsils removed. "Rob isn't even here today."

Throwing her hands up in the air, Sierra pulled the one thing that worked every time with Hudson, tears. "Well, I know that now but I didn't know it before and I walked all the way over there in my Gucci heels. No one could tell me when he would be back and when I headed back here, my heel twisted, and I almost fell."

"Are you alright, Sierra?" Hudson asked, being polite and trying to diffuse the argument that was brewing between them.

"I just twisted it a bit right here," Sierra said lifting her leg and ankle toward their boss.

Felicity wanted to make gagging noises but figured Hudson wouldn't approve. She couldn't believe he was dumb enough to fall for Sierra's fake injury. But she had to give it to the woman, she was an expert at getting attention and getting out of work.

Trying to get them back on the actual important topic of video footage, Felicity walked around her desk to stand next to Hudson. "Look, I just wanted to make sure we had original video from the nonprofit organizations that are receiving awards. I organized them in order of importance."

Sierra looked offended. "Felicity Storey, they are each important."

Felicity shook her head. "In order of importance to our conference, like the one who won nonprofit of the year and will be getting the large cash award, needs to be filmed first. Then the top five who also get cash prizes for their triumphs should be filmed second. That way if we do run out of time, which looks like might happen, we'll at least have something to work with. We can always use the stock footage available online that you suggested earlier for the rest."

Felicity of course didn't like that idea, but it would come down to time.

"I was going to call the rest of them today," Sierra didn't miss an opportunity for a hair flip and made sure to step closer to Hudson so he could smell her strawberry shampoo.

Felicity was getting claustrophobic as she stood next to Hudson and the tall woman took another step closer. Felicity took a big step back and Hudson grinned. He knew she had an issue with small spaces, even though she refused to admit it.

"I can have Ira clear my afternoon," Hudson said.

Sierra beamed from the idea of him clearing his schedule until he added, "We'll pull our resources. Sierra will focus on booking everyone for this afternoon and tomorrow. And I can go with you Felicity to get the footage you need for the video."

Sierra reached out to touch his forearm and Felicity stared at her and then at him. He didn't cringe as she would have liked but he didn't react positively either. Basically, he didn't have any reaction, just looked at Sierra as she spoke. "I think we're forgetting here who has built a huge social following. I mean, I am an influencer and probably should be there when you film."

Hudson nodded. "Your experience is worthy, Sierra. But we'll get all the raw footage, and you will be an integral part of putting it all together including the clips sent out to the donors prior to the conference.

Felicity wished she'd been filming that conversation. It was sublime because Sierra couldn't have known her words would backfire into her having to actually work some extra hours.

Nodding in agreement, Felicity added, "I can upload all the videos so you can work on it at home if you need to Sierra. I know it takes a long time and they're super important."

Sierra shot her a cold look and then smiled calmly. Felicity was certain the woman was plotting her slow and painful death, but it would be worth it after watching this whole thing go down the exact opposite of what Sierra had wanted.

Felicity flitted around her own desk, grabbed her bag and keys, before asking Hudson, "Should I drive?"

"I have a new driver who started today. We'll use him so we don't have to worry about parking."

Felicity nodded. "Okay, I just need to run into the break room to grab my lunch and I'll be ready."

Hudson shook his head. "I didn't bring lunch, Miss Storey, and I can't imagine you have enough in there for both of us. We'll stop for lunch. My treat."

Felicity shrugged like it wasn't a big deal, but she knew that Sierra was ready to kill her which made it that much sweeter. Karma was a bitch, and it was a great life lesson that Sierra needed to learn sooner rather than later.

When Ira walked back into the office, Felicity could see he was upset about something before he covered up his expression. Hudson told him about their plans, and she saw the sly grin spread across Ira's face when Hudson mentioned that Sierra would be staying there so she could book all the rest of their appointments with the nonprofit groups. He suddenly looked pleased, and Felicity understood he appreciated as much as she did the irony of it all.

It was perfect. Except now she was worried that something was going on with her sweet new friend Ira and she hadn't paid close enough attention. As she and Hudson walked out front to meet his new driver, she sent Ira a text.

"Please don't worry about meeting Evie if it's too much trouble. We'll figure something out on our own. You seem to have a lot on your mind. Let me know if I can help in any way."

Once she sent the text, she looked up to see Hudson watching her. "Something wrong, Miss Storey?"

"No," she answered. "I was just rescheduling something with a friend." She climbed into the large Suburban SUV. Hudson held the door for her and then walked around to the other side to sit beside her.

"This is your show, Miss Storey. You tell Bryce where we need to go."

Felicity had never ridden in a taxi much less had a driver. Unless her mother or Evie's parents counted.

Pulling out her list, Felicity crooked her head to the side. "Bryce, how long have you been a driver? And how do you handle a parking space where another car is already there with their blinker on?"

Hudson laughed at her and then told Bryce to ignore those questions.

Felicity shrugged before giving Bryce the address for their first appointment.

In the past, the nonprofit groups knew they were in the top rankings but wouldn't find out if they won until the conference was over. The wait wasn't necessary because the votes were already cast, and the winner already known amongst their group. So, Felicity had another suggestion. "Since you're coming along today, why don't you announce it to them in person? We'll get their honest reaction on camera and share it with the donors' group at the conference."

Hudson's expression didn't give anything away and she wasn't sure if he was happy or mad until he spoke. "I love that idea. Someone usually calls them once the conference is over but hearing it and seeing it are two different things. You came up with that idea yourself?"

"I wanted to ask you but there wasn't enough time. I figured if you said no then it wouldn't matter because we're still going to video everyone today and tomorrow." She handed him some questions to ask the groups and asked if he wanted to do all the interviews or if he wanted her to conduct some of them.

The plan was to interview the winning group first telling them they made the finals so they could capture their reaction on video. Then they would announce that the group won the whole thing for their hard work and contribution to helping others.

They could then edit the video footage, adding in music and creating a whole emotional event to share with the donors' group at the conference in Vermont. It would surely motivate them to give even more in the upcoming year. Plus, it would be meaningful to the groups to meet someone from the Frost family in person instead of just a phone call.

Felicity had already set up all the appointments with those groups and Hudson watched her roll with the details as they pulled into the location for *Grace at the Greenlight.*

The director greeted them at the front door and as Felicity suspected, she was surprised to meet Hudson Frost in person. Talking fast as she showed them around and introduced them to a few volunteers, it was obvious they made her a bit nervous.

There were six people volunteering and Hudson made sure to speak to each one personally. Felicity explained that *Greenlight* was chosen as a finalist and Hudson wanted to meet them in person because of the great job they were doing.

Excitement filled the air, but they were understaffed with volunteers that Wednesday and they had to talk and work at the same time. Felicity kept her small video camera rolling as they talked about their programs and what they were able to do with the money donated by The Frost Group.

She loved how grounded Hudson was in the moment and how personable he became after just a couple of minutes. Felicity asked them to stand together so she could take a photo. As soon as they did, she asked one of the volunteers to pop open the cannister of confetti when Hudson leaned forward and told the director they had won the first spot.

Hudson looked like he might get emotional when the director cried but pulled it together after he gave her a hug. The excitement in the room vibrated as they immediately discussed how many more people they could help with the added donation.

Goosebumps covered Felicity's arms as she swallowed back tears. But it didn't slow her down while she took great candid pictures along with video.

Before leaving, Hudson ordered coffee and beignets for the group because he said they needed the caffeine and sugar to fortify them for the rest of the day. The entire visit took over an hour and Felicity suddenly realized there was no way she could have done this on her own. Especially since they were taking twice as long as she'd predicted and needed to rush to the next place.

"I don't think we can visit with each of them as long as we did there. We won't be able to get to everyone on my list today if we do," she said but Hudson shook his head.

"I'm afraid you've created a monster, Miss Storey. I won't be rushed."

She grinned as she tried to organize who was where and what time they could reasonably make it to each location. The next three stops were Second Harvest Food Bank, St. Michael Special School for children, and Lakeview Shepherd Center- A day center for seniors. All diverse nonprofits but the honest care the volunteers provided and the way they adored Hudson was a sight to behold. He couldn't help himself when he bought lunch for all three groups, including all volunteers, kids, and seniors at each place.

When they got back in the car, she laughed at him. "How are

you going to afford to do this again next year if you keep giving so much away?"

She could see Hudson was a bit embarrassed by her praise. "You let me worry about that, Miss Storey. Where to next?"

The next business was going to be her heart. It was a shelter for animals and Felicity admitted to Hudson that she always wanted to save them all and bring them home with her. She tried to bolster her feelings but when they pulled up, Hudson helped her down out of the large car before asking her if she was going to be okay.

The weather had gotten worse, and they each wore raincoats, but he also pulled out a large umbrella. "I'm fine. These places are just amazing. I'm so glad they made the top five."

Hudson wrapped his free arm around her as he covered them with his umbrella. "Stay close, Miss Storey. I'll help you make it through this one."

He was so sweet sometimes that she didn't know what to think or say. And when they got inside, she wasn't sure who was going to save whom.

Chapter Twenty-Three

Beckett Young met Felicity and Hudson at the door while he was holding and feeding a teeny-tiny newborn kitten. Hudson looked at her and whispered, "Be strong," as he reached out to hold and feed the kitten himself.

She watched as he nuzzled the little thing close to his chest like it was something he did all the time. *Who was this man and what had he done with her grumpy boss?*

Hudson didn't waste any time telling Beckett that they were in the top five of all the businesses they helped and would receive a monetary bump in their annual donations for all the great work they were doing.

Felicity almost missed getting the video because she was so overwhelmed by her boss and his enthusiasm for animals. When Beckett told him that it would be a great help because the van they used to help transport animals from kill shelters had broken down, she couldn't miss the look on her boss' face. Hudson immediately told him he wouldn't have to use the money for that because he would buy the shelter a new transport vehicle.

They spent another hour walking through the facility so

Hudson could see what else they had improved upon but also asked what were their immediate needs that weren't being met. All the while, Hudson held that kitten.

Again, he bought Beckett and all the volunteers dinner, and if Beckett hadn't told him that the kitten already had a home, she was certain Hudson would have adopted him.

When they got back into the car, he looked over at Felicity who was grinning like crazy. "What?"

"You love animals." It wasn't a question.

"What's not to love? He answered as if it wasn't a big deal, but she knew differently. Her ex didn't like cats, dogs, birds, or any animals at all which was the reason she didn't hesitate when she saw the picture of Winston.

"You love people too. Like really love them." She stopped looking at him because she was either going to cry or kiss him and she wasn't sure she wouldn't do both.

"I'm starving. You hungry? Let's go eat, Felicity," he said before telling Bryce to take them to Superior Grill on St. Charles Avenue.

They sat by a large window overlooking the street and ordered drinks. When the waitress came back, they ordered their food, and each ran to the restroom to wash their hands and clean up a bit from the rain they'd been in and out of most of the day.

Hudson was back at the table before Felicity, and she admired how handsome he was sitting there in the fading light of day. Of course, he was handsome in the bright sunlight too, but she tried not to think about it.

He smiled at her when she had a seat. "I don't know why my father never handed out these awards in person before but it's a lot of fun. I think he would really approve."

Felicity grinned as she took several large sips of her water. "I'm not so sure he would approve if he knew how much money you spent on food and then a van for the animal shelter."

"Don't forget the added kennels," he said as he dug into the chips the waitress brought to the table.

"Yes, and the ten additional kennels." She couldn't help but look at him differently. A man who loved animals was sort of her spirit animal.

"The van was important to their business, and I couldn't just let them try and function without a vehicle to pick up animals from kill shelters."

Felicity had tried to volunteer at the animal shelter near her college but the one time they let her go to a kill shelter to pick up two dogs, she came pack with seven. They flipped out and fired her. She argued that they couldn't fire her because she was a volunteer and the director pointed her to the door after he told her that he unvolunteered her.

She didn't think that story was relevant now, so she kept it to herself as he stared at her.

"Tell me how you ended up with Winston?"

Felicity laughed. Was this man her boss or her friend? Could they honestly be both? "Someone put him on Craig's List. Siberian Husky for a hundred dollars with his picture."

"Why do I get the feeling there is a longer story in there?"

She cut her eyes at him as she broke a chip in half and dipped each side into salsa. "Because you stalk my YouTube channel."

"I wouldn't call it stalking. I'm just a fan. Of the dog." He kept a straight face, but the smirk was there.

"I was going through a bit of a rough break up. It happens. Anyway, I couldn't stop thinking about that cute face and why would anyone want to get rid of a full-blooded husky for a hundred dollars?

"Evie Mae freaked out that I would go alone to follow up on a Craig's List ad. She said when it's too good to be true then it's fake. She made her older brother go with me and it was probably a good idea. We drove out to the location and there was just a single-wide trailer on some property that needed to be mowed and there he was tied up outside in the unbearable heat." Felicity wiped the salt off her hands. Thinking of what her precious dog had been through and how he probably wouldn't have made it if she hadn't saved him, dissolved her appetite.

"Mitch had a gun in the back of his shorts but honestly, he's a huge guy and no one in their right mind would want to mess with him. When we knocked on the door, a middle-aged woman came out and met us."

"So, you knew he was yours the minute you saw him?"

"He actually claimed me," she said with a smile. "The woman who lived their opened the door and barely said hello before he chewed through the rope, she'd tied him up with and came barreling toward me. I braced myself just in time and when he put his paws on my shoulders, I hugged him back.

"She told us some crazy story about her sister had him but he was too much for her. It was probably all a lie. He was twenty-five pounds underweight and when I gave him a bath that night, he was covered in ticks, fleas, and mites. The vet said he probably wouldn't make it because he had heartworms and I cried. She treated him at half the cost and Mitch even pitched in to help me."

"You dated Mitch?"

Felicity shook her head. "Gross. He's like my brother."

Hudson nodded but she didn't miss how he stared at her.

"The treatment was no joke. Winston had to have meds for six months and was basically sedated during that time to keep his heart from racing or he could've had a heart attack."

Hudson nodded. "I remember that was when you started your channel, right?"

Felicity grinned. Ira had told her that Hudson had watched all the videos. She hadn't been certain that was true, but hearing him talk about them, made her realize he not only was a fan, he'd paid close attention.

"I wasn't sure he would make it through and wanted to document how important it is for us to be stewards of these incredible creatures. I swear he's my angel on earth. Sent just for me. I was going through a difficult time, and he loved me hard." Hudson watched her carefully and if she hadn't been talking about Winston, she might have been self-conscious.

"He's a smart dog though. You trained him a little bit every day and I think he'd do anything for food," Hudson said.

Felicity remembered when she first got him how he would hide his food or bury treats immediately instead of eating them. It took her months to make him understand that he would never go hungry again.

"He does love his treats. He's a healthy weight now and his coat is super shiny too."

"Built for snow, I hear?"

Felicity shrugged. "My vet said they acclimate somewhat, and he does swim in Evie's parent's pool, in the winter. One day I hope to take him to see snow."

"He's a special one."

"Yes. Winston is the best thing that has happened to me in a long time."

The waitress brought their food and when she left them alone, Felicity watched Hudson for a minute. "I know that Sierra said she's allergic, but my vet said if someone is allergic to dogs then Huskies are usually the worst for you. And honestly, she did not sneeze once. I was wondering if Fridays could still be bring your mascot to work day?"

Hudson laughed. Sierra had pretty much admitted that she'd lied about the allergy thing. But he would press the issue with her Thursday just to be certain.

"We'll see, Miss Storey."

Felicity nodded as she thought about how Winston charmed everyone, even her boss, who she now understood loved animals. They would start with Fridays but as soon as he agreed then she would push for Mondays too.

It was after seven when they pulled up in front of the office. Felicity thanked Bryce for the ride and began to tell Hudson she would see him tomorrow as she climbed out of the SUV.

He shook his head as he got out and met her at her door. "Miss Storey, it's late and I'm not going to let you just walk to the garage by yourself."

Felicity nodded but didn't know what to say. Her ex-boyfriend never walked her to her car or to her door after a date. Honestly, she couldn't remember any boys she'd gone out with treating her that way. She was starting to like Hudson Frost and she needed to calm down. He was her boss, and this was just work.

They walked through the building and got into the elevator without talking but after she pressed the button for the parking garage, she didn't miss how he smirked.

"What?" she asked squinting her eyes over at him.

"I was just worried you were about to press the stop button," he said and wiped his brow.

She shook her head and tried not to laugh. "You think that's bad, wait until I get on an airplane for the first time."

He stopped smiling and stared at her. Sierra had told him that Felicity hadn't flown before, but he wasn't sure she was telling him the truth. Still, he'd offered his private plane just in case. But he now needed to know the truth. "You've never been on an airplane, Felicity?"

She shook her head avoiding his stare.

"But you knew this job required you to travel?"

She shrugged. "There are lots of ways to travel, Mr. Frost. It could have just as easily been by car, bus, or train."

"Bus?"

Felicity grinned and when the door of the elevator opened, she almost skipped out into the parking lot. The garage was mostly empty and as the cool night air blew across them, she crossed her arms to keep warm.

She was glad she wasn't alone and when she turned around to tell him that, he was standing awfully close.

"You think your pretty funny don't you, Miss Storey?"

"Humor is a very underrated quality, Mr. Frost."

He stepped even closer, and she could feel his body heat. She tried not to lean into him and quickly closed her eyes before she did something crazy like hug him.

When he reached over and gently tucked her windblown hair behind her ear, she opened her eyes to see that his pupils were dilated just like hers. "It's late, Miss Storey. If you wouldn't mind, would you shoot me a text and let me know that you made it home safely tonight?"

Felicity nodded because she didn't trust her own voice at that moment.

Hudson reached around her and opened her door so she could get in and when she sat down, he told her to be safe before he closed it for her.

She quickly started her car but before she backed out, she looked over at him and he held his phone up to remind her to text him when she got home.

Biting her bottom lip, she wished she'd said something smart-alecky back to him, so she didn't seem so desperate but at that moment she was a bit hopeless for him.

As she headed across the long bridge home, all she could think about was how he had held that kitten and tried to take care of all those people who took care of others.

Why did he have to be a spoiled rich kid like her ex boyfriend? She'd learned the hard way that she ultimately didn't have anything in common with those types of people and it was best that she stopped the daydreaming about her boss right then and there. But why did he have to go and buy a van for the animal shelter and bottle feed that kitten? He was not playing fair.

Chapter Twenty-Four

A wet cold dog nose under the covers forcefully nudged Felicity awake Thursday morning. "Just a minute, Winston," Felicity said and his response was a loud howl to go outside. "It's a good thing you're cute, mister," was all she could say as she slipped on sweatpants over her sleeping shorts and tennis shoes.

They made record time around the block as it began to rain. When they ran back into the small pool house, Evie dragged herself around the kitchen trying to wake up too.

So, Felicity put on her happy face as usual and tried to pep her friend's mood up. "Who wants to own a food truck and make her coffee business dreams come true? We do!" she said, and Evie shook her head.

"I said, who wants to make their coffee business dreams come true?"

Evie Mae weakly said, "We do." And Felicity laughed. "That's right. Now let's get these pastries loaded into the car so you can get there before the morning rush."

Evie growled at her which made Winston howl. It was a game

he liked to play, and he proved he could be the loudest one in the room each and every time. When Evie leaned down to pet him, he licked her nose and Felicity couldn't help but love that her best friend loved him too. It had been touch and go in the beginning because he was a bit feral but Evie eventually warmed up to him and now was basically a co-parent.

Felicity hugged Evie and loaded Winston into her friend's car before she rushed back inside to get ready for work. She and Evie were up until almost one and it was wearing them both down. She would have to spend time this weekend baking extra treats so they could get ahead. Otherwise, Evie would have a rough week ahead.

Traveling would be difficult for them all and it overshadowed how excited Felicity had initially felt when she heard about the picturesque ski town with tons of snow.

When she pulled into the office garage, she looked around and noted that like last night there were hardly any cars in there. She wished she could have just spent the night sleeping at her desk. But she was a dog mom now and apparently a part time baker.

Felicity heaved the bag of coffee supplies over her shoulder as she headed into her office. It was quieter than usual which was saying something since she was always one of the first to arrive.

This morning no one else was there yet and she checked the clock to see that it was only a quarter after seven. She had made it across the bridge in record time. Double checking her office, she saw Hudson's light still off, and was a bit surprised that she had beat him there.

It had to be her greenlight morning working in her favor. Whenever she drove across town and didn't catch any red lights, it made her feel like her day would be a little bit better. And it must be true since that morning she could get set up without being rushed.

She hummed *We Wish You a Merry Christmas* as she headed into the break room to begin brewing coffee for the office masses.

If she didn't hit her goal that morning, then she would surely have the full amount of money to pay Sierra back tomorrow. But she wasn't so sure she could stop the coffee business now that everyone loved it so much.

Betty, Charline, and Loretta were the first one's in and they chatted for several minutes before Hudson walked in. "Good morning," he said and his voice was a bit gravely like he'd just woken up.

The older women all left after that, leaving him alone with Felicity. "I wasn't sure you would make it in for coffee this morning, Miss Storey."

Felicity shook her money can and grinned. "You best believe I'm not going to miss an opportunity to get those outrageously expensive shoes paid off."

"Right. But you know, it's okay if you need a little more time." Hudson grabbed some napkins and didn't seem to look at her when he talked about the money for Sierra's shoes. Was he still aggravated about the whole incident?

"To be honest, Sierra hasn't said a word about them to me. She probably thinks I forgot or something. But the Storey women have integrity, and I would never skip out on paying for them."

Hudson nodded at her and without another word left the break room. He had been wonderful and considerate the night before and she was silly to think there was more going on between them. It only took the light of day and a brief conversation about Sierra and her ridiculous Italian shoes to bring them both slamming back into reality.

A large group filled the break room and took Felicity's mind off of Hudson's mood swings and the ever-lingering shoe debt hanging over her head. She sold out of everything, holding back a cup of Joe and a blueberry muffin for Ira. But when she walked back to her office, she saw that he wasn't in yet and Sierra was standing in Hudson's door flirting with him.

"The snow is so lovely up there this time of year. My parents took me when I was in grade school, and we spent all of winter break skiing and snow sledding. It is magical," she said as she twirled her strawberry blonde hair and did a little wiggle thing as she talked. She was wearing a tight sweater dress and another pair of expensive-looking high-heeled boots. Sierra did have style and Felicity wondered if what she was feeling toward her all that time was a bit of jealousy.

Felicity had never been jealous of anyone before and loved to cheer fellow students or employees on when they did a wonderful job. She would laugh and say, "You can't compete with me because I want us all to win."

Evie would tease her and say, "It isn't a contest if everyone wins, Fe."

Instantly, she wondered if Evie's morning had gotten any better when she got to the coffee truck. While Sierra continued to chat it up with Hudson, Felicity sent her best friend a quick text and received one right back. "Much better, thanks. Baby Shark must not like the rain because he didn't show up first thing this morning."

Felicity felt relieved that Evie was having a better day and after she quickly counted her coffee money to see that she was only thirty dollars away, she did a little dance of her own sitting at her desk. She would pay Sierra off in the morning and that would put the whole incident behind her, it was definitely a greenlight day.

But when she looked up, she saw Sierra watching her. "What was all that about," she asked as she twirled her pointer finger at Felicity.

"I don't know what you mean."

Sierra rolled her eyes. "Whatever. Do you have time to go through the emails this morning?"

Felicity didn't understand why Sierra didn't like to answer the emails, but it was obvious that she didn't. Sierra found a way almost every morning to hand them off to Felicity. They were equals in the office hierarchy, but Sierra didn't miss a chance to push things onto Felicity's to-do list. Still, Felicity liked her job and answering emails was the easiest thing they did there.

While she was quickly going through email, Ira walked in with his head down. He had always been good natured, and his behavior lately was concerning Felicity. She watched him log in to his computer before he realized she'd put a cup of coffee and muffin on his desk.

Looking up he mouthed, *thank you,* to her and then put his head down again to type. Next, he was up and in Hudson's office with the door closed.

Felicity looked over at Sierra who also had an eye on Ira, and when he closed the door behind him, she rolled her eyes. "He's so grouchy in the morning."

That wasn't at all the way Felicity saw him and she hoped she would get a chance to chat with Ira soon. But he walked out of Hudson's office and grabbed his things, including the coffee and muffin.

"See you Monday," he said avoiding looking at them as he left.

Felicity jumped up to follow him but before she made it around her desk, Hudson stepped out of his office. "I'm afraid I need to change our plans for today," he said looking at her and then Sierra. "You made the rest of the appointments, Sierra?"

She stood up, "Yes, of course, and I'd love to be the one to go with you today and video everything." It was so obvious that Sierra had worn that dress and those boots because she thought she would be with Hudson all day. She ran her hand down the waist of her dress as she tried to make eye contact with their boss. But Felicity was too worried about Ira to care. He'd said he would see them Monday and it was only Thursday. Was he sick? Was something going on with his family?"

"I can't leave the office today and honestly, Felicity has the whole interview, video, and picture thing down. You two go together. I'll have Bryce drive you again today, Felicity."

"Yes, sir," Felicity said but Sierra flopped back down in her seat. While she pouted, Felicity followed Hudson back into his office. "Is everything okay with Ira?" she asked.

Hudson stared at her, and she wished she knew what the heck he was thinking. "It's none of your concern, Miss Storey."

"Yes, sir, Mr. Frost," she responded and did not miss how his eyes hardened and nostrils flared a bit at her. She didn't care. He made such a point of saying how Frost Manufacturing was a family, but he seemed to turn that emotion off whenever he wanted. They'd spent a great deal of time together and he had no reason to be so cold toward her. Maybe it wasn't any of her business, but she was concerned about Ira.

Felicity walked back to her desk and pulled out her phone to send Ira a text. "Hope everything is okay, sweet Ira. If you need a friend to talk to then just give me a call."

When she finished, she saw Sierra still sitting at her desk pouting. "You ready to go? I would like to get back as soon as we can so I can finish the emails."

"I'm not really wearing the proper shoes to go run around town with you," Sierra said as she gave Felicity one of her grand hair flips. "I'll stay here and take care of the emails today. You can go."

Felicity was already frustrated at Hudson, and she'd had enough of Sierra telling her what to do. "Who died and made you the boss?" she said staring strawberry not shortcake down. At least she could stare down at her since she was sitting. Standing, Sierra had at least five inches on her.

"I'm not going. It's raining and my boots are suede."

"But if Hudson was going, you were all for it. Am I right?"

Sierra shrugged, "Duh."

Felicity grabbed the folder and her camera and stormed out the door. Sierra and Hudson were both foul and they deserved to spend the day with each other. She didn't need their help. She didn't need anyone's help.

She climbed into the SUV with Bryce and together they mapped out the city and made a plan of how to get to all the locations before the end of the day. It would take her a bit longer on her own, but she was happy to not have to deal with her spoiled boss and even more spoiled coworker.

But the longer she sat there and thought about them both, the angrier she got. They ruined her greenlight day and she really deserved to have one.

As Bryce pulled into the first location, she sent Hudson a text. "The resident prima donna didn't want to get her suede boots wet, so she decided to hang back at the office. I sure can't afford another pair for her, so she's all yours, Mr. Frost. Hope you two have a wonderful day!" She sent it before she could talk herself out of it and then switched her phone off so he couldn't respond.

The rain poured down and Felicity put her raincoat on, tucking her camera and folder inside so they wouldn't get wet. It might be miserable weather, but she didn't mind the rain and the thought of how angry Hudson would be when he couldn't give her his rebuttal made her laugh.

Those two deserved each other, she thought and then frowned. The Hudson Frost who she'd spent time with yesterday and a whole Sunday working at the coffee truck with was incredible. It was too bad he couldn't act like that when anyone else was around.

Instantly, she thought about her ex-boyfriend. Troy Brooks treated her differently around other people too. *Jerk.* And she'd been so smitten with him that she hadn't noticed it until it was too late.

Chapter Twenty-Five

W hat was up with rich guys and their Dr. Jekyl and Mr. Hyde personalities? Who had time for that nonsense? She could barely keep up with her one life and she sure wouldn't treat people differently depending on who they were around. You either liked her or you didn't. Simple.

Walking into the clean surroundings of a wonderful nonprofit that worked tirelessly to provide shoes for the elderly, Felicity forgot all about the grumpy people at her office.

She made it her mission for the day to put others first, and after each location, she sent pictures to Hudson to remind him of what was truly important.

By two in the afternoon, she was starving and asked Bryce to drive by City Park so she could take a quick break. As she got out of the car, she saw that she had six missed calls from her boss, but she didn't bother to call him back. If it was important, then he could tell her when she returned to the office.

Sitting on a stone park bench, she watched several young mothers and their children playing a game of duck, duck, goose.

Her mother had always been super busy, and she couldn't remember a single time that they went to the park or played a silly game. Still, she'd had a good life and nothing to complain about. But she sure would like to have a different lifestyle for her children, maybe like those happy little moms and toddlers in the park.

Felicity laughed as a little boy ran as fast as he could and slid into a spot before the goose tagged him. Pulling out her sandwich she told herself that sitting alone to eat the brown bag lunch she'd packed while watching some cute kids play didn't make her pathetic.

Troy Brooks had told her she wasn't the marrying kind and she agreed when she slapped him across his face. He'd said that they'd had a great time in the sack together, but she was a good time girl, not someone he could bring home to meet his parents. But he had brought her home to meet his folks. They went for Thanksgiving break and spent the weekend afterward with them too.

It was obvious that his mother didn't really like Felicity, but she couldn't figure out why. Then the last night they were there, she overheard his father who'd had too much to drink tell his son that he understood he had needs. "Sexual needs. But just because you bed her doesn't mean you have to wed her."

Felicity sat at the top of the staircase and listened as Troy's mother spoke. "She was raised by a single mother, Troy. Does she even know who her father is? She's a mutt."

It had hurt to hear what they had to say about her, but Felicity had always understood you couldn't put a filter on your parents and their opinions. But when Troy didn't stick up for her, she'd been destroyed.

She ran back upstairs to the guest bedroom and cried for an hour. When she pulled herself together and returned downstairs,

Troy acted as if nothing had happened. He even continued to date her back at school for another week.

When she walked in on him with another girl in his bed, he used all his parents' words against her.

Evie was there to pick up the pieces. Then Evie's mother and brother came too. Felicity's mother didn't know she was dating anyone much less how serious they were. She had told Felicity from the time she was thirteen that she had to stay away from boys until she got out of college. And she meant it too. There was no way she could tell her mother what had happened. But the Shepard Family had rallied around her and once she found Winston, things got much better.

Felicity watched the little boy run around the circle again but this time a dark-haired girl caught up to him. They both laughed and now he was it. Felicity loved kids but she was pretty certain they wouldn't be in her future. She was going to be a dog mom. Especially since she wasn't going to date anyone ever again. She smirked as she picked up her trash and headed back to the SUV.

Bryce stood outside of the vehicle and talked on his phone. Looking serious when she walked up, he quickly held it out for her. "It's Mr. Frost. He says he's been trying to reach you."

Felicity grinned and walked right past Bryce to get into the backseat. Looking confused, the driver told Mr. Frost that she couldn't take a call right then, but he would tell her to call him back. Felicity gave Bryce a thumbs up and when he got off the phone, she thanked him for covering for her.

"Don't worry, Bryce. I'll text him." She was feeling invigorated. Maybe from the awesome sandwich or from thinking about her last relationship failure. She was stronger after going through something like that and sometimes she had to remind herself that she could handle anything. Certainly, a little crush on her boss that wasn't going to go anywhere. Besides, Hudson Frost was a little too smug for his own good. Not getting what he wanted exactly when he wanted it, might just do him some good. Of course, it could get her fired too, but she refused to think about that. She was resurrecting her green light day and he would just have to wait because she had a long list of nonprofits to visit and photograph before the day was over.

It took the rest of the afternoon and early evening for Felicity to finish. She'd tried to get done faster but there were a lot of people on the list, and it wouldn't be fair to not give each of them the same amount of attention. It was after six and she was truly wiped out. Proud of all the work she'd done, including videos and still pictures, Felicity had everything they needed for the conference and additional social media posts.

She thanked Bryce as he dropped her in front of the building. It would take a few minutes for her to gather her things from the break room and her desk so she sent a text to Evie that she would be there a little after seven to help at the coffee truck. The nights at Espresso to Geaux were slower and she didn't mind taking a turn especially since the next week she'd be off to Vermont.

As Felicity walked off the elevator, she had her head down in her phone and walked right into an angry Hudson Frost. "Sorry," she said not realizing it was him at first.

"Miss Storey, when you are on the clock for Frost Manufacturing and I call you, you are required to answer. Is that clear?"

"Yes, sir, Mr. Frost," she answered and then turned to head toward the break room.

"I'm not finished," he said in a cool voice that seemed to echo in the hallway.

Felicity instantly could tell he was past angry and to be honest, might truly let her go. So, she turned around and gave him her full attention. "Yes, sir, Mr. Frost," she said but instead of stopping there, she added, "What is it that you needed today that couldn't wait." *Shut your mouth, Felicity Storey,* she screamed in her head.

"In my office, now," he responded and for a second she wondered if she should in fact go with him or perhaps make a run for it. Thankfully, her rational side won out and she slowly followed Hudson into his office. As he had a seat behind his desk, she stood and waited for judgment.

He pulled out his phone and began to read in a monotone voice the text she'd sent him that morning. "*The resident prima donna didn't want to get her suede boots wet, so she decided to hang back at the office. I sure can't afford another pair for her, so she's all yours, Mr. Frost. Hope you two have a wonderful day!* Exactly, what did you mean by sending that text to me?"

Felicity had sent that text while she was angry and honestly, hadn't remembered it sounding quite that bad. "I apologize, Mr. Frost. I was a bit upset at Sierra for refusing to help me with the video today." Thankful she'd managed to control her words, Felicity stopped talking before she said too much.

"And?"

"And what?"

"Why would you say she's all mine?"

Suddenly, her filter was off and her mouth running. She rolled her eyes. "It's obvious that she likes you. That's the whole reason she didn't want to go today besides the fact that the rain might ruin her new boots. She wanted to be near you." Felicity shrugged. She knew she sounded ridiculous, but exhaustion won out.

"And what does that have to do with me? Do you think I've encouraged that behavior? I'm her boss. I-I wouldn't date an employee."

Felicity nodded. Did he know she had a crush on him too? This was so embarrassing and worse than she could have imagined. "Sorry," she said as she lowered her head, wishing this conversation was over.

"Just so we're clear, Miss Storey, what is it that you're sorry for?"

For falling for you and all your kitten loving behavior, she thought. Biting back a smile over her ridiculous thoughts, Felicity tried to answer without any humor in her voice, "I'm sorry for not answering your calls or calling you back today. It won't happen again."

"And I'm not interested in Sierra and I'm not encouraging her behavior."

"Yes, sir, and that," she said and that time a smirk came out.

"Do you want to tell me what's so funny?" He didn't look angry anymore and Felicity had a full on smile now.

"Nope. I sure don't," she answered honestly.

Hudson shook his head and thankfully wasn't going to fire her tonight.

"Mr. Frost, just so you know, there isn't anything in our company handbook about dating another employee."

"And you would have a reason for looking that up because-"

"No reason."

"It's late. Go home, Miss Storey."

Felicity nodded and turned to walk out. Feeling a bit lighter than before, she gathered her things in the break room in record time. But as she headed toward the elevator, she could see Hudson holding it for her.

Was he going to walk her to her car again?

She got into the elevator and pressed the button for the garage. "Isn't Bryce taking you home?"

He nodded but kept looking straight ahead.

"Then what are you doing?"

"You know what I'm doing."

"Walking me to my car?"

"Yup."

She didn't miss how flippantly he'd answered her. *Was that because she'd done the same thing to him?*

He purposely walked with her and then held the door open, but she could see the way he was checking out the condition of her vehicle. "Miss Storey, when are you getting this car repaired? Your front bumper looks like it is going to fall off?"

She walked around to the front of her car and realized one of the giant tie wraps that she'd used had broken off. After putting her things into the backseat, she opened the trunk and pulled a couple of new plastic ties out and used them to secure the bumper.

"Your insurance company denied paying for the accident and I only have liability. No biggie. Evie's brother, Mitchel, will get me a used one when he can and until then, these things last like almost two weeks." She shrugged and then got into her car.

When she drove away, she saw Hudson Frost rubbing the back of his head and she laughed. Hudson Frost had been born with a silver spoon in his mouth and had probably never used tie wraps to repair a car in his life.

#Chapter

Dressed in his best red Christmas bandanna, Winston sat next to Felicity as she happily handed out coffee in the break room. She'd made the thirty dollars she needed plus another twenty to cover the supplies and insisted on giving it away the rest of the morning.

"Happy Fri-yay," she called it, and the entire office was jolly by the time they'd visited her and received their cups of cheer.

Hudson was one of the last to make it into the break room and she'd already put back a salted caramel muffin and coffee for him. But when he walked in and saw Winston, he raised that judgey eyebrow at her.

Suddenly, she remembered he'd actually said, *'I'll get back to you,'* about mascot dog Friday. She was pushing her luck and started to regret it.

"Here's your coffee, Mr. Frost. And a perfectly made muffin not one of the misshaped leftovers like I usually bring."

Still, he looked at her.

"I should have sent a text to make sure bringing him in today was still okay," she added a little nervously and he noted that he couldn't remember her acting nervous before except maybe in the elevator.

"It's okay, Miss Storey. You know I like having him around. I was a bit distracted this week and didn't get a chance to discuss it with Miss Colson. He can stay with me until we determine whether or not she is allergic."

"Thanks," she said and her larger than usual smile was back.

When Loretta walked in and Felicity greeted her with "Happy Fri-yay!" and then the older woman said it back, he shook his head. He'd never heard the older woman say more than a few words and she never spoke louder than a whisper. But this morning he watched her high-five Felicity and then told her about her grandson flying in for Christmas.

He stood there drinking his coffee astonished that he'd known Loretta and most of the current employees since he was in school and would come in to work with his dad during the summers and holidays. Yet in less than two weeks, Felicity Storey with some freshly brewed coffee and reject pastries had become personal friends with almost everyone.

When Loretta left, Felicity looked up to see Hudson staring at her.

"What?"

He shook his head. "Happy Fri-Yay?"

"You better believe it," she said shaking her coffee can full of cash and coins.

Hudson nodded and knew he would have to talk to her about Sierra's shoes that day, but he would avoid it as long as he could. "Come on, buddy," he said to Winston who didn't hesitate to follow him out of the break room and down the hallway.

Felicity got to her desk before Sierra showed up and began downloading all of the videos and pictures she'd taken the day before. Sierra could handle the emails and then they would spend the rest of the day editing the raw footage for social media and their conference needs.

It was eight-thirty when Sierra strolled in and went straight to Hudson's office. She let out a short scream when Winston ran over to greet her, but Hudson quickly called the dog back to him. By the time Felicity was in the doorway to help run interference it wasn't necessary.

"I can't believe you brought that dog to the office again. I told you that I don't like dogs."

Felicity had her hands on her hips, "No. You actually said you were allergic which is a totally different thing."

Hudson interrupted before Sierra could get things really going. "Sierra, are you allergic to dogs?"

Strawberry not shortcake shook her head, making certain that the wavy curls in her long tresses swirled around her shoulders. "I spoke to my mother, and she said it was cats that I'm allergic too." She then giggled and shrugged.

While Sierra preened in front of Hudson, which seemed to be her regular morning routine, Felicity grabbed her coffee can of money and handed it over in front of Hudson. "Here, Sierra," she said proudly. "This is the full three thousand five hundred dollars for your shoes."

Sierra rolled her eyes and handed the can back to Felicity. Then she looked at Hudson expectantly. He slowly stood up.

"Can we discuss this at the end of the day, please," he said, and Felicity nodded thinking he was talking to both of them. But when Sierra shrugged and went back to her desk, she wasn't so sure.

Why wouldn't Sierra take the money? Had Hudson told her not to take it? She didn't know what to do with herself. She'd been so proud to finally have the debt paid off and evil Sierra would even take that away from her?

Hudson watched as Felicity looked like she was about to burst. She was practically vibrating as she stood there. When she turned toward him, he was ready for her to speak her mind, but she leaned forward through gritted teeth and said, "I knew she wasn't a dog person."

And then stormed back to her desk.

He tried not to laugh at her, but she was the cutest woman he'd met in a long time and some days he could barely keep his amusement to himself. Sure, she'd been insubordinate but he'd never known a woman to be more head strong, confident, or funny.

Felicity Storey kept him on his toes and how she continued to work at both this full-time job and her coffee truck when clearly she needed some serious rest, he would never know. But she didn't ask for anything and was tenacious to a fault. It was the reason he would wait and talk to her after work about the expensive Italian shoes or she might just walk out for good.

Hudson opened his bottom drawer and gave Winston a piece of chicken jerky, his favorite type of treat, and then walked into the outer office to discuss conference ideas with both his ghostwriters.

Surprisingly, Sierra and Felicity got along for the majority of the day. They laughed over some of the pictures used for the gallery bulletin board at the conference. Then agreed on some movie soundtracks for the special conference dinner where they used the clips Hudson and Felicity filmed together.

He ordered lunch in for the entire office and watched as more than half the staff said, "Happy Fri-Yay," to Felicity which seemed to get under Sierra's skin.

Still, it had been a great day and even though Ira was out, things were running smoothly. After five, Hudson walked into the outer office to find Sierra gone for the day and Felicity sitting at her desk adding clips to his social media while she had her sock feet resting on Winston.

As soon as Winnie saw Hudson though, he wiggled out from under her and ran his way. "Hey, Win. You need a treat?" he asked, and she followed them into Hudson's office.

"Traitor," she said to Winston as he sat and then spun around for his chicken jerky treat. "Now I understand why he likes you so much."

"Treats are a strong motivator, Miss Storey," Hudson said and she saw that twinkle in his eyes she'd liked so much.

"Why do you think I hand out coffee and pastries in the morning, Mr. Frost."

He laughed aloud at her comeback. "Touché."

Felicity bit her bottom lip to hold back a grin as she slipped into one of the chairs in front of his desk. She still didn't have her shoes on and for some reason he found that really attractive. She had so many outside obligations, yet never rushed out of the office at the end of the day.

"Okay, spill the beans, Hudson. I've tried to be patient but when Sierra left today, I couldn't say or do anything. I tried to give her the money again, but she refused to take it. It's not in my nature to take something for nothing and I can't work with her if she has this over my head. The Storey women do not accept charity."

When she finally finished her rant, Hudson got up and

closed his office door. Instead of sitting back in his large leather chair, he sat in the seat next to her so he could face her.

"I'm afraid you aren't going to like what I have to say, Felicity," he said, and she noted that he used her first name. This was serious or he would've said Miss Storey in his smirky voice.

"Just tell me. I can take it," she said, and he wasn't so sure she could.

"You didn't ruin her shoes on purpose, and I wasn't sure how long it would take for you to pay her back. Let's face it, Miss Colson can be a handful sometimes. So, I had the payroll department give the money to her out of petty cash."

Felicity stood up. "What?"

"You heard me."

"If that were true then why wouldn't you have just told me that back then?"

"It is true," he said staring into her eyes. What she didn't know was that they didn't have a petty cash fund until he put four thousand dollars down and called it that. He swore the employees in payroll to secrecy and then waited to try and figure out how to handle things with this feisty woman.

"I pay my debts, Mr. Frost."

"I have no doubt that you do, Miss Storey."

She stood there silently for a moment and he smiled because he could see her brain working through all the facts. Then she lowered her eyes at him. "What else does petty cash cover?"

"Petty things, Miss Storey," he said.

She crossed her arms in front of her chest and stared at him. She wasn't going to get anything else out of Hudson Frost about the money, but thirty-five hundred dollars was a ton of cash. "Should I donate this money to the petty cash fund then?"

Hudson stared at her. That was a fortune to her and still she didn't think she should keep it. "Miss Storey, that money would buy a lot of kibble for our boy here."

Felicity gave him a nod and sunk her teeth harder into her bottom lip as she looked over at Winston. Hudson had no idea but that much money would pay all the interest they owed Keller Shark for the month.

It was obvious that the whole situation was disturbing to Felicity. As she walked toward his door, he saw the glum look on her face. Without thinking he stepped to the door before she could walk out. And when she looked into his eyes, he wanted to hug and kiss her more than he had the other day. He put his hands on the door instead.

"It just feels wrong for me to keep this money, you know. I caused her shoes to be ruined and I've worked so hard to make the extra money so I could pay it back."

Hudson continued to stare into her eyes. She was even more beautiful on the inside than the outside and he needed to calm the hell down when he was around her. "I should have told you sooner, but I have no doubt that you can make good use of that money. Perhaps for the coffee shop? Besides, you earned it."

"K," was all Felicity said as she walked past him to sit at her desk and put her shoes on. But Hudson didn't want her to leave feeling deflated. She was the woman that had the entire company smiling all day.

"I wanted to tell you that you did some remarkable work this week, Felicity. I saw your social media posts and the video for the conference looks great so far."

Felicity's face lightened when she looked up. "Pics are my thing. I have a gift," she said, and he didn't miss how her cheeks brightened a bit as she smiled about that.

"You make great coffee and pastries, write, take photos and videos, and keep up with social media for your company and mine. I'd say you're great at just about everything you do, Miss Storey."

He'd caught her completely off guard and there was no

denying it when she seemed taken aback by the compliment. Winston stood by her side, and he wondered if the dog picked up on her sudden mood change too. It surely seemed like they were in sync.

It took her about sixty seconds to recover but then she smiled slyly. "Sounds like I'm fabulous and kind of like you have a crush on me, Mr. Frost."

His face froze for a beat while their eyes locked onto one another. "I'll walk you to your car, Miss Storey," was all he said in response, and she laughed as they headed toward the elevator.

Chapter Twenty-Six

The weekend flew by with satisfied customers enjoying holiday coffees and desserts at Espresso to Geaux. Felicity and Evie Mae also baked up a storm each night to get ahead of the upcoming week.

Felicity tried on tons of clothes before she finally settled on what she needed for her trip to Vermont. While Evie tried to tell her that she needed more layers just in case it was colder than expected.

"My suitcase, your suitcase, is already busting at the seams and I can't bring more than one without getting charged extra," Felicity said as she peeled off the last sweater and shook her head. "Winter clothes are exhausting. How do people put all this stuff on every day?" she complained.

Evie laughed at her and shook her head. "You're going to see why they wear that many clothes. And I'm here to tell you that your Southern blood is thin." It was obvious to Evie Mae what was really going on. "Look, Fe, I know you and you're worried about flying. There is nothing to stress about. It's going to be fine."

"How do you know that?"

Evie smiled at her best friend who had never been on an airplane before and wasn't too keen on small spaces. "Didn't you say you're flying on Frost Manufacturing's private plane? I'm sure you can bring more than one suitcase and it's going to be super comfy compared to coach on a commercial airline."

Sitting on the end of the bed with a puffy coat in her hands, Felicity took a deep breath. "What if I freak out?"

"Listen, my mom doesn't like to fly, and she has one drink on the flight to just take the edge off. She swears by it."

Felicity had really never been much of a drinker, but she would make an exception when flying. Especially since she had to go with Sierra who would be zero help in an emergency.

While folding all of Evie Mae's winter clothes back up, Felicity needed to have a heart to heart. "Evie, I need to tell you something and just hear me out before you say anything because it has a happy ending, okay?"

Evie sat on the end of the bed to listen. "Things didn't go so well in the beginning at Frost Manufacturing. You know Strawberry not Shortcake? Well, she's apparently a social media influencer for clothes or something on the side and I accidentally spilled coffee on her Italian leather boots. They cost $3500 and-"

Evie stood up, "If you tell me that I have to go out with Baby Shark now because of that chick's boots, I'm going to lose it."

Felicity shook her head. "No. I have been going in extra early for the last two weeks so I can run a little coffee service out of the break room. You know all those muffins and cookies that weren't good enough to sell at the coffee truck? I've been handing those out too. I don't charge anyone but they order a coffee and dessert then make a donation so its technically not a business. However, in two weeks, I've made all the money to pay her back."

"Wow, Felicity. You're only doing that in the morning and made that much money?"

"I know it sounds crazy, but people heard what the money was for and I think, well I know, some were giving me more than what a coffee and muffin would cost in the wild. I think Hudson even put a couple of hundred-dollar bills in there at least once but maybe twice."

"You said it has a happy ending? I guess you've paid her?"

Felicity shook her head. As she explained it to Evie Mae, she realized that Hudson was putting more money into her donation can even after he had the payroll department pay Sierra back from the petty cash fund. "That's the thing, I tried to pay her Friday and Hudson told me that it was an accident. He used the company's petty cash fund to pay Sierra over a week ago."

"You're saying we have thirty-five hundred buckaroos to go toward our December interest payments?" Evie was on her feet and barely holding in her excitement.

Felicity laughed. "Yes! Can you believe it?"

They both hugged each other and jumped up and down. It was the best thing that could have happened for them with this interest nonsense and would ease their financial problems considerably.

Evie's face was glowing with happiness and Felicity felt much better after telling her friend the truth of what had happened. "I'm sorry that I tried to keep it from you, Evie. I was ashamed for being so careless and I just wanted to spare you from worrying about it."

"We're in this together and you don't have to go through anything alone."

"I know. But I saw how much Isaac Keller has annoyed you, and I couldn't add to that when I leave all of this behind and go to my job in New Orleans, Monday through Friday."

"Are you kidding? I feel bad because you work full time there and then come home and work here too."

Felicity and Evie hugged each other again. They needed to

have that talk and remind each other that they were a team, and they would get through all of this together. "Are you sure you're going to be okay all week without me? I know Winston can be a handful."

"Mitch has already offered to come and take him as often as I want, and you know we all love him. My dad said he will walk him in the mornings. My cousin, Kate, is going to work all week because she gets out of school at noon. Plus, Mitch and Kate offered to work Saturday so I get my first day off and let's be honest, I'll need to bake. So, no worries, okay? I've got this!"

Evie crooked her eyebrow at her best friend. Felicity always looked out for everyone but herself. And there was no doubt she was worried over her upcoming trip. "It's pretty exciting that this time next week your conference in Vermont will be almost over. You're going to see snow and sit by a fireplace drinking eggnog or something else delicious."

Felicity nodded. Evie was right. "I'm just a little overwhelmed about the getting there part. Plus, my coworker spends most of her time getting out of work and what if I can't pull this off by myself?"

Evie rolled her eyes. "Since when have you not pulled something off? You're my go-to-girl when I need a plan executed which is why you're the one with the job. You're too gifted to just run the coffee truck with me."

"Whatever." Felicity zipped up the suitcase that Evie lent her and changed into her sleeping shorts and a sweatshirt.

Evie tucked away all the winter items that Felicity didn't need but before she went to bed, she added, "I love that you're humble, Fe, but it's true. You have a gift and everything you set your mind to doing, gets done in some incredible way."

She hugged her best friend because if she knew anything about Felicity, it was that she was an overthinker and would spend half the night contemplating what Evie had said, the coffee shop, her new job, the conference, and the upcoming trip.

The next morning, Felicity woke up before her alarm. She'd fallen asleep with Hudson Frost on her mind and how he'd said something similar to what Evie had said about her gifts. Of course, she'd known Evie most of her life. But Hudson had only known her for a couple of weeks and what was he doing paying that close of attention to her?

Walking Winston in the freezing cold that morning, she still had her boss on her mind. Clearly, she paid a lot of attention to him too, but that was different. She had just started at Frost Manufacturing and needed to figure him out in order to do a great job. How else would she answer emails and write speeches if she didn't know the man?

Later that morning when she got to the office and set up her coffee service, she plugged in her twinkling Christmas lights and hummed *O Holy Night* as she brewed coffee. She'd made gingerbread cookies and used holiday muffin cups to put a little more *Fa La La* into everyone's Monday morning. Especially since she wouldn't be there to make coffee for the rest of the week.

The break room was buzzing over her new holiday offerings and as everyone put more donations into her coffee can, she reminded them that she'd already paid her debt to society and only needed to cover costs at this point.

Still, when she got to her desk, she counted out two hundred dollars. Were her work friends worried about her having enough money for this trip? It seemed they all thought Sierra had spent an enormous amount of money on her wardrobe for the conference. Charline and Janice, both told her that she needed to really dress up because the attendees were some elite wealthy business owners from around the world.

"I'm set. Evie had tons of sweaters and winter clothes for me to borrow. I even have a pair of suede boots lined with fur."

Kathryn joined them in the conversation and crooked her head when Felicity told them what she'd packed. "Honey, you can't wear leggings and a sweater. You're going to need an evening gown and heels for that dinner."

Felicity took a deep breath when she realized that maybe she hadn't understood the term business-casual winter-lodge-apparel. She tried to put on a brave face as the women explained how important this conference was to Hudson and that the man who she'd never seen sweat over anything, truly worried about pulling this event off each year.

"I leave tomorrow," she added, and all three women tried to soothe her.

"I'm sure what you have is going to look great. You look great in everything," Janice told her.

Kathryn nodded. "It's going to be freezing and boots with fur will be perfect."

Then Charline leaned in and tried to whisper but spoke louder than usual. "We've heard a handful of the attendees are rich single men and we don't want you to miss an opportunity. You never know Felicity, you might just find your man there."

Felicity looked up to see Hudson staring at her. He looked a bit irritated, and she quickly looked at her watch. It wasn't eight o'clock yet and she had five more minutes before she needed to pack up the coffee service.

She half smiled at him. Perhaps he just needed coffee? Saying good-bye to her older friends, she stepped behind her cart and made him a cup of coffee. "I have Christmas muffins, and highly recommend the pistachio. It's Evie Mae's specialty. Or the gingerbread."

He thanked her for the coffee but declined the treats. He looked like he had something to say to her, but he turned and walked out of the break room as swiftly as he'd walked in.

Grouchy is back, she thought. Why did that bother her so

much? Shaking her head, she made Ira a cup of coffee and set aside several gingerbread cookies and a couple of muffins for him to choose from as she slowly put her coffee supplies away.

Ed ran in at the last minute and apologized for being late. "I won't make it without your coffee all week, Felicity, you have to take pity on me," he said making her laugh.

"Gotcha covered, Ed," she said pouring the last bit of coffee up for him.

Heading to her desk, she was happy that Ira would be back today. He'd sent her a brief text that he was fine, just had some personal things to take care of that weekend. She wasn't sure if he would ever tell her what was going on, but he could certainly enlighten her about her wardrobe needs for that week.

She walked into her office to a smiling Ira who was already on the phone. He winked at her when she set his coffee and treats down on his desk. But before she had a chance to sit down, Hudson yelled, "Miss Storey, I need to see you in my office!"

Sierra walked in as Felicity was being summoned and behind her back said, "Uh-oh."

Chapter Twenty-Seven

~∾~

Felicity had a notebook and pen with her, but also carried one of the Christmas muffins and gingerbread cookies. Hudson had always taken a treat with his coffee, and she'd hoped that sugar would soothe the beast.

However, the way he was looking at her, she didn't hand over anything, just sat on the edge of the seat in front of him.

"Miss Storey. I couldn't help but overhear your conversation with the other ladies in the break room this morning." He paused for effect. "This conference is one of the most important events of the year and means a great deal to my family as well as the attendees. Your image is a reflection of Frost Manufacturing."

Felicity clicked her pen nervously, click-click-click. Perhaps he'd been standing in the break room longer than she'd realized. "I'm sorry, Hudson. I mean, Mr. Frost. I didn't have time to go shopping and the clothes that I packed aren't that bad. I mean, maybe they aren't as dressy as Sierra's, but I can repack and possibly add some formal attire. I was thinking ski lodge and business casual, but I'll get it together."

He stared at her for what felt like forever. "Miss Storey, this isn't a matchmaking event."

"What?" *What did he mean by that?*

"There will be wealthy attendees and I have no doubt that some of them might flirt with you," he said, and she suddenly realized he seemed uncomfortable.

"I don't know what you think you heard in the break room, but I'm not going there to meet someone or find a date. That's not even on my radar. How could you think that about me? I thought you were paying closer attention than that, Mr. Frost." Felicity handed over the treats she'd made and then turned and walked out.

She needed to stop thinking they were friends and remember Hudson Frost was her boss and the CEO of Frost Manufacturing. He also seemed to run hot and cold with her and she wasn't a fan of that whatsoever.

As she sat at her desk, Sierra stared at her. "Are you okay?"

Felicity couldn't remember Sierra ever caring about anyone in the office. "I'm fine."

Looking at Ira who was still on the phone, Felicity turned back to Sierra. "What are you wearing this week for the conference? I'm worried that I might have packed a little too casually and well, I could use some help."

Sierra was thrilled that Felicity wanted to talk clothes with her. "Finally, I've wanted to discuss this with you for a week," Sierra said beaming.

They were as different as two people could be, but Sierra had her strengths. "I take pictures because you never know how something truly looks until you photograph it."

Felicity restrained herself from laughing at that comment. She'd mistakenly thought Sierra was kidding but she was seriously pulling out her phone and pictures.

When Felicity saw the outfits not only for the conference but also for their travel day and workdays prior to the conference, she realized she was in trouble. "Thank you, Sierra. Truly," Felicity said and immediately sent a text to Evie.

911... the clothes I packed are not fancy enough. What am I going to do? She asked her friend.

Evie laughed that Felicity's text was about clothes. While her friend had always cared about how she looked, she wasn't one to be 'styled' and it was going to thrill Evie's mother to no end to be able to finally help her.

A few minutes later, Evie Mae responded with, *Don't worry. I have messaged Kristy and she is on it.*

Felicity leaned back in her desk chair. It was only eight-thirty and she'd learned everything she'd packed wasn't good enough, been called into the boss' office, and now had to do final edits on the main video for the conference before presenting it to that same grumpy boss. At this rate, she'd never make it to Vermont without having a full-on panic attack. Of course, she'd never had a panic attack before, but she'd never flown either.

It was late afternoon when Hudson was ready for the final presentation. Sierra agreed to finish the emails, while Felicity put her finishing touches on their video. It seemed that letting Sierra share her fashion knowledge made them friends now and Felicity at least felt better about having to travel with her.

Ira had been overly busy all day but joined them in Hudson's office for the big reveal. Felicity stood at the screen and explained how Hudson would give his speech and then start the production. As she pressed the remote and stepped to the side for it to play across the screen, Hudson stood and motioned for her to have a seat in his chair. Sierra strangely didn't notice, but Ira smiled at her as she sat in the leather chair still warm from Hudson's body heat.

Felicity watched as all three of them laughed when appropriate and looked heartfelt when expected. Their reactions were honest, and she knew she'd nailed the work.

Ira clapped and stood up when it was done. "Best we've ever had," he said. "But, of course, I knew it would be."

Sierra was overcome with emotion. "Wow. Just wow."

Hudson grinned but didn't say anything until Sierra and Ira left the room. "Excellent work, Felicity," he said.

She was proud but still she didn't miss how he'd held praise. "Why do you always wait until no one is around to say nice things to me? Is it just me or do you not praise anyone in public?"

Taken aback by her remark, he stepped to stand in front of her. "What do you mean?"

"I don't know how to make that clearer. You're a great man and do a wonderful job here. I only want to make you proud for hiring me. But you act differently toward me in front of others. Sierra actually was worried for me this morning when you called me into your office. There was no mistaking that tone of voice you used. I was in trouble, and everyone knew it." Was she being too personal? This wasn't like her, and she regretted saying anything although she meant every single word of it.

Hudson closed the space between them and reached for her hand. "I apologize. It wasn't my intention to hurt your feelings." Again, he looked like he wanted to say more.

Felicity swallowed hard as she felt his warm hand hold hers. "It-It's okay. My feelings are fine," was all she could say.

Hudson led her into the outer office. Letting her hand go when they reached the door. When he cleared his throat, Sierra and Ira both looked up.

"I don't think I was clear before and I want to make sure that there is no confusion, I am very proud of the work done for this conference and specifically the incredible video that Felicity produced." He then turned to head back into his office but before he walked away, he winked at Felicity.

She grinned like a fool and then bit her bottom lip to make it stop. Was it obvious that she was feeling something for the boss? It was his fault because he kept sending her mixed signals. It was not because she'd been alone for so long and missed male attention.

Sitting down at her desk, she double checked the itinerary for their trip and watched Ira walk into Hudson's office and close the door. As soon as he left the room, Sierra began talking about flying private and how she'd always wanted to see The Frost Family plane.

Felicity's head spun as she thought about flying for the first time. She would have a drink like Evie's mother and then be fine. *Right?* She could feel her heartbeat pick up but before she could freak out, Ira returned and knocked on her desk twice, making her look up at him.

He smiled slyly but didn't say anything before Hudson followed behind him. "So, it turns out that I have a meeting tomorrow in Connecticut."

"Darn," Sierra said and then covered her mouth like it was a mistake. "Sorry, I was just looking forward to flying private for the first time."

Felicity's mouth went dry. She was really going to have to do this and there was no getting out of it. Private or commercial, it didn't matter. Both would fly them straight to the scene of the crash.

"Are you alright, Felicity?" Hudson was staring at her.

"Great," she said but no one thought she meant it.

Ira smiled at Felicity warmly as he added, "No need to worry. Hudson is going to ride with you two to Vermont and then take the plane to his meeting."

Hudson nodded. "I'll only be there for the afternoon and then fly back home late that night. But if anything happens or you two run into any trouble in Vermont then I'll be close"

Sierra was happy again as she packed up her things for the day. The clock didn't tick past five before she headed out each day but this time, she did pause a moment.

"Should we meet here at the office or at the airport in the morning? I don't want to leave my car, so I'll be dropped off early either place."

"The airport is fine, Sierra," Hudson answered before she quickly headed out.

Felicity hadn't thought about her car and didn't really have anyone available to drop her off early in the morning. All her friends worked, and it was a long drive across the bridge round trip for any one of them. She was quiet as she worried about what to do with her car and how much it would cost to park it at the airport.

Ira sat on the edge of her desk. "What's on your mind?" he asked, and she looked up with that brave face she wore all the time.

"I can park at the airport, right?" she asked and instantly felt silly. "I mean, I haven't flown before and Sierra, not wanting to park there, threw me off. I just mean, there isn't something special that I need to do to park there, right?"

"Besides sell a kidney? No," Ira laughed. "It costs a fortune to park there for a week."

Hudson nodded, "I'll actually be in Maisonville tonight. Staying at my parents' place. You can ride with me," he offered.

Ira stood and nodded. "Problem solved." He told Hudson he would email him the documents he needed for the Connecticut meeting in the morning before he told them both goodbye and safe travels.

Felicity slowly began to pack her things, double-checking her to-do list so she didn't leave any conference materials behind. She didn't acknowledge Hudson was still standing there and watching her.

When she finished, she looked up at him. "Do you need me to do something else before I head out?"

He smiled and shook his head, no. "Are you worried about the flight?"

Shrugging, Felicity tried to minimize her fear. "I'll be fine. Just need to stop over-thinking it, you know."

Holding out his arm for her to walk through the doorway first, she smiled that he was going to walk with her again.

"What are you doing tonight?" he asked as he pressed the button to call the elevator.

"I always stop by Espresso to Geaux on my way home. See if Evie needs me. But tonight, I want to spend some extra time with Winston. You know, I've never left him overnight before. And Evie's mom has apparently picked out some clothes for me, so I'll need to repack."

She always had ten times more things to do than anyone else he knew. "I'm meeting my parents at seven for dinner. Want to join us?"

Chapter Twenty-Eight

Had Hudson actually asked her to have dinner with him and his folks? Felicity shook her head, no, as she thought of an excuse. "I usually stay at the coffee truck past seven and I don't know how long it will take with Evie's mom. She's never helped dress me before and I don't want to mess up the whole image thing at the conference."

She knew she was rambling but memories of meeting her exe's parents over a year ago rang out in her head. She wouldn't be good enough and instead of cheating on her and dumping her, this time she'd be fired from a job she liked and needed.

"Alright, no pressure. You'd mentioned that you wanted to meet them at the Christmas party and since that didn't work out then I figured tonight would be a possibility."

Did he look disappointed? Again, she was worrying over nothing. As the elevator opened up and they walked across the garage to her car, he opened her door. "I'll pick you up at seven in the morning, okay?"

"Thank you," she said as she shoved her bag into the passenger seat, and he gently closed her door. Rolling down her window, she looked up at him. "Thanks for the dinner invite too. Maybe it will work out next time," she said and didn't miss how his eyes lit up as he nodded at her.

By the time she pulled into the parking lot where the Espresso to Geaux truck was parked, the fog had rolled in pretty thick. It gave everything a bit of a romantic, yet scary vibe and she smiled when she saw Evie Mae and her cousin Kate standing at the window helping customers. Their faces were lit up from the Christmas lights they'd hung all around.

When she joined them inside, they laughed and talked about some students from the high school theater class coming by and singing songs from their Christmas Program. Apparently, the small crowd there joined in, and it felt like a flash mob serenade.

Evie Mae gave Felicity a hot tea and explained the days her brother and Kate were going to fill in while Felicity was away in Vermont. It was sweet how everyone offered to step in and help them in their time of need.

It wasn't something Felicity was used to before she met Evie Mae and her family because she and her mother didn't have anyone else. But there was a comfort there that was hard to put into words.

Evie explained to Felicity that her mother had already put together all her outfits and the necessary makeup and hair products she would need for her trip. They only needed to run in and grab it all when they got home. It was such a relief for Felicity and the three of them laughed, talked, and waited on clients for the next couple of hours.

A little after eight, as Felicity stepped back into the truck from her long walk with Winston, she heard Evie Mae chatting her head off with a customer. Apparently, Winston instantly recognized the voice too as he bolted out the back door before, she got it closed.

"Hey, buddy," Hudson said catching Winston before he

jumped up on his mother. Felicity scolded her dog when she rounded the corner and saw him next to Hudson. "I apologize," she said to Hudson's mother when she saw the stunning older woman.

Hudson proudly introduced his mother and father to Felicity. "Mom and Dad, this is the woman I've been telling you about, Felicity Storey. Felicity this is Calista and Harry Frost."

Calista Frost smiled warmly at Felicity. "It's so nice to meet you, Felicity. We've heard such wonderful things."

Harry bent down to ruffle Winston's fur. "Who's a good boy?" he said to Winnie and then stepped toward Felicity. "He's a great dog. We love your videos."

Felicity was taken aback. Hudson had mentioned her to his family? And shown them her videos? "So nice to meet you both," she said and reached out to shake their hands.

Harry Frost leaned in. "We can't wait to see what you've done for the conference reveal video. Hudson couldn't stop talking about it tonight over dinner."

"Thank you. Thank you so much, sir. Honestly, the work you and your wife have done to help others inspired me."

Evie handed over all of their coffees and dessert and Felicity told them it was on the house, but Hudson's father insisted on paying them. Then he added money to their tip jar too.

"I love that enterprising spirit, young ladies," he sipped his coffee and grinned even bigger. "Great coffee. This whole thing is brilliant," he said waving to their coffee truck and the patio set up.

Calista agreed and they talked for a few more minutes as they walked toward their giant SUV. "Hudson says you've never flown before and I want you to know that it does take a little getting used to, dear. But try not to worry, okay. Our pilot has been flying for twenty-five years and he would never take off if the conditions weren't excellent." She turned to look at Hudson.

"You take special care of her. It's overwhelming the first time if you aren't inclined for that sort of thing."

"Yes, ma'am. Of course," he answered his mother lovingly.

She hugged Felicity as her husband opened her door but before she climbed inside, she added, "I heard there is going to be a lot of snow this week. Dress extra warm."

Felicity smiled at her and watched as Hudson's father helped his wife into the large car. They were everything she hadn't expected and then maybe what she'd hoped.

Hudson waited for his parents to get into the SUV and then turned toward her. "It doesn't look like you've been home yet, Miss Storey?"

She was still wearing her work clothes and he'd changed into jeans and a black sweater. He looked incredible in suits but there was something about him in casual clothes that made her have to catch her breath.

"Owning a business is no joke, Mr. Frost," she replied giving him her most confident look.

"So, I hear," he said, stepping closer and she saw how his eyes dilated. "You going to be alright traveling tomorrow?"

"You still picking me up in the morning?"

"Of course."

"I'll be great then," she said, and they both stood there locked onto one another but neither of them touching. Winston took his nose and nudged Hudson's hand and then hers. Winnie didn't understand why no one was giving him attention. They both laughed and then bent down to love on him together. It was a moment that neither would forget.

After he and his parents left, she slowly walked back into the coffee truck. Kate was the first one to say something. "Holy moly, is that your boss? He is a hottie! How can I get a job there?"

Evie Mae just watched the exchange between her seventeen-year-old cousin and Felicity for a minute before she sat down and stared at her best friend.

"What?" Felicity asked.

"He talks about you to his parents?"

Felicity shrugged. "I'm sure they meant about work."

"His mother knew you had never flown before and told him to look out for you. That didn't seem to be about work. And the way he stood so close to you out there, I was pretty sure he was going to kiss you."

"Winston sure likes him too," Kate added.

"Yes, well, he bribes Winnie with treats that he keeps in his desk drawer. And I'm sure his mother was just being nice. He wouldn't kiss me," Felicity said but honestly, she'd felt like he wanted to kiss her a couple of times. And to be honest, the idea thrilled her more than a little bit.

"He's going to fly with you tomorrow too? When did that happen?" Evie wasn't going to let it go.

"Apparently, he has a meeting in Connecticut tomorrow, so he is going to tag along and then take the plane."

Kate and Evie both looked at each other and said, "uh-huh," and "That's convenient."

Smiling at them teasing her, Felicity hadn't even considered that Hudson might have planned that trip on purpose. But perhaps he didn't want his employees to travel alone together since they hadn't gotten along so well in the past?

She changed the subject to coffee, which always got Evie Mae distracted and a couple of hours later they headed home.

It didn't take long for Felicity to try on the clothes Mrs. Shepard picked out for her. She removed all but one of the items she'd packed before and filled her suitcase to the brim with the dress clothes and shoes.

Staying up to bake only until midnight, she laid in bed for an hour staring out the small window at the night sky. She had no doubt that Evie Mae could manage the coffee truck business without her, and Winston would be loved by the whole Shepard family. But she was already homesick, and she hadn't even boarded the metal menace that was supposed to defy gravity and fly her to beautiful snowy Vermont.

Winston kneaded his front paws into Felicity's arm as he slept next to her, and she tried not to tear up over leaving her dog for six days. He would be fine. She would be fine.

Four hours later when Felicity woke up, she smiled that in her dream Winston was playing in the snow with her. She would scout out this place in Vermont and perhaps next year, take him to see snow.

At six o'clock on the dot, Hudson pulled up to the Shepard family home and walked back to the pool house for Felicity. Not surprised when Evie Mae, Winston, and Felicity all were running around like they'd been up for hours. *Did they ever sleep?*

"Hey there, Winston," he said as he ruffled the sweet dog's fur with both hands. "You already walked him?"

Felicity nodded as she tried to wheel her suitcase out the door.

"Here, I've got that," Hudson said as he reached for her bag and said, "Good-morning to Evie."

Evie grinned at him and Felicity as she handed over two to-go cups of coffee. Felicity gave her best friend a giant hug and then her dog a hug and a couple of kisses on the head before she walked out with her hottie boss. Smiling at the comment Kate had made the night before.

She didn't miss how he opened her car door before putting her suitcase into the trunk. He had no doubt learned those chivalrous manners from his father. Could they be that different from her ex's wealthy family? They certainly weren't pretentious and seemed genuinely happy to meet her.

Lost in her thoughts, Felicity jumped when Hudson reached over and patted her hand, "Penny for your thoughts."

She shrugged. "Just thinking about all the things we need to do when we get to Vermont."

"Are you sure? You aren't still worried about flying are you because I can assure you that it's perfectly safe."

"A huge structure made of metal, lifting all of us up thirty-thousand-feet supported solely by air will never make sense to me on a primal level. Save your logic and facts, Mr. Frost." Felicity meant those words, but she was touched that he genuinely seemed concerned for her. And as of last night, when he showed up at Espresso to Geaux with his parents, he no longer was acting differently in private with her. He had no problem being thoughtful and funny in front of his mom and dad or her best friend.

Could Hudson Frost honestly be so different from Troy Brooks? She needed to protect her heart because at that moment she was feeling rather vulnerable.

Chapter Twenty-Nine

It didn't take long for Hudson and Felicity to board the plane and before Sierra got there, he took the time to show her around. He introduced her to the pilot and the steward who would take care of them, letting the team know it was her first time flying and that she was a bit nervous.

Normally, it would irritate her for someone to think she was weak in any way, but Felicity had put herself in this position. Not to mention, Hudson was being attentive which won him a few more points that morning.

When Sierra boarded the plane wearing tight black pants and a gold silk shirt, Felicity immediately looked down at her clothes. She was wearing a thin black cashmere sweater with skinny gray plaid pants. It was a smart outfit that looked great on her, but Sierra could go from work to a dinner party in what she wore. She also had a beautiful camel color coat with a cobalt blue scarf that made her hair stand out.

"Where's your coat, Felicity," Hudson asked.

"You did bring a coat?" Sierra added as if Felicity didn't feel self-conscious enough.

"Of course, it's in my suitcase," Felicity said annoyed that Sierra felt the need to chime in.

Then Sierra added, "You're going to need it the minute we get off the plane. How could you not think to carry it with you?"

Before Felicity could get really wound up, she realized they were in the air, and she gripped the arms of her seat.

"Gotcha. You were getting so mad at me for nosing into your business that you didn't even think about take-off," Sierra laughed. So, were they going to be friends now?

Felicity kept her death grip on the ends of her armrests when Hudson put his warm hand over hers. "It's okay. We are in the air already and we'll level out soon. Hold my hand if you're nervous."

Didn't he know that holding his hand would make her even more nervous? But between him and Sierra both trying to distract her, she had to admit, it wasn't as bad as she'd thought.

Then the steward brought her a mimosa and she drank it down quickly making Hudson and Sierra smile at her. When they had another round, Felicity asked him to hold the orange juice and once she drank it, she felt calmer. *Day drinking was apparently acceptable on a plane.*

Hudson held her hand for longer than was necessary and Sierra looked over several times, but Felicity didn't know what to say. She liked holding his hand but was pretty certain it would be a problem for Sierra and the work they had to do together that week.

The third mimosa sans orange juice, lasted for the rest of the trip because Felicity, Sierra, and Hudson talked the rest of the way or at least that was the way Felicity saw it.

Sierra told them about going snow skiing every year and Hudson also had been snow skiing a ton of times with his family. Felicity admitted she'd always wanted to see snow in person and would give anything to take Winston one day.

"Why didn't you just bring him?" Sierra asked.

Felicity motioned her head toward Hudson as if he couldn't see her and he smiled. "Maybe next time," he said in that bossy voice of his and Felicity grinned at Sierra.

He was definitely more relaxed on the plane with them, but that CEO demeanor was always hanging close where he could use it when necessary. However, there was no doubt that he was very fond of Winston.

The steward checked on them one last time and gave Hudson a nod before he left them to get buckled himself for landing. Felicity, again, was unaware until she heard the landing gear under the plane. She immediately grab Hudson's hand.

"We'll be on the ground in a few minutes. See, it wasn't that bad at all," he said using that deep calming voice of his but still she held his hand tightly and then closed her eyes so she couldn't see the ground getting closer.

"Did you get us a rental car, Felicity?" Sierra asked.

Felicity's eyes popped open. "No. But I booked everything else. You could've rented us a car, Sierra."

"Well, I guess you'll need to summon us an Uber driver," Sierra said as she admired her long painted nails.

Before Felicity could snap back at Sierra, the plane touched the ground and began braking. Sierra winked at Felicity who realized she was being a snit in order to distract her again.

Hudson leaned in and told them that Ira had booked them a driver ahead of time. He added that it was a good thing since they both had drank from New Orleans to Vermont.

He walked off the plane wrapping his coat around Felicity until her luggage was brought around and she could dig her own coat out. But before she could put it on, light snow began to fall.

"Oh my," she said not noticing the cold because it was too beautiful to matter at that moment. "It's incredible, isn't it?"

Hudson didn't miss the way the driver looked at Felicity and that was all he needed to urge him to change his plans. He called Ira and asked him to reschedule his Connecticut meeting then he walked over to Felicity and held her coat out for her so she could cover up.

Escorting Felicity and Sierra to the hotel, Hudson gave the driver a large tip and told him they wouldn't need his services after all. There was challenge in the man's eyes, but Hudson didn't move a muscle until the man thanked him for the tip and then got in his car and left.

It was there at the hotel that the two women noticed Hudson was not, in fact, heading out on the plane to go to his meeting. He grinned and said he was concerned about the hotel accommodations and wanted to make sure everything was set before he left.

There was no need to tell them he would go to Connecticut another time or handle the meeting online instead of in person. He didn't want to miss Felicity seeing the grand Hotel for the first time, and his mother was right, it was his duty to watch over her on this trip. Even if Felicity didn't realize it.

The moment they walked into the hotel, Felicity was all smiles. There was a large fireplace with a fire roaring inside, plus plenty of Christmas decorations to go around.

The manager had done extra for the large event, and it was obvious they were squared away for the wealthy guests that were coming. "This is incredible," Felicity said and even Sierra was a bit giddy.

"It looks even better than I remember," Sierra agreed, smiling at Felicity.

It seemed the two were going to get along fine together and so he offered to buy them lunch before he took off. Sierra insisted on changing her clothes and freshening up first. So, Felicity agreed that she needed to do the same.

Hudson was pleased that by the time they'd finished eating,

Felicity was stone sober and focused on their conference tasks. She pulled out her checklist and together, she and Sierra went point by point, making a plan for the rest of the afternoon.

For the first time in a long time, Hudson didn't want to think about work. But he hadn't prepared to stay the week in Vermont and needed to go back to New Orleans because electronic manufacturing didn't slow down in December.

He planned to return Thursday evening and be ready for the conference Friday. By Sunday night, he could relax and get to know Felicity better.

Ira admitted he knew Hudson liked Felicity the first day when he interviewed her for the position. Ira had managed all the other interviews and it was the first time Hudson had stepped in to talk to anyone.

When Hudson planned the Connecticut meeting so he could fly with her to Vermont, Ira suggested at the end of the conference and weekend that he should ask her to dinner. There wouldn't be a more romantic setting than his family's home in Vermont overlooking the snowy mountain.

From the moment Ira mentioned it, Hudson couldn't get the idea out of head. If he'd prepared better, he would take her to dinner before the conference and spend the week with her organizing the event.

He actually hugged Felicity before he left and reminded her that he was a phone call away if she needed anything before he returned Thursday evening.

The afternoon had been a whirlwind as Felicity and Sierra worked hard to meet with the caterers, servers, hotel manager, and Reindeer sleigh drivers. They put together welcome baskets for the attendees that would be delivered to their rooms before their arrival Thursday.

Snow continuously fell all afternoon and Felicity insisted on sitting by the window with their cheese pizza to go over the rest of the conference details. She'd changed into the one and only original outfits she'd packed, black leggings and a white super soft sweater and when Sierra walked in wearing her fuzzy slippers, they both laughed.

Wednesday would be easier, as they only had taste testing with the caterer in the morning. Then the rest of the day they would decorate the beautiful ski house where Hudson would host the big dinner event.

"You know, my mother has been friends with Calista Frost for years. Really good friends," Sierra said, as she drank her diet coke.

"And you've never gone out with Hudson?"

Sierra shook her head. "I had a serious boyfriend all through school and Hudson wasn't even on my radar until I moved back home."

"That's why you wanted to work for Frost Manufacturing?"

Sierra shook her head. She didn't look like she wanted to talk about it but kept going anyway. "I was a wreck after my breakup. We'd lived together after college, and I helped support him while he went through graduate school. Big mistake putting all your effort into someone else instead of yourself. Afterward, I moved home, lived with my parents and wouldn't do anything except lay by the pool."

"I'm sorry. I had a bad break up too. We didn't live together but I thought he was the one until he cheated on me. Told me I was a fun time but not someone he would marry. His family has money and big fat egos."

Sierra nodded like she understood. "At least he didn't cheat on you with his best friend."

"My best friend, Evie Mae, doesn't think you can be close friends with the opposite sex."

"I agree with Evie, but he wasn't friends with a girl, and they'd been secretly sleeping together the entire time we dated."

Felicity didn't know what to say but seeing Sierra's decent side was a relief. She'd rarely met anyone that wasn't redeemable, and her coworker had skirted the edge of good and evil. Knowing that she was still just heartbroken made a lot of sense to Felicity.

"Have you ever thought about getting a dog?"

Sierra laughed. "Girl, I couldn't take care of myself. I sure shouldn't be trusted with an animal."

Felicity shook her head. At least, Sierra was honest. She suddenly felt really bad for her and it was girl code to try and help her. "Do you want me to try and talk to Hudson about you?"

Sierra smirked. "That ship has sailed. I've never seen Hudson look at a woman the way he looks at you."

"What?"

"At first, I thought the whole *I've-never-flown-before* thing was a ruse. At least until I saw you in action. But the way he held your hand and watched over you with that creepy driver."

"What creepy driver?"

Sierra shook her head. "You do need a keeper."

"I thought we were going to be friends but if you say things like *I need a keeper* then forget about it." Felicity could take care of herself. She'd been raised by a strong mother and Asha Filatova Storey was no weeping willow.

"Friends? Really? I dated my ex for so long that I don't have any friends." Sierra moved to the edge of her seat. "I meant those comments about Hudson in the best of ways, Felicity. Seriously. He's a good guy and you two would make a great team."

Sierra stood up and then shocked Felicity even more when she hugged her before going upstairs to her room. She was still heartbroken over her ex-boyfriend and for the first time, Felicity felt like she really understood her. She wasn't a mean-girl, she was grieving.

As Felicity cleaned up their dinner trash, she considered what Sierra had said about Hudson. *Did he really look at her in a special way?* She was just hoping they could be friends because she needed that job. Was there a possibility of something else? And was she ready for more?

Chapter Thirty

Oh, my goodness. No wonder he isn't staying at the hotel with us," Sierra said as she exaggerated fainting on one of the giant leather sofas. "You know, I'd heard his family owned one of these large places, but this is beyond-."

"Your expectations?" Felicity finished Sierra's sentence. The massive home was up on the mountain and looked more like a ski resort lodge instead of a private home. There was already a fourteen-foot Christmas tree in the center of a wall of windows and the lights had been put on, but nothing else was done.

"This place is stunning but nowhere near ready for our guests. We shouldn't have taken so long with the chef and baker," Felicity said trying not to get too worked up. She couldn't help being a control freak whenever there was a big project or task. Usually having to talk herself down and follow her lists, because she always made a task list.

"Tsk, tsk," Sierra said with her legs propped over the arm of the sofa. "This is all we have left to do today and then we are free to drink cocktails and sit in the sauna."

"I don't know how much decorating you've done, Sierra? But this is the largest place I've ever had to help decorate and did you see those boxes in the garage? We should have hired some help. This is going to take us all day and that is if we work at breakneck speed. I say we turn on some music and get the big ladder out for the tree first."

The edge in Felicity's voice made Sierra nervous. "You really think it's going to take that long?"

"We also have to test the video and lighting for Hudson's big presentation. The desserts are coming in the morning and the food by midday. There is no time to spare."

Sierra took off her shoes and they went out to the garage to find that every tub was labeled- Tree, fireplace mantle 1, 2, & 3, Stairwell railing, kitchen island, etc.

Felicity turned on the large gas fireplace and Sierra turned on classic Christmas music. They worked nonstop until four that afternoon. "I think I hear a phone," Sierra said and Felicity checked her back pocket and then looked all around the empty tubs and boxes for where she might have lost her cell phone.

"I haven't checked it all day. Have you?" Felicity asked as she searched through tissue paper.

Sierra shook her head, no. "You had me so worried we wouldn't get this done that I completely forgot about checking messages or email."

The buzzing started again and that time, Sierra lifted a stack of tubs to find Felicity's mobile phone underneath. At the same time, she grabbed her own phone out of her purse to find that it was dead.

"Oh no, I have twelve missed calls and seventeen text messages," Felicity said and Sierra put her hand over her mouth.

They hadn't meant to check out for so long, but the decorating was a lot of work. Sierra sat next to Felicity as she looked over the text messages. There were several from Ira asking them about the weather conditions. Then several from attendees scheduled to arrive tomorrow night, also asking what they'd heard about the potential weather event.

Felicity and Sierra both looked at each other. "What event?" Sierra asked.

"I have no idea. We need to finish this up and get back to the hotel. They quickly began gathering all the empty tubs and boxes and stowing them away in the storage room off the garage. Felicity swept the floor as Sierra grabbed the cordless vacuum and they made short work of the mess.

When it was all cleared away, they stood back and admired their work. The place was stunning. Once they tested the video equipment they could head back to the hotel.

Sierra set it up as Felicity called Ira.

"I thought we were going to have to send a search party out for you," he said half-joking and half-serious.

"Sorry, Ira. Neither of us had our phones as we decorated this behemoth house. What's going on?"

He explained there was a weather alert for the area. A possible blizzard was going to hit on Friday.

"I've never been in a blizzard before and probably wouldn't be a good judge," Felicity said. Here let's video chat so you can see what we see.

Two minutes later, Ira's handsome, smiling face filled her phone screen. "See, Ira, it's snowing but it doesn't look like it's any worse than it was yesterday."

Felicity held her phone up at the window so he could see out. "It's beautiful here though and I'm sure it's going to make for an amazing conference. Especially when the horse drawn sleighs bring everyone here from the hotel."

Sierra agreed and he noticed that the two women were getting along which he found unusual. No one got along with Sierra. Next, Felicity showed him the house and how amazing everything looked with their decorations. Ira congratulated them for getting it done so fast and told them he would stay on top of the weather channel for them as well as reach out to attendees so they wouldn't worry.

"Sometimes these things aren't as bad as the weather channel predicts. Let's hope that's true this time," he said, before promising to check in again in a few hours before he hung up.

"That's just crazy," Sierra said. "It's a ski resort and it's supposed to snow. One year when we were here, we got thirty-six inches of fresh snow, and everyone cheered because the skiing was going to be great. It's not like they aren't prepared for this sort of thing. Not like when it snows in New Orleans and the city shuts down."

Felicity sure hoped Sierra was right. It took another hour for them to set up the video and video screen and then evaluate the sound. It was finally perfect, and they were both wiped out when they headed back to the hotel.

Ira had rented them a four-wheel drive jeep and they were thankful to have it on the icy roads. Sierra drove slowly and they both remarked that it was a good bit worse than earlier that day.

Still thinking things weren't going to get too bad, they had all their hopes dashed the moment they walked into the hotel. It was complete mayhem.

People were everywhere, some checking out, others complaining about this or that and the hotel staff were running all about wheeling carts of supplies. Something was definitely coming and neither Sierra nor Felicity had been prepared.

Sierra began emailing attendees and making a list of who had canceled and who would give them an answer in the morning. Felicity went to talk to the hotel management to verify their emergency weather plans and to find out if they could in fact, house their attendees longer should the weather come in hard and fast.

By eight that night they were in a holding pattern until the weather forecast could definitively say yes or no to a blizzard. That news wouldn't come until six the next morning.

Felicity nor Sierra could eat because of stress and when they realized they wouldn't know anything until morning, Felicity bought junk food out of the vending machine. They shared, cheese filled crackers, honey roasted peanuts, and chocolate chip cookies along with a diet coke.

"Dinner of champions," Sierra said as she finished off the cookies. "Two weeks' worth of work in the gutter."

Felicity tried to remain positive. "Not necessarily. We need to both go to bed thinking this will work out positively. My best friend, Evie believes you can manifest your own positive outcome if you try hard enough. And I have to say it has worked for her so far."

Sierra nodded. "All I want to manifest right now is some sleep. I'll set my alarm for six if you want to try and sleep in until seven."

They each headed to their rooms and Felicity laid in bed looking at pictures of Winston that Evie Mae sent to her earlier that day. She would love to see her dog, but hoped things turned around for the conference. They had worked so hard and even though it wasn't her fault, she didn't want to disappoint Hudson.

It was near midnight when she got a text from him. "You alright, Miss Storey?"

Grinning that he was sending her a text, she tried not to think too hard about what it meant. "I'm always good. Just having a little weather thing today but no doubt it's all going to turn around in the morning."

"Ever the positive thinker."

Felicity laughed at that one. She could think of all the negative behavior he'd witnessed from her which told a different story. But she liked that he saw her in an optimistic light.

"I positively cannot wait for this whole conference thing to start."

"Me too," Hudson typed and then, "Get some rest, Felicity. Either way, tomorrow is going to be a big day."

"Good night," she typed and then she sent a text to Evie to kiss Winston for her.

The next morning, Felicity woke up to someone knocking on her hotel door. It sounded a bit frantic, and she nervously looked out the peep hole before opening. It was Sierra.

As soon as she opened the door, Sierra walked in. "Bad news. Seriously, shocking news. A hundred-year blizzard is barreling toward us and the airport will be closed in two hours."

"The airport is closing this morning?"

"Yes. Look, throw your stuff into your suitcase and let's make a run for it. I got us two standby tickets and if any of these tourists don't make their flight, it's ours for the taking."

Sierra might as well be speaking a foreign language. Felicity didn't know what all of that meant, but she did trust her crazy coworker when it came to getting the hell out of dodge.

They were both packed and loaded into the Jeep in less than twenty minutes. The roads were much worse than last night and although it should've taken them twenty to thirty minutes, it took a full hour to get to the airport safely.

Felicity was shaking and pulling her luggage along. They would have to carry on their suitcases, and she had to throw her body wash and shampoo out at the TSA check in area because they exceeded the size of liquids permitted. *What the hell was that all about?*

The airport was a mess and there were already people sleeping on cots and Felicity tried not to look around at the hopeless faces on many of the travelers.

She and Sierra waited and waited until the last flight to leave the airport was up. There was one spot open, and they were certain when the airline worker called the man's name three more times that he would show up at the gate. But he didn't.

Sierra offered for Felicity to take the seat, but Felicity wasn't so sure she could fly without someone she knew next to her. "What if I freak out? To be honest, with that snow out there, I'm not so sure I trust the pilot."

Laughing at Felicity, Sierra gave her a big fat hug and told her to take the jeep. "Remember we parked it in the long-term parking lot and the key is in the wheel well. Go straight back to the hotel. Promise?"

"Yes, mom. I got it," Felicity said. "Text me when you get home or at least to your next stop."

The two women hugged again and then went their separate ways.

Felicity waited a moment to make sure the plane was going to actually take off and it did. Then she hurried to the jeep. She'd never driven in snow, and it took a little practice to get the hang of it but she went slowly like Sierra showed her. Halfway back to the hotel, her phone rang, and she knew better than to answer it but she couldn't help herself.

"Where are you?" Hudson asked and she instantly picked up on his tone. "I'm in the jeep, top down, and heading to the beach. Where do you think I am?"

"You are supposed to be at the airport."

"I was and now I'm not."

"Look, I'm driving in the snow in a jeep with snow tires. I've never done either one of those two things."

"What?"

He sounded like he was freaking out and Felicity told him to take a chill pill and she would call him when she got back to the hotel. The only problem was that when she got to the hotel, it was locked up tight. There was a sign on the door that said it was closed due to inclement weather.

Felicity wheeled her suitcase back across the frozen parking lot and shook her head. "Inclement weather, my foot. This is a natural disaster," she said aloud to absolutely no one.

She looked around the parking lot and realized there was only one place left for her to go. She only hoped she could remember the way to get there and that her dodgy cell phone service would hold out.

Chapter Thirty-One

Felicity only thought the roads from the airport to the hotel were treacherous. The jeep slid sideways across the road not once, but four times as she tried to make her way up the mountain to Hudson's home in the whiteout conditions.

She memorized the roads and the turns to Hudson's place before she started out. However, those road signs weren't visible any longer, and some of the turns she made were on the wrong side of the road because she could no longer make out the roads at all.

Shaking and relieved to finally have made it there, she wished she'd had the garage door opener, so she didn't have to go back out into the frozen squall.

She dragged her heavy suitcase through the blinding wind and snow that she had thought was so beautiful at first. And found the food they'd ordered for the event was left in large plastic bins by the front door. Well at least she wouldn't starve to death. *How long could blizzard conditions last anyway?*

She made her way inside, dragging her suitcase first and then all the food bins. But once she closed the door, she stopped suddenly. The decorations she and Sierra had put up were absolutely stunning and in the middle of her disastrous day, it felt almost magical to be in this incredible space.

She took a moment to breathe and then got right to work, unloading all the food items and putting them away. Next, she found the nearest bedroom, the giant master suite that included a fireplace, and threw her suitcase onto a chair so she could dig in it for her comfiest clothes. It was easier said than done since she'd removed most of what she'd originally packed. She put on her fur-lined leggings and sweater but couldn't help but look over all the beautiful clothes and shoes that wouldn't help her in a blizzard. Still, she was a bit sad not to get to wear them at the conference.

Suddenly, she was sad for all the work and effort she'd put into making it a successful event. The work was now all for nothing as Christmas was right around the corner and there would be no way to reschedule the event.

Pouting for a few minutes, she took her wet clothes and hung them over the side of the master suite bathtub. Putting on her fur-lined boots, she laughed because she'd thought Evie Mae was crazy giving her fur-lined anything. But now, she was more grateful than ever to have them. She checked her phone for service, but it was still out.

What else did she have to worry about in this type of weather emergency? She tried to think. It was nothing like the severe weather she was used to. Sure, if there was a hurricane, she'd need water, a flashlight, food provisions. But with snow, there was water everywhere, she just might have to melt it. She searched for a flashlight as that still seemed like a good idea and charged all of her electronics including her spare battery. Did a big house like that have a generator? If not, she would have the fireplace for heat. As long as she could get it lit without the electric igniter.

Just in case she couldn't figure that one out, Felicity went ahead and lit the grand fireplace. It was made of stone and that rock went all the way up to the ceiling. It truly was beautiful.

Next, she went to the kitchen and made herself a cup of hot chocolate with tiny marshmallows. It had always been her favorite. She also dug through the food bins until she found some gingerbread cookies. They weren't as good as she made, but they were still good.

She snuggled up on the couch in front of the fire and watched the snow fall as she ate her cookies and drank her hot chocolate. It was so strange to be stranded, in a blizzard by herself in Vermont, and she tried not to feel so homesick as she thought about how long this ordeal might last.

This was only her third day away from home, but she missed her best friend and her dog. It hadn't been so bad before when she was busy but now that Sierra was gone and there wasn't anything else for Felicity to take care of, she didn't know what to do with herself.

She searched the house for supplies, just in case she lost power, and came back to the living room with several warm blankets. As she watched the snow continuously fall, she fell asleep on the sofa. Somewhere in the middle of the night, the power went out and the huge house was freezing. Felicity wasn't sure what had woken her up but figured it was all the natural sounds that occur when there isn't any power.

She went back to her suitcase and put on layers of the dress clothes she'd brought. Laughing at how funny she looked, she then pulled all the covers off the master bed and brought them back into the great room. Making a super plush pallet on the floor, closer to the fireplace, it didn't take long before she fell asleep again.

It was morning when she woke up and the power was still out. She wrapped one of the blankets around her as she went to look out the large windows at the snow still falling. It had to be four or five feet deep out there, and she wondered how anyone would ever get down those roads now.

Checking her phone, there was still no service and she hated to admit how isolated she felt but it was true. And she wasn't someone who liked to be alone. She searched the house thoroughly this time and found a great collection of books.

After picking out six books that looked good, she then went into the kitchen to rummage through the food. She was starving. Of course, she would love some coffee but wasn't quite sure how to do it without a coffee maker which used electricity.

She laughed that if she got really desperate, she could always suck on some coffee beans. For the rest of the morning, she read a book and napped.

When she woke up, she could've sworn the snow was slowing down and she walked to the large bank of windows to look out again. It was even worse, maybe six or seven feet deep and she teared up that it might be spring before anyone got to her.

She felt foolish for getting emotional. Then Felicity thought she heard a dog bark which made her full-on cry because she didn't want to spend Christmas at this beautiful house in Vermont alone.

Suddenly, she saw the reflection of some flashing lights and thought, well that's it, delirium has set in. Because the only thing she could think of out there in the snowy wilderness would be a UFO. Then she laughed that she would welcome aliens, so she didn't have to spend another night there alone.

When she stopped laughing, she heard that dog bark again. She was sure of it and even though she missed him, it sounded like Winston. What if there was a poor dog stranded in that weather? Running to put on her shoes and coat, Felicity peered out the front door. There wasn't anyone out there and so she stepped out onto the portico near where the walkway would have been had the snow not covered it completely.

That was when a large piece of machinery came over the hilly driveway and the lights blinded her. She tried to shield her eyes but still she couldn't make out who or what it was and what if they were up to no good? She was a woman out there all on her own without any way to protect herself or call anyone for help.

She turned to run inside and that was when she thought she heard her name.

It was official, she was going crazy. She stepped closer to the door but before going inside, she turned to look one more time. And there was Hudson Frost stomping his way through the snow to get to her and by his side was her own dog, Winston.

Felicity put her hands over her mouth and swiped at the tears that rimmed her eyes. She'd never seen anything more wonderful than those two trekking through the heavy snow to get to her. Hudson was moving almost as fast as Winston and after her dog jumped up and hugged her, Hudson wrapped her up in his arms. "You had me so damned worried," he said holding her tightly.

"I had myself pretty worried too," she responded through her tears. It took them several minutes to get the snow cleaned off well enough to walk past the entryway. Hudson got Winston a bowl of water and then asked, "Why isn't the generator on?"

"All I know is the power went out last night and nothing kicked on, so I guessed you didn't have one."

That was when he noticed all the clothes she had on. "You look warm," he said. "And festive."

They both laughed and she shook her head. "The first time I see snow and get caught in a blizzard. Don't make fun of me, Mr. Frost. I was trying to look professional for the conference and didn't bring snow monster clothes."

He hugged her and kissed the top of her head. "Let me see if I can get the generator on and get you warm, Fe."

The kiss was so natural and then the way he used her nick-name that only her mother and Evie Mae called her, Felicity had to force her emotions down. She followed him in the direction of the garage as he said, "Sometimes, the generator is temperamental."

Felicity watched as he went out a side door of the garage to another covered area. He took a wide shovel to push some of the snow back so he could stand in front of the huge generator that must power the whole house. She didn't know what he was doing but he seemed to know what was needed as he removed a panel and got to work.

It only took him five minutes and it started working. It was the most beautiful things she'd ever seen when the whole house lit up. But then he gave her that hot grin, and she ran into his arms and kissed him the way she thought he was going to kiss her so many times.

When he took over and picked her up off the ground to move them back inside, she thought she would melt. He kicked off his boots and carried her to the couch where he explored her mouth and then chin and neck. But she had on three layers of clothes, and it was impossible to disentangle her from them all in that position. When he pulled back to see her face she was flushed and smiling.

She was biting her bottom lip and he wanted to do that too. He needed to slow down. Possibly shower and eat before things went any further.

Felicity sat up and reached for his hand. Winston was half asleep in front of the fireplace and she saw how exhausted Hudson looked. "I can't believe you're here and brought Winston too. How? I didn't think anyone could fly into the airport. And those roads are impassable. I should know since I drove off them more than on them in that four-wheel drive jeep trying to make it here. Yesterday."

He grinned as he held her hand. "There was nothing going to stop me from coming, especially after I found out that you were all alone up here. Ira called the hotel and found out that they'd closed and didn't let anyone stay even if they had been stranded by the storm.

"I figured you'd make your way here."

She couldn't believe what he was saying. *Nothing would stop him from coming for her?*

Could Hudson have said anything more romantic at that moment to her? Holding back her emotions, Felicity tried to stay on track as she said, "That still doesn't tell me the how."

Chapter Thirty-Two

I wanted to surprise you with Winston and then the whole blizzard warning happened. Evie still encouraged me to do it and so I picked him up yesterday and we flew into Hartford, Connecticut."

Felicity ruffled Winston's fur and kissed his head. "How did he do on the plane?"

"Evie called the vet who gave him something to help him relax. He slept most of the way."

"Did he freak out when he saw the snow?"

"That's the thing, it wasn't snowing there yet. I rented a four-wheel drive truck and headed this way. It normally takes a couple of hours but once we hit the Vermont state line, it was slow going. I made it as far as a few blocks from the hotel and that was when Jim, the snowplow driver, saw us. He brought us all the way up here."

"Wait. You flew in yesterday?"

Hudson grinned. She didn't miss much.

"How long were you and Winnie stuck in that truck?"

"We had to stop around three this morning, but I had some provisions and kept the heat on us."

Felicity couldn't believe he'd slept in a truck all night trying to get to her. She launched her body into his and their lips collided. When they came up for air, he gently pushed her hair off her face. "Worried about me?"

She didn't miss a beat. "Yes. If anything had happened to my dog while he was in your care, you would've been in huge trouble."

Hudson laughed. "I sure hope you have some food around here. The beef jerky is long gone and neither of us ate much on the plane."

Grinning, she kissed him again. "The good news is that we have all the food you could possibly eat. The bad news is that you have to pay for all the conference food, and we didn't even get to have the conference."

Hudson followed Felicity into the kitchen with Winston howling behind them. He didn't want to miss out and he'd heard the word food mentioned several times.

Feeding Winston fresh turkey meat as he also ate some, Hudson watched as Felicity made him a sandwich and gave Winston a plate of something that looked like turkey potpie.

"I know you're disappointed about the conference," he said watching her make a pot of coffee. He may have been starving but it was still early morning, and she didn't have power until a few minutes ago.

"We worked so hard, and I know it means a lot to you and your family. I'm sure the attendees were looking forward to it too." She looked sad as she talked about the conference.

"It isn't all for naught, Felicity. We can do a virtual meeting when we get back and, of course, show them the video footage."

Once she made her coffee, they took their food and drinks

into the great room to sit in front of the fireplace. "I'm thinking you need to reschedule the conference as a springtime event after this anyway," she said.

Hudson laughed and told her that she might be on to something with that idea. After they ate plenty of food, they took Winston outside for a quick run and bathroom break in the snow.

He didn't want to go back inside but Felicity was freezing so they tempted him with a treat to get him to follow.

Felicity went into the bedroom and peeled off all the layers of dress clothes she was wearing. There was a glorious heater in the bathroom and so she took a long hot shower and washed her hair. It took some time for her to blow her long hair completely dry, but she felt so much better when she slipped into her sleeping shorts and a black sweater.

It was overcast outside and if it weren't for all the Christmas lights, then the house would have seemed dark. It was perfect for them to get some much needed rest and when she returned to the great room, Hudson was freshly showered too, and wearing gray sweatpants with a flannel shirt.

Winston was asleep on the pallet that Felicity had made in front of the fireplace, and she smiled that if she had to be stranded anywhere, at least they were together.

Hudson walked straight to her and wrapped a thick blanket around her body, pulling her into him. When she looked up at him, he gave her a warm kiss. "I was wondering what was taking you so long," he said as he ran his hands through her long hair.

"Did you miss me?"

He pulled her into his body even tighter. "Something awful."

When they kissed again, there was so much heat that she pushed the blanket to the floor. She didn't need it. She only wanted him, and she pulled him on top of her on the sofa. Her hands were under his shirt, and it felt like fire everywhere she touched.

Hudson liked her hands all over him but they'd both been through a hellish twenty-four hours, and he wanted this to mean more. She already meant something to him.

He rolled over to his side and wrapped an arm around her waist to pull her in closer to him. Kissing her forehead, he leaned back to look into her eyes. "I haven't been with anyone in a long time, Fe."

Had she heard him correctly? If she were being honest with herself, he was the most incredible man she had ever met. Who wouldn't want to be with him? Hudson Frost could have anyone he wanted.

She leaned into him. "Bad breakup?" she asked, avoiding his face. *Please say no.*

He lifted her chin to look at him. He shook his head and admitted, "No. Workaholic."

Felicity hugged him tightly. He really was too good. She admitted that she'd only had the one serious boyfriend and that had ended over a year ago.

Hudson played with her hair as he told her all about the first year he was CEO, and how difficult it was for him to iron down all the processes his father had already put into to place.

Then he admitted how he spent the second year, making changes to those processes so the company would be even more efficient and profitable.

"It took all of that, so I felt like I belonged as the leader," he confessed.

Felicity kissed him sweetly on the lips. "And you are doing an incredible job too. I could see how proud both of your parents are of you."

She sheepishly confessed, "Your so good at your job that I spend every day just wanting your approval."

He kissed her on the forehead and then lips. "Fe, you are incredible. You blow me away everyday with your creative ideas and the way you answer emails or rewrite my speeches. You make me look better. You've also won over the entire staff with your coffee and treats. I tried so hard not to show favoritism toward you and perhaps, I didn't give you enough positive feedback?"

Felicity shook her head. "You're a great boss. Honestly, it's in my DNA that I always feel like I'm not doing enough. Evie Mae, my therapist, says that it's because I have Daddy issues."

Shrugging it off like it wasn't a big deal, Felicity smiled at him and then turned over on the couch. She'd said too much. Hudson wrapped the blanket over them and pulled her back into his front. But he had no intention of letting her off the hook. She'd opened that door and he was going to walk right inside.

"Why do you have issues with your dad?"

She laid there for a long time and just when he thought he should ask her again, he heard her take a deep breath and then let it out before she began to explain. "My mother was a knockout with blonde hair and blue-green eyes."

Hudson whispered, "So you get your eyes from your mom?"

"Yes. But she was blonde and smart. She spoke English but also Russian and lots of boys were enamored with her. But she met Franklin Storey in college her sophomore year. And he was going places."

"You told me she had to drop out because your grandparents got sick?"

"That's right. She took care of them, and Franklin went on to graduate from law school. Once he became a lawyer, he found her again. Her parents had passed away and she was barely making it as a secretary in New York. They got married and she worked two jobs to help pay off his school debt. Debt is a horrible thing to my mother, and she is all about living within her means. Anyway, she got pregnant with me and still she worked. She wanted to buy a house to make a home for her family.

"She had the down payment by the time I was one and bought a small house in Brooklyn. She said he never warmed up to the idea of being a father. Maybe because I wasn't a boy. But when I was four, he left us."

Hudson didn't know why but he'd thought her father had died by the way she avoided talking about him. "Do you remember him?"

She nodded. "I remember him sitting in the living room of our house and not speaking to me. It was like I was invisible. Anyhow, he filed for divorce but in the court papers, he demanded the house and somehow, he won. We were kicked out and that was when my mother moved us to Maisonville. She never got any money from him, and she's never owned another home again.

"She deserved better. It was so unfair because she always worked really hard. One day, I plan to buy her a home."

"Your mom never remarried or dated?"

"No to remarriage but she's had dates. No one she'd ever bring home and I don't think she would trust anyone again."

"Do you ever see him?"

"Never. He's never attempted to reach out to me for one single birthday or graduation. Nothing. We just weren't that important to him."

"His loss."

"Thanks. But as a kid, when you have a parent out there who doesn't want anything to do with you, you think you're not enough. Especially when there are things like Daddy Donut Day at school and you're the only kid without someone. I mean, there were other kids whose parents were divorced but the dad still came to stuff like that or a grandfather. But of course, I didn't have grandparents, so no one for grandparents' day either."

Hudson had both parents, and both sets of grandparents too. His mother was a teacher, and he didn't miss out on any of the special school events.

"But I don't really have issues. Those bring a special someone to school days ended in elementary school and I would sit with Evie Mae and her dad or grandparents. Truly, I think it all made me stronger and able to take care of myself."

"No doubt," Hudson said, and he kissed her on the top of her head again. She snuggled into him, and he'd thought she'd fallen asleep when she began talking again.

"It was for all those reasons that my mother warned me to stay away from boys until I graduated college. She never liked it when I had a date for homecoming or prom in high school either. Sometimes, it felt like a cultural difference because my grandparents had an arranged marriage and she pretended to lean into their culture when it suited her cause. When I started dating Troy Brooks, I couldn't tell her. Especially when it felt so serious. He pursued me, and I believed he cared about me."

She rolled over toward Hudson so she could see his face when she told him about Troy's family and how she overheard them talking about her. When she told him that Troy had cheated on her and then what he'd said to her, she saw Hudson's jaw clench.

He lifted her chin so he could kiss her lips. "It was after that when you found Winston?"

"It was because of what had happened that I desperately wanted Winston. When I saw his picture, he looked so alone and that was how I felt too."

Hudson pulled her hands to his mouth and kissed them. "My parents taught me that things are going to happen beyond our control in this life. Our power comes with how we react to those things."

"That's pretty powerful," she said remembering the tragedy

that his family had been through. They were remarkable people to have turned things around in such a positive way.

She leaned into him and then it hit her. "Hudson? Is this where the accident happened?"

Chapter Thirty-Three

Hudson kissed Felicity's forehead. She didn't miss much. "We didn't live in this house, but yes, it happened on the trails near here."

After all they'd been through, his family still kept a home in this town and decorated it every year. That was why they held the conference in Brownsville, Vermont. It was to honor their first-born son who had passed away there.

Felicity couldn't stop the tears that fell, and Hudson hugged her tightly. It was another moment for them, and it was intense.

They didn't talk anymore after that but held each other until they fell asleep together. It was dark when they woke up to find it had stopped snowing.

Winston barked to let them know he needed to go back outside for a moment. Hudson put on a full body snow suit and took the sweet dog out for a little longer than Felicity could have done with her short wool coat.

When he returned to the house, she'd heated some dinner and they ate together sitting on the floor in front of the fireplace. "So how long do these blizzard things last? I've never been away from my mom for Christmas. I mean, I would be okay, but I hate to think of her all alone."

Hudson reached out to squeeze her hand. He knew Felicity would be okay because he would see to it. But he sort of loved how she looked after her mother. "It's going to be at least a few days before they can plow the roads around here. But as soon as they do, then we can get to my truck and then to the airport. I promise to get you home for Christmas."

Felicity had only known Hudson for a few weeks, but she knew he was good for his word. He would do everything in his power to get her home. And until then, she would enjoy their time together and the slower pace that didn't exist outside of the snowstorm area.

They slept in the great room together on the sofa with Winston on the floor next to them. The next day after walking Winston and eating breakfast, Hudson found a monopoly game, a large puzzle, and some uno cards. They played games, talked, and laughed for the entire day.

He shared stories of his childhood and some of the antics he played on his father around the warehouse at Frost Manufacturing. It was made even more funny since he was now running the entire operation.

Felicity told him about growing up with Evie Mae and some of the pranks they played on her older brother. It was amazing that Mitchel had anything to do with the two younger girls anymore with how they got him into trouble.

The sun came out an hour before sunset and they took Winston on a walk together. Hudson held her hand and pulled Felicity in for a kiss multiple times under the guise of warming her up.

They worked together in the kitchen and then sat by the fireplace to eat before popping a movie into the DVD player. It was a film from the eighties that was filmed in the area, called Funny

Farm with Chevy Chase. Felicity had never heard of it, but it was funny and had them both laughing.

It was late when they went to bed and Hudson pulled her into the master bedroom where he'd remade the bed with fresh linens and lit the fireplace.

Felicity winked at him as she climbed under the covers and started throwing her clothes out from under the blanket. For every item she took off, he matched her. The only difference was that she was covered under the blanket, and he was standing in the open room. Hudson Frost may be a workaholic, but he sure didn't miss leg day at the gym or any other day. His body was a work of art, sculpted and strong. Felicity was hot just looking at him and more than ready when he came to bed.

He climbed under the covers with her and then slowly kissed her entire body. Purposeful and attentive with his hands and mouth, Hudson had Felicity begging him to make love to her and he did over and over again through the night.

The next morning when Felicity woke up, Hudson was already up. When she walked into he great room, he was sitting on the couch reading a book as Winston slept on the sofa next to him.

"Good morning, sleepyhead," he said with a smile.

Felicity's hair was mussed up and he thought she looked perfect. She whispered, "morning," as she stumbled to the coffee pot. Hudson jumped up and made her a cup of Joe just the way she liked it before he gave her a sweet kiss and guided her to the sofa next to him.

Felicity didn't know he even knew how she took her coffee. "Winston and I already took a walk this morning but if you want to go out again, we could try this afternoon?"

"Sure, that would be great," she said as she leaned into his hard body. She felt settled next to him in a way she had never felt before in her life. It made her nervous and she tried to not screw this up.

Felicity was quieter and reflective thinking back to how the last few weeks were like slow foreplay between them. She loved the banter and he'd been wonderful to her last night. She dared to say he was magnificent in bed and it had been the best sexual experience of her life. But she didn't speak in hyperbole, and she didn't want to blow up his ego. Especially if this had been just a one-night thing or blizzard fling for him.

He lifted her chin to make her look him in the eyes, "You okay, Fe?"

She gave him a saucy smile, "Yes. Just tired." It wasn't long until she laid her head on his shoulder and fell back asleep.

Hudson covered Felicity up with a blanket and eased her into a more comfortable position on the sofa next to him. She was beautiful when she woke up in the morning and he couldn't help but think about making love with her until the early morning hours.

He already cared for her more than was probably normal in such a short time. But he didn't want normal. He wanted extraordinary and Felicity Storey was nothing short of amazing.

Perhaps she was just tired. She certainly had earned a few days of rest with the schedule she kept every day. He would let her sleep as much as she needed and then they would go out for a long walk with Winston, and he would get her to talk to him.

It was early afternoon when Felicity woke up again. She had a fluffy blanket over her, and the fireplace was still going but she didn't see Winston or Hudson anywhere.

When she sat up on the sofa, she felt a bit woozy from sleeping so long. She needed some calories and stood up to run to the restroom and then to get something to eat.

Just as she heated some turkey potpie which was honestly the best thing the caterer made, Hudson and Winston came bounding into he house. Had they gone running in the snow?

Hudson was laughing and Winston was thirsty. "Hey," she said, and Hudson walked over and kissed her hard on the mouth.

"He's such a great dog. We just spent an hour all over the mountain and he saw a deer and took off after it. The next thing I know, they are playing tag with each other, and he chases her for a while and then she would chase him. It was incredible." Hudson looked so young as he laughed and told her the story. He then pulled out his phone and showed her the video. It was hilarious.

"Hungry?" Felicity asked and Winnie howled at her. "Okay, boy," she said and then winked at Hudson. "How about you? Are you hungry too?"

Hudson nodded but offered to help her. She pointed at the barstool and told him to sit down. Once she heated up more potpie for them, she sat next to Hudson to eat.

"It's still freezing out there, but the sun seems to be melting the snow each day. We might be able to get out of here tomorrow."

Felicity hugged him tightly. "That would be so great. I bet Evie Mae and my mama are freaking out."

Hudson kissed her and she sat back down to finish her food. After they cleaned the dishes, he told her about the redwood sauna that his father had installed five years ago. He led her to it and then they stripped down to their underwear and climbed inside.

It didn't take long before it began heating up and as his body began to glisten in the heat, Felicity couldn't help but feel hot on the inside. She wiped her mouth with the back of her hand and didn't miss how Hudson's eyes were heavy with lust for her.

She leaned over and licked his shoulder but before she could get on her knees to tease him further, he kissed her and pulled her into his lap.

Where last night was slow and purposeful. This was hot and fast paced. The sauna was no joke, and they wouldn't have lasted in there if they'd taken too long.

Felicity headed to the shower with Hudson right behind her. By the time they were dressed and in the living room, it was almost dark.

Hudson found another movie and they laid together on the sofa to watch it. But when Felicity rolled over toward him, he kissed her forehead, nose, and then lips. "Can I get you anything?" he asked lovingly.

"I've got all I need right here and now," she said and then when she thought better of it, he felt her body stiffen.

Hudson kissed her hard on the lips. "Don't hold back from telling me things like that, Fe. You have to know how much it means to me when you say things like that. Don't ever regret it. Okay?"

She stared into his eyes. Was he serious? Could this be as real as it felt to her? How could anyone ever be sure?

It was as if he understood what she was thinking. "I know this is moving kind of fast but it's real for me too. I'm not going anywhere," he said, and Felicity seemed to tremble a little before she hugged him tightly and held on.

"If you're having doubts or you're worried about anything, let's talk about it. Okay?"

Felicity looked up at him and kissed him hard on the mouth again. How could he know all the right things to say to her? It was amazing and still made her worry even more about losing him. She cared about Hudson Frost and when all this was over, would they still be able to work together?

He kissed her forehead and then asked again, "Do you want to talk about it, Felicity?"

Instead of telling him her feelings, she told him about Isaac Keller and what he was putting them through with the ridiculous loan she and Evie signed.

She didn't mean to tell him all the details of how they'd been taken advantage of, but it spilled out as she avoided her emotions.

Hudson sat up straighter and she could see him putting his CEO face on. "How much have you paid him so far? And how is it accruing?"

She told him everything and he shook his head. She and Evie had built a really nice little business but wouldn't be able to make a profit until something was done about the loan shark who was taking advantage of them.

"I'll need to see that contract," he told her, and she agreed to get him everything he needed.

"But you can't tell anyone, especially Evie Mae's family or my mother. I tried to talk Evie into at least telling Mitchel, but she was worried he would go after Isaac Keller. Mitch can be a hot head sometimes."

Hudson agreed but he decided not to tell her that he wanted to go after Isaac Keller for hurting them too. Instead, he would get his lawyers involved.

The baby loan shark wouldn't see him coming until it was too late.

Chapter Thirty-Four

It was Tuesday afternoon when the snowplow made it up the mountain to Hudson and Felicity. The driver waved to them as they walked toward the road with Winston chasing a ball.

Leaving the small ski town would be bittersweet because they'd both slept and relaxed more than maybe ever before. The love they'd made there may not transfer into their real world lives and Felicity felt that cut a little deeper in her soul.

Hudson cleaned the snow off the jeep and loaded Felicity's luggage into the back while it was warming up. Winston was excited as usual to get to go anywhere with them and the Jeep was another adventure for him.

They were able to make it down the mountain road safely enough in the four-wheel drive Jeep, but Hudson wanted to take the truck he'd rented the rest of the way. It was heavier and would manage the road if things got dicey.

It took three hours to make it to the airport, but once they'd hit the state line, their phones worked again. Hudson called his pilot so he could gas up the plane and be ready for them. Then he called his parents.

Felicity called her mother and then Evie Mae. Once she told them they would be home soon, she sent a text to Ira explaining the same thing.

It almost didn't seem real when they settled onto the plane and headed home. Winston was antsy until his medicine kicked in and Felicity joked that maybe she should take some of it.

Instead, she wiggled close to Hudson, and he held her hand or had an arm around her the entire time. She was still nervous, but he talked to her during the take-off and kissed her while landing to keep her distracted.

It was after midnight when Hudson pulled his SUV up to the Shepard's House and he hated to let Felicity go. He carried her luggage and walked her and Winston to the door of their little home.

"Would you like to come in and see my bedroom?" she asked. She didn't want him to leave either and it did something for him.

"I need to go into the office tomorrow," he said, and she suddenly remembered it was Wednesday. "Oh, gosh, I'm sorry. I guess I'll see you in a few hours."

He pushed her against the front door as he kissed her hard on the mouth. "You will not show up at the office tomorrow, Felicity Storey. Do you hear me?"

She laughed and shook her head. "You're not the boss of me," she said, and he loved that smart mouth of hers.

"Let's go to bed," he replied and followed her inside so they could at least get a little rest that night.

The next morning, neither of them woke up when Evie opened the bedroom door. She left Felicity a note and took Winston to work with her. She didn't know exactly what was happening, but her best friend deserved some happiness and if she had found it with her new handsome boss then good for her.

Hudson and Felicity didn't wake up until ten that morning. They found the note from Evie and then he picked Felicity up and threw her over his shoulder like a fireman. Hauling her back to bed to remind her that they were back at home and things had not changed between them.

Another hour and half later, they showered and dressed for the day. Giving her a very long kiss goodbye and then another, Hudson headed across the bridge to the office and Felicity drove to the coffee truck to help Evie and discuss everything that had happened over the last week.

Evie was all smiles. "So, you and the hottie CEO are together-together?"

"Yes. I think so," Felicity said thinking back to how he explained that to her as he slowly made love to her for the third time that morning.

They worked together the rest of the day and it felt like old times before Felicity had to work for Frost Manufacturing.

While she shared details of her time with Hudson to Evie Mae, she didn't admit telling him about Baby Shark. They laughed and talked about everything else that day and night at Espresso to go and it hadn't come up. But it was important that Evie heard it from Felicity that Hudson was looking into the legality of the contract and she would tell her best friend tomorrow.

Besides, if Hudson could help them then that would be fantastic, but if things had to stay the way they were then she could know that at least Felicity had tried.

That night, Felicity and Hudson talked over the phone but for the first time in almost a week, they slept apart. He was in New Orleans, and she was in Maisonville, and it felt like they were a million miles apart.

She was worn out from being on her feet all day and he had a ton of catch-up work from being out of the office for so long. It wasn't ideal but Felicity reminded herself that it was real life, and she would see him in the morning at work.

Hudson had spent the morning going over the contract that Felicity and Evie Mae had signed with the crook, Isaac Keller. There were so many things wrong with it that Hudson couldn't discuss it with her over the phone. He wanted to talk to her in person about never signing a contract without having an attorney look it over first.

He called his attorney and they met with Isaac Keller in person that afternoon. It didn't go well. Keller was an idiot. Keller argued for ten minutes that he had some leverage with Evie Mae and Felicity, but they showed him how it was illegal for him to charge the amount of interest that he charged them as well as the twenty-five percent ownership clause that supposedly would go into effect in January. He stormed out of their office, slamming the doors behind him and causing a scene.

Hudson and his attorney drew up the papers to sue Isaac Keller on the girls' behalf and gave him very little choice on how to do the right thing.

But Isaac Keller had to cool off so he could see the reasoning there. They told him he had twenty-four hours.

Thursday morning, Felicity got to the office early to brew coffee, and everyone was thrilled to see her. She handed out muffins and cookies with each cup of Joe and she was extremely happy to be back.

Half the staff called her Elsa from the Disney Movie, Frozen and she laughed that she'd felt that cold when the power went out.

Ira walked in and gave Felicity a big fat hug and told her that she wasn't allowed to leave again. When Sierra got there, she also gave Felicity a hug. She felt a bit like a rockstar.

By 8:30 in the morning when Hudson wasn't there, it took

Felicity by surprise. She sent him a text and he sent her back a form response, *Sorry I can't talk right now.*

Ira explained that Hudson had several meetings that day and then had her explain how things went down with the blizzard. She spent half an hour explaining everything to him and Sierra but still no Hudson.

He sent her another text apologizing for missing her all day, but he got caught up in meetings and it couldn't be helped.

She was disappointed but went home knowing that he had at least tried to get back to the office and that they would definitely see each other the next day.

Of course, Friday was a half day since Christmas fell on the weekend but still, she hoped she could spend some time with Hudson.

When she drove up to the coffee truck, the look on Evie Mae's face was pure unadulterated anger. She rushed in to see what was wrong with her and that was when Felicity realized that it was directed toward her.

"What have you done, Felicity?"

"What?" she asked but Evie was too upset to even speak to her. "I can't talk to you right now. Go home. I'll see you when I get there."

Felicity was too tired to argue. She took Winston with her and headed to the house. She wasn't home ten minutes before her mother showed up and then Evie's parents.

What was wrong with everyone?

"Tell us the truth?" Felicity's mother, Asha said. "Who is this Isaac Keller, and did you sign a contract with him or not?"

Felicity didn't know what to say. Had Evie told them? Of course, she didn't. If she had, then she would have called Felicity. Neither one of them wanted their parents to know.

Much to their unhappiness, Felicity refused to discuss anything about her business with Evie unless Evie was home.

After quizzing her for over an hour, they made a plan to come back when Evie got off work.

Felicity tried to call Hudson but didn't get an answer. She baked muffins and cookies as she waited for Evie to get home, but she didn't get in until after midnight. She shook her head instead of talking to Felicity and went into her bathroom to shower. It was almost one in the morning when she came out and confronted Felicity.

"We had a pact. We've actually had one since kindergarten. How could you, after we both agreed to sign that contract, how could you go behind my back and tell someone?"

"You have to understand Evie. I trusted Hudson and he was going to help us get out of the high interest rate Baby Shark was charging us. He swore to me that he wouldn't tell anyone. Especially our families."

"Well apparently, he couldn't be trusted and they are freaking the freak out. Evie shook her head and stormed off to her bedroom, slamming the door.

Felicity tried to call Hudson again, but he didn't pick up. She left him several messages and when she didn't hear back from him, she went to bed upset.

Things weren't the same now that they were back home. And now Felicity questioned if Hudson felt differently now that they were back too.

The next morning, Evie Mae was gone before Felicity woke up. That never happened and Felicity felt terrible. She had to get to the office, but she really wanted to sit and talk to her best friend to sort this out.

After making coffee at the office, Felicity found out that there were only a few people coming in the day before Christmas Eve.

She walked into her office and saw that Sierra was out until after the holidays. When she knocked on Hudson's closed door,

Ira answered and told her they were in a meeting. He then closed the door again and she officially felt shut out.

The longer they were in there the more hurt she felt. Then she got angry. Why was Hudson avoiding her? None of this made sense. And why would he tell her mom or Evie's parents about their contract with Isaac Keller?

If he didn't want to be together now that they'd returned to New Orleans, he could've just told her. He didn't have to hurt her in such a personal way.

As it slowly approached Noon, Felicity cleared her desk and packed up her personal affects. When Ira finally came out, she was fuming.

Ira gave her a hug and wished her a Merry Christmas. She barely spoke to him as he left because she was so angry at their boss.

Once she shut down her computer, she stormed into his office to find him on a video call. She stood and stammered for several minutes but when he couldn't break free, she turned around and left.

She'd shared her secrets with him, and he hadn't guarded them. He worked all the time and obviously, could not make time for her in his real world.

She scribbled furiously on a notepad and taped the letter to his door.

I told you that no one could know about the contract with Isaac Keller. I trusted you and now everyone is upset with me, and I don't know how to fix it. This is too much. Don't bother calling me back. I quit!!!

She practically ran out of the office before her tears took over. She had to find a way to make this right with Evie Mae and it would have to start with talking to their parents.

Chapter Thirty-Five

Felicity sat in Kristy Shepard's garage hair salon and poured her heart out. Evie Mae's mom had been a perfect friend to Felicity her entire life and if there was anyone that could help correct the situation, it was her.

She washed and then blew out Felicity's hair as she cried and told her how happy she'd been with Hudson while snowed in at his home in Vermont.

"Now it's all over and I quit my job," she cried some more. "How could he betray my trust like that and how do I find these horrible guys? Am I a magnet for bad boyfriends?"

Kristy kissed the top of her head and then turned the chair around to show Felicity her stunning hair. It made her half smile as she wiped away the last of her tears.

"Honey, you are a beautiful, intelligent, talented woman and you will find the right guy someday. We all have to kiss a few frogs first," she said smiling sympathetically at Felicity.

"You met Mr. Shepard in the tenth grade," Felicity said seriously. Neither one had kissed anyone else, ever.

Kristy sat on her stool and smiled at Felicity. "Now tell me all the details about this contract. We can call a lawyer and try to stop- what did you say his name was again?"

"Isaac Keller but we call him Baby Shark," Felicity cried again. "Evie Mae is never going to forgive me."

Kristy Shepard hugged Felicity and told her not to worry about Evie Mae because she would always love her no matter what.

Drying her tears, Felicity told Evie Mae's mother the whole sorted tale of how Isaac always had a crush on Evie in College and would hang around even though Evie refused to go out with him. He jumped at the chance to loan them the money and that was the beginning of all their troubles.

By late afternoon, the entire Shepard Family and Felicity's mother gathered together to discuss the loan Isaac Keller held over the girls' heads. Mitch and his father offered to go talk to Isaac privately, but Kristy and Asha told them that wouldn't be necessary.

If they put all their savings together, they could pay off the loan in its entirety and the girls could make payments back to them instead.

Felicity endured a lecture from her mother about debt and then from Mitchel about borrowing money from a loan shark. It was what she deserved for getting into a mess like that but also because she told Hudson about it before her family.

Now that she had a plan, she had to go to Espresso to Geaux and talk to Evie Mae. They all agreed to let her go first and talk to Evie, but she only had fifteen minutes because they were coming right behind her.

"We've got your back Fe," Kristy said. "And Evie Mae's, so you girls have nothing to worry about."

Felicity knew Evie Mae well enough to know that she would be angry about the whole family getting involved but she didn't see any other choice. Especially since she'd quit her job.

She drove up to the coffee truck and was surprised to see only a few people in line to get coffee. It was the day before Christmas Eve, Evie liked to call it Christmas Adam, and freezing outside.

When she walked up to the back door, she took a deep breath before walking inside. Evie Mae would have to understand. This was for the best and their families would help them.

But when she opened the back door, there was Evie Mae hugging Hudson Frost. She didn't stop long enough to ask any questions. She just ran out of there and got into her car. Before she could get it started, Hudson was there at her window.

"Come on, Felicity. Talk to me," he pleaded.

She shook her head, no, but replied, "I don't know what that was all about, and I don't need to know."

She trusted Evie Mae. It was Hudson that she wasn't so sure about.

"Please, Fe. Talk to me," he said again, and she got out of the car.

She had hurt in her eyes, but her words were angry. "What are you doing here? Haven't you done enough?" She put her hands on her hips and he saw the fire in her eyes. "I trusted you. I told you things I've never told anyone else before. And we aren't home a day before you tell the one secret, I asked you to keep? I made love with you- a bunch of times."

Hudson leaned down so they were face to face, but Felicity rolled her eyes and turned her head. She was stubborn and so cute when she was angry. "Fe, look at me."

She refused and then turned her head in the other direction, avoiding his eyes. Hudson picked her up and threw her over his shoulder so he could take her back into the coffee truck. It was then that Evie's parents, Mitch, and Felicity's mom, Asha pulled up in the parking lot.

They saw Hudson carrying Felicity toward Espresso to Geaux and all hurried out of their cars and over to the girls.

Everyone talked at once with Brennan and Kristy asking Evie Mae what was going on, Mitch telling Hudson to take his hands off Felicity, Asha Storey asking Felicity who Hudson was and Winston who had been napping began to howl.

It was utter chaos and exactly what having a large family was like when there was a problem to be solved. Hudson put two fingers up to his lips and whistled loud enough to make Winston stop.

Everyone else stopped too and stared at him. He patted Felicity's bottom before he set her down. She was even angrier than before, and he winked at her like he wanted his own Dateline special. And everyone in that small food truck would help her bury his body.

Hudson instantly put on that charming smile that made people listen to him. And Evie Mae walked over to put her arm around Felicity. "It's okay. Hudson's got this."

Everyone looked at Evie and then stared at Hudson again. "I'm not quite sure how this all got so convoluted, but when my girlfriend Felicity told me- "

He didn't get to say another word because Felicity stomped her foot and glared at him. "I am not your girlfriend."

"Yes, you are," he said grinning and Evie Mae laughed too.

The whole food truck vibrated as The Shepard Family and the Storey women were all ready to jump Hudson Frost. Evie put her hands up to try and calm them down. "Just listen to the man. I promise this has a happy ending."

They looked at her curiously and then glared back at Hudson for a third time. He hoped it was charmed. "As I was saying, my girlfriend and I had a lot of time together while snowed in at the house in Vermont. When she told me what had happened with Keller and that contract, I called my attorney. We gave him twenty-four hours to make the appropriate changes, or we would take him to court."

Evie leaned forward, "But instead, Baby Shark sold the contract to Hudson, and he wiped out the exorbitant interest and we now only have to make the normal loan payments back to him."

"What?" Felicity asked. Brennan and Kristy both shook their heads and the whole crew started talking again.

Evie Mae shook her head and pulled Felicity outside with her. She hugged Felicity and apologized for getting so angry when all her friend was trying to do was help them out of a bad situation. "Hudson wasn't the one who told our families. It was Isaac Keller who called your mother and mine saying that we were trying to weasel out of our business loan."

"He didn't?"

"Yes, he did. Hudson's dad is friends with the New Orleans chief of police, Ollie Morales, and he is going to launch an investigation into Baby Shark and his dad's businesses. I don't think we will hear from him again."

Felicity rarely didn't have something to say but Hudson had fixed everything for her and Evie Mae. When she looked over, he was leaning against the back door with Winston by his side. Her mother and the Shepard's were all still talking inside the food truck.

Evie hugged her and then walked over to Hudson to hand him something before she stepped back inside to get their families to settle down. After all, they had a business to run.

Hudson walked over to Felicity and smiled. She cut her eyes at him before giving him a half grin. "You never asked me to be your girlfriend."

"I figured it was understood, Miss Storey."

"Well, you figured wrong, Mr. Frost."

He leaned forward and she saw the sparkle in his eyes. "Will you be my girlfriend Felicity Storey, forever and ever?"

She crooked her head and tried not to laugh. "You need to

know that as long as you're my boyfriend, when I call you then you are obligated to answer."

He laughed at her using his words from when she hadn't answered his calls a week ago. Then he reached into his pocket and pulled out the mistletoe that Evie had handed to him.

Holding it over his head, he grinned at her, "As long as we are following the rules, I think you owe me a kiss."

Felicity grabbed his tie and pulled him in close so she could lay one on him. Hudson reached around her waist and pulled her body into his. And when they finally came up for air, everyone was staring at them.

It was going to be an eventful Christmas and a most joyous New Year, Evie thought as she clapped for her best friend.

Felicity took the mistletoe and threw it at Evie Mae who caught it in both hands. It wasn't a wedding bouquet, but the sentiment was the same. She was next.

About the Author

LISA HERRINGTON is a Women's fiction and YA novelist, and blogger. A former medical sales rep, she currently manages the largest Meet-Up writing group in the New Orleans area, The Bayou Writer's Club. She was born and raised in Louisiana, attended college at Ole Miss in Oxford, Mississippi and accepts that in New Orleans we never hide our crazy but instead parade it around on the front porch and give it a cocktail. It's certainly why she has so many stories to tell today. When she's not writing, and spending time with her husband and three children, she spends time reading, watching old movies or planning something new and exciting with her writers' group.

Connect with Lisa, find out about new releases, and get free books at LisaHerrington.com